W9-CBU-691

KILLING TIME

Key Lessard slipped out of the timber and belly-crawled for a hundred yards, easing up onto a slight rise. He lifted the .308, sighted in the bar lights of the sheriff's squad car, and pulled the trigger.

The slug blew a fist-size hole in the lights, sending bits and pieces of plastic and glass flying.

"Jesus Christ!" the sheriff yelled, looking wildly around him. "Dammit, Key, I know that's you out there. Cain't we talk about this, partner? You've got to see our side of this thing!"

Key had never seen it fail. Hate groups were all the same. Cowards when the chips were down. He raised the .308.

It was a good day for killing.

BOOK YOUR PLACE ON OUR WEBSITE AND MAKE THE READING CONNECTION!

We've created a customized website just for our very special readers, where you can get the inside scoop on everything that's going on with Zebra, Pinnacle and Kensington books.

When you come online, you'll have the exciting opportunity to:

- View covers of upcoming books
- Read sample chapters
- Learn about our future publishing schedule (listed by publication month *and author*)
- Find out when your favorite authors will be visiting a city near you
- Search for and order backlist books from our online catalog
- Check out author bios and background information
- Send e-mail to your favorite authors
- Meet the Kensington staff online
- Join us in weekly chats with authors, readers and other guests
- Get writing guidelines
- AND MUCH MORE!

Visit our website at
http://www.pinnaclebooks.com

BLOODLAND

BY WILLIAM W. JOHNSTONE

P

Pinnacle Books
Kensington Publishing Corp.

http://www.williamjohnstone.com

PINNACLE BOOKS are published by

Kensington Publishing Corp.
850 Third Avenue
New York, NY 10022

First Zebra Printing: November, 1986

First Pinnacle Printing: March, 1999
10 9 8 7 6 5 4 3 2

Printed in the United States of America

Dedicated to Lace—with long overdue apologies.

Death is afraid of him because he has the heart of a lion.

Anonymous

Pride, envy, and avarice are the three sparks that have set these hearts on fire.

Dante

Prologue

He was twenty-three years old when the Vietnam War ended for him in 1973. He had entered the army at seventeen. A year later he had completed NCO school and one year after that had entered OCS. He had graduated at the top of his class. He had never told anyone at Benning he could have had an appointment to the Point if he had wanted it.

Now he had gone through nearly ever type of dirty training the army could toss at him. He went through it, picked it up, and tossed it back at them. He had endured some of it, enjoyed some of it, and grown and matured as the training shaped him.

He was a captain in the army's Special Forces, commanding a spook team, when he decided to call it quits. He knew with a soldier's insight and no small amount of bitterness, that the U.S. was not going to allow its fighting men to win the war in Southeast Asia.

And that pissed him off mightily.

He felt as if his country had let him down.

Which it had.

He was on his way home when he realized he was

not ready to go home. He didn't know if he would ever go back home. He was restless and filled with ill-concealed rage. He was trained to kill with his hands, his feet, a rolled-up newspaper, a stick, a knife, a gun, explosives.

He possessed no skills for the civilian job market.

He was still in uniform when he deplaned in San Francisco. He threw his green beret into the bay, changed into newly purchased civilian clothes, and boarded a plane for Paris. In Paris he enlisted in the French Foreign Legion. He was wounded two and a half years later and got out of the Legion. He drifted to South America and was involved in dozens of little no-name brush wars. He sent most of the money he earned to a stock brokerage firm with instructions to play it high risk and reinvest any profits. They got him in on the ground floor of computers and earned him several hundred thousand dollars.

What to do with it? they asked, after tracking him down in Central America.

Make me some more money! he telexed back. It was just a game to him.

They made him some more money.

He barely got out of Nicaragua alive; came close to meeting the same fate as several other American soldiers of fortune: Dead. He drifted to Africa and knocked around, doing what he did best — fighting.

He drifted down to South Africa but didn't like what was shaping up there. He went to the Mideast just to see it all blow up.

It became so confusing there not even the so-called experts could tell what side was fighting whom, and for what reason.

He woke up in a Beirut hospital and was told by a gentleman from the U.S. State Department it was time for him to head on back home. Back to Nebraska.

He had asked why.

Because your mother died about six months ago. The family's been looking for you.

BOOK ONE

THE HOMECOMING

Chapter 1

He hadn't been home in fourteen years. Had never seen several of his nieces and nephews. Hadn't voted in any election in over a decade. Politics and politicians made him nauseous anyway. The outcome of the Vietnam war still rankled him.

It wasn't that he hadn't thought of going back to see his mother and father and sisters and brothers. It was just that whenever he did make plans to return, a war always got in the way.

And now he was—

How old was he? He had to think about that.

Thirty-seven.

Most people his age had kids in high school. Or were married. Or had been. Key Lessard had never married.

Key had loved well but not wisely. He smiled. Oh, he'd been in love. Especially that first time, back in high school. Wow! Had he ever been in love.

He tried to recall her name. Jesus! What was her name?

Was was probably right. Surely she had married by now. Probably had three or four kids. Hell, she might even be a grandmother. For sure, she had married a farmer.

He grinned. Rosanna Emerson.

Yeah. That was it. Pretty, pretty Rosanna. Class of '65.

Twenty years ago. *Twenty years ago!*

And then later, while in the army, there had been—

No! He would not think of her. She came too often into his thoughts as it was.

He shook his head, chasing her away. He thought instead of Rosanna. When he'd flown back home after his first tour in 'Nam, Rosanna and he had had a very awkward meeting. She had shown him her engagement ring. What was the guy's name? Oh, yeah. Skip Gerris. Pretty good ol' boy, too. Damn good tailback.

And I was a pretty fair country linebacker, Key mused. No, he corrected that. Not fair, damned good. Good enough to have had several offers from colleges and universities.

Turned them all down and joined the army.

He hadn't watched a football game in more years than he cared to remember.

Television was still a rarity in many of the countries Key had fought and lived in.

Despite it all, Key still thought he had made the right choice. He would change nothing.

Except for—

Again, he fought away her memory.

Key cut off Interstate 29 and crossed the Missouri River into Nebraska City, taking Highway 2 into Lincoln. Warm summer air fanned him through the open windows of the Grand Prix he'd bought in New

16

York City.

Key had not owned a car since he was eighteen. Never had a need for one.

The crops looked good as he drove the highway. Key did own land.

Ten years back, when his father decided to break up the farm and dole it out to his kids, he had given and sold the land to his four kids. Key had arranged, through letters, to lease out his land to his brothers and sister; more specifically, to that dip-shit she'd married.

He didn't want to think about Lester Kidd, either. God, how could Claire have married that creep?

Key recalled the last time he'd heard from his father. His dad had said a lot of men were losing their farms. Taylor Lessard hadn't gone into much detail as to the why of it, just that it looked bad. Real bad. And when was Key coming home?

Waves of shame washed over him. Fourteen years was just too damned long to stay away. No excuses for it.

And now Mother was dead.

Damn! He pulled into a motel in Lincoln and checked in. He hid a smile as he filled in the registration card.

What name to use?

He had about a dozen he was known by, in various parts of the world.

He signed his Christian name. Key Lessard.

He once asked his father why he had named him Key. His father had told him he liked the name, that's why.

Back in New York, Key had bought, in addition to

17

the new Grand Prix, all new clothing. Three suits, a couple of sport coats and slacks, some jeans and sport shirts, new shoes and Wellington boots. He had bought new luggage; nice leather luggage. A traveling briefcase bar. He'd seen one like it in a movie one time and had always wanted one.

In his twenty years of war, Key had never owned many nice things.

He had once possessed —

He shook her mental face away one more time. "Goddamnit!" he said. "Stay away!"

But he had always wanted to buy nice things for his parents. He kept sending money home, instructing his mom and dad to buy something for themselves. TVs, living room and bedroom suites, carpet — hell, spend it on anything you like.

He wondered if they had.

Probably not.

Opening his little briefcase bar, Key built a Crown Royal and water over a couple of small pieces of ice. He sipped his drink and then showered and shaved. He looked at his reflection in the door mirror.

What he didn't need was one more bullet or knife scar. Wounded four times in 'Nam. Twice in the Legion. Four more times as a merc. He'd picked up that knife scar on his leg down in South America. That knife scar on his chest in Africa. He shook his head. Lots of mileage on a thirty-seven-year-old body.

He finished his drink, dressed in slacks and pull-over knit shirt, and walked outside to sit poolside.

Many of the young ladies were firm and shapely, their swimsuits barely covering the essentials. A

18

couple of the ladies—Key guessed them about nineteen to twenty-two years old—openly flirted with him. He smiled but otherwise ignored them.

Other than the supposed instability of many Vietnam combat vets, their unpredictability and so forth and so on, there was something else most were very hesitant to speak of: The twisted and bent sex drives. Not twisted or bent in a perverted way. But the oftentimes inability to function sexually. Passion and/or lust could lie dormant for weeks, even months, then come in waves. The shrinks tried to explain it, but most combat-torn vets learn early on how to work shrinks, many of them never telling the truth to a noncombat asshole with ten dollar words. And when the passion/lust was not there, *nothing* could bring it. Nothing.

"Don'ttouchmegoddammitleaveme*alone*!"

That's tough for a woman to take. Key had never heard of one who could tolerate it for very long.

She couldn't.

Aw, shit! Key thought. She tried. She really did. In her own way, she did. But Key, at the time, was a knock-around-the-world professional soldier, and she was a very rich, very classy lady. No hope from the start. None at all.

He gritted his strong, even, very white teeth. He had smoked cigarettes until he was thirty, then quit. Not that he particularly gave a damn what was printed on the side of the pack. If people wanted to kill themselves, that was the individual's business. It was just that Key had been out in the field and couldn't get any smokes.

He sat by the pool for a few moments more,

thinking what to do next. It was far too early to have dinner. If he ate now, he'd wake up in the middle of the night ravenous. He didn't want to go into the bar—he hated barrooms. Always some loudmouthed craphead who wanted to start some trouble. Some town bully who thought he was bad.

There was, as Key knew well, a great deal of difference between bad and tough. And Key knew, too, that in many cases, the loudmouthed bullies who thought themselves bad were just tough. Not bad.

Being bad was a completely different story.

Key was both tough and bad.

He stood six feet, two inches. Two hundred and fifteen pounds. Trim waisted, big chest, wide shoulders. Solid. There was not a conventional weapon of war in use throughout the world that he was not an expert with. From pistol and rifle and explosive to 155 howitzer. And everything in between. He held no belts in exotic hand-to-hand fighting techniques. But he was expert in any most could pronounce. Key was utterly ruthless in a fight. He would give no quarter—ever. Fighting was his business. And Key was a good businessman.

His eyes were gunsmoke grey. His hair was worn short, the dark brown peppered with premature gray. His wrists and hands were huge. The fingers blunt-ended, the knuckles scarred.

Not that he would hit a man with his fists—unless he just absolutely had to. Only a fool uses his bare, unprotected fists for a weapon. The hand is such a complex piece of engineering; so many little bones to break. Hurts, too. A better way is the balled fist brought down on an opponents' neck, or onto the kidney. The knife edge of the hand onto the neck, or stiffened fingers into the softness of the throat. The fingers gouging out an eye. The feet and elbows are also excellent weapons.

There is no such thing as a fair fight. Not in Key's mind. There is a winner and a loser, and that's all. There is only one rule in fighting: Win.

At any cost to the opponent.

But Key rarely lost a fight. He couldn't remember the last fight he'd lost. He never started a fight and tried his best to stay away from unnecessary fighting. Fighting was his business. And Key kept a neat profit and loss sheet; the loss column almost void of figures.

And if by chance Key did lose a fight he was pushed into — well — strange things happen at night. Knives flash, a silencer huffs, an arrow sings.

Those who kill for pleasure are sadists. Those who kill for money are professionals. Those who kill for both are —

Mercenaries.

Key Lessard was a mercenary.

One of the best.

Chapter 2

Key carefully knotted his tie and stepped back, inspecting his reflected image.

Conservative suit, conservative shirt and tie, polished, lace-up shoes. He should have looked like a very successful business executive.

But he didn't.

The burnt-in tan gave him away. Years of dust and winds and sun and sweat had hardened his features. Gave him a very slight permanent narrowing of the eyelids. That scar on his forehead. The piece of ear missing. Not a very big piece but noticeable.

Crap! he thought. I still look like the stereotyped Hollywood merc.

Key was not a handsome man in the classic pretty-boy sense. He was square jawed and hard eyed. He did not smile often. There had been damn little in his life to smile about.

Unless one smiles at death and pain. Many of whom could be placed directly at the feet, or hands, of Key Lessard.

He did not now and had not for years given a damn what present style dictated. He wore the clothing that was comfortable to him at the time. He wore his hair short because it was easier to take care of in the field.

There was something about him that made most men very uncomfortable.

He turned off the bathroom light and walked toward the dining area. He ordered a vodka martini on the rocks, prime ribs, salad, and baked potato.

As he took the first sip of his drink, he was conscious of eyes on him. He tried to ignore the sensation. Finally he turned his head to look at the man staring at him.

Guy looked familiar. From a long time ago.

The man began to smile. He pushed back his chair and walked toward Key's table. He held out his hand.

"Key Lessard! Man, it's been years."

Key rose to take the hand. Soft hand. Old memories flood him, the past reaching out to shine through faded memory clouds. "Whit Lockley. You're right. It has been years. Twenty years."

Whit asked Key to join his party. Key accepted the invitation. Not because he and Whit had been that close in high school—they hadn't—but he did so out of curiosity.

He remembered Whit's wife, Linda, a very petite, very pretty blonde. Cheerleader, Key recalled. Nice legs. The others at the table were entirely forgettable, but Key mentally tucked their names away. The men were bankers in Lincoln. Pale faced and fleshy. Soft hands.

"Man, you look great!" Whit said. "You must work out every day."

"Yes, I do."

Whit looked paunchy. Far too much out of shape

for a man not yet forty. He smiled and patted his belly. He grinned. "My chest kind of slipped, Key."

Indeed it had.

"What is your profession, Mr. Lessard?" one of the women asked.

Linda smiled.

Key shifted his eyes. One of his qualities was his bluntness. He never pussy-footed around an issue, instead facing it head-on. "Some people call me a soldier of fortune. It's a nice word for a mercenary."

Conversation did not lag. It just stopped.

Finally, one of the bankers said, "You're joking, of course, Mr. Lessard."

"No. I fight for money." He did not add that he always fought on the side of freedom and democracy. Let these people think what they wished. Key really didn't give a damn. "I left Beirut about three weeks ago."

"*How* did you leave it, Mr. Lessard?" the banker asked.

Key sipped his martini. "In ruins, mostly."

Whit rubbed his face to hide his smile. Linda laughed openly. Whit said, "Let me bring you all to date on Key. Or," he corrected, "as much as I know about him. Key turned down half a dozen football scholarships and went straight into the army from high school. Next we heard of him, he'd been commissioned. Went into the Green Berets. Commanded a . . . let me get this straight: an A-Team, right, Key?"

Key nodded. Yeah, Whit, he thought. Want me to tell some before-dinner stories about 'Nam? I got a thousand of 'em. Leeches, snakes, sweat, blood, pain.

American political betrayal.

And back home, it was take dope, drop out, and call servicemen baby-killers.

Whit said, "Then there was a hitch in the French Foreign Legion. After that, Key became, ah, shall we say, an open market commodity. Ah, rather an expensive item, so I'm told."

"Who told you?" Key asked.

"The FBI."

Key laughed at that.

"You find that amusing?" one of the Lincoln bankers' wives asked.

"Hysterical."

Whit's face sobered. "Key, I'm sorry. I have not said a thing about your mother. Forgive me?"

"Certainly. I didn't know she was dead until a State Department official informed me in Beirut."

"Practically the entire town turned out, Key," Linda said. "She was truly loved."

Key nodded. "How is Dad?"

"He accepted her death," Whit said. "But like so many farmers, he's coping, struggling."

"I keep hearing that."

"If they'd stop behaving as children and run their farms like a business, they'd all be a whole lot better off," one of the Lincoln bankers said.

Key glanced at the man. Had that been malice in his voice? Surely not. "Children?"

"What do you know about farming, Mr. Lessard?" the other banker asked. It was not unkindly put.

"I was raised on a farm," Key said. "But that was twenty years ago."

"It's changed."

25

"Speaking of change," Linda said, "let's change the subject. I hear enough of this in Lewiston." She touched Key's arm with light fingertips. "Are you home to stay, Key?"

"I don't know, Linda. Perhaps. I know I'm tired of war. But that's all I know. And that feeling might well pass. Probably will. It's what I do best."

"Your mother framed your Medal of Honor," Linda said. "She was very proud of it."

"I wondered what happened to it."

"Speaking of behaving as children," a banker's wife said.

Key smiled, looking at the woman, knowing what was coming. He kept silent, waiting for the woman's vocal outrage at his profession.

"Now, honey," her husband said.

"No." she shook her head. "Guns and war. The cowboy mentality. Our cowboy president. Brute strength. Might is right. America, right or wrong. It's sickening."

Key got the impression he was listening to and looking at a suppressed, slightly over-aged flower child. Carefully manicured and coiffeured, who, after venting her speen about those nasty horrible dirty soldiers, would return to her two hundred thousand dollar home, with all the security money could buy, and close the door, shutting reality out.

Rave on, baby.

"Shirley . . ." Linda said.

"Let her talk," Key said, after declining Whit's nod at his empty martini glass. "That's the beauty of this country. Free speech. I've fought in countries where a citizen could be put to death for speaking against the

26

government. I chose a rather strange—to some people, the majority, I suppose—lifestyle. I'm accustomed to defending it."

"Thank you for that, Mr. Lessard," Shirley said. "My brother was, or is, a POW in Vietnam. And for what?"

"For what? For a politicians' war," Key said. "Wars should not be dictated to or run by Congress. That's why we have the military, with its professionals. There should be an amendment to the Constitution forbidding Congress from having anything to say or do about the running of a war. We could have won the war in 'Nam very quickly if the liberals had stayed out of it. It was a moral war. I will go to my grave believing that."

It was obvious to Key that at least half of those at the table did not agree with him. He wondered if any of them had ever heard a shot fired in anger.

"Would you have used nuclear weapons, Mr. Lessard?" the other banker's wife asked.

"No. Five hundred pound bombs would have been quite sufficient. A never-ending wave of B-52s. I would have destroyed North Vietnam. To win a war, ma'am, one must inflict so much pain and suffering on the enemy it becomes unbearable. It must reach the point where the enemy has but two choices: Surrender or die. Eventually, that is how this nation will have to deal with the mounting problem of terrorism."

"It doesn't bother you that innocent people would have been slaughtered?" Linda asked. "The very old and the very young?"

"Of course it bothers me. But didn't innocent

27

people die in London, Berlin, Dresden, Hiroshima, Nagasaki. Certainly they did."

"One man's terrorist is another man's hero," Linda said. "Or something like that."

"Very true," Key said. "In the Mideast, nearly everyone involved has a point. Right and wrong is so twisted it's nearly impossible to untangle. I was getting ready to pull out of there when I got hit."

Shirley looked at him. "Hit?"

"Wounded."

"Oh."

Key looked at Whit. "I knew your father ran the local bank, Whit. Are you in the banking business?"

Did the man suddenly appear slightly uncomfortable? Key thought so. Odd.

"I'm president of the bank, Key. One of the banks in town, that is. Lewiston has grown quite a bit since you left."

"It must have. You sound apologetic, Whit."

"Defensive, Key, is the word. A lot of farmers are blaming the banks for their troubles."

"I've been reading and hearing about the farmers' troubles. Not much, but enough to know there is a problem in this country. Is it as real as it sounds?"

"Here we go," Linda said with a sigh.

Whit joined her in a sigh. He nodded his head. "Yes, and no, Key. Like the Middle East problem, or situation, it's very complex. And there is no short-term fix." Again he sighed, heavily. Dropped his eyes. Lifted them again to meet Key's eyes. "You might as well hear it from me, Key. Your brother-in-law, Lester Kidd?"

Key nodded.

28

"My bank has foreclosed on his farm, the property—everything. It goes to auction Monday. Ten o'clock."

They did not speak of farming after that. They chatted of small things, old friends and old times. After the meal, as soon as he could, Key excused himself and walked back to his room. The news of Lester's losing everything did not come as any surprise to Key. What made him mad was that was Lessard land, deeded to Key's sister, Claire. And Lester had pissed it away.

Lester always had been an asshole.

Key noticed two of Lincoln's less-than-admirable types hanging around the parking lot. Key stayed in the shadows, watching them. They looked in their late teens, early twenties. Punks. One of them carried a pry-bar in his hand. Key did not think he was going to use it to open a large bottle of beer.

Key deliberately scuffed his feet on the concrete. The two spun around. Moonlight glinted off the expensive Rolex on Key's left wrist. Showed the fabric of the tailored conservative suit.

An easy mark for mugging.

Not quite.

The punks looked around them. The shadowy parking lot was quiet and empty; most were in the dining room or watching TV. They circled Key, one to his right, the other to his left.

"Toss your wallet on the ground, man," one punk said. "And slip off that watch."

"You can tell time?" Key asked. "Will wonders never cease? Next you'll be telling me you both can read and write. That would be more than I could

29

bear."

"A real smart-ass, huh, Jimmy?"

"You got it, Robert. *Now!*" he hissed.

Jimmy tried to fake Key out while Robert swung the pry-bar. But when Robert drew back his arm to swing, Key stepped in close, blocking the blow with his left arm and driving his right elbow into the nose of the attacker. Blood spurted as the nose shattered. When Robert's head snapped back under the force of the blow, Key lowered his elbow and drove it into the softness of throat. Gagging and gasping for air, the craphead hit the parking lot.

Key spun and kicked high, the point of his shoe striking the second dip-shit under the chin. The sounds of teeth breaking off and bone shattering filled the air.

"Nothing like a bit of exercise after dinner to settle the food," Key said. He walked to his room and notified the front office what had taken place. He waited for the cops to arrive.

The police were amused but, being professionals, they had to hide that amusement.

"Key Lessard," the field sergeant said. "I read about you a time or two."

"Don't believe everything you read," Key said with a smile.

"There isn't a mark on you," the youngest of the cops noted aloud.

"Just lucky," Key said. He looked at the sergeant. "It won't do a bit of good to press charges; you and I both know that. Just get them out of here." He wrote out the farm's address and gave it to the sergeant. "I can be reached there when some asshole lawyer wants to sue me for violating the civil rights of those dickheads."

The cops laughed. The cops and the civilian all knew where each was coming from.

Alton County lay some fifty miles west of Lincoln, wheat and corn country. Cattle and hogs. America's heartland, so the saying went. But the heart was in trouble. It needed some radical surgery. But a bypass was not the answer.

People had been bypassing the problem for too long.

And Key certainly did not know the solution to the problem.

The previous evening, after Whit's announcement, the topics of conversation never touched on farming. Key could see and sense that Whit was unhappy and troubled about taking Lessard land. But Whit had a board of directors, and Key knew enough about finance to know that someday the principal had to be paid. One simply could not go on living on borrowed money and repaying only the interest. And that applied to the government of the United States as well. It was like, in a way, relying on luck in combat. Luck certainly played a part, but skill and caution were numbers one and two in staying alive.

Key drove with the windows down. It would be much hotter later on in the summer—harsh winters and hot summers—but for now, the weather was warm and pleasant. And Key was experiencing some butterflies in the pit of his stomach. About the same as when he made his first jump.

He had mixed emotions about this homecoming. He had heard other career combat men speak very unkindly of "going home."

Not very many homecomings they had spoken of had proved to be happy ones. Key could believe that. What in the hell did any of them have to talk about? They would meet old classmates whose lives were now centered around mortgages and leaky roofs and braces for the kids' teeth and crabgrass and The Club and playing grab-ass with someone else's wife.

The mercenary community is a relatively small one: Everybody knows everybody else—where they've been working, how it was, how much they got paid. A solid respect builds.

Flashing lights in the rearview cut off his slight silent musings. Key checked his speedometer. Fifty-five. What the hell?

He pulled over to the shoulder of the road and parked, cutting off the engine. He got out and waited while the highway cop radioed in something. He had temporary tags on the Grand Prix. Maybe that was it.

The cop got out and walked toward him, stopping at the Grand Prix's back bumper.

"Keep your hands in plain sight, Mr. Lessard. Don't make any quick moves."

"All right," Key said, as pleasantly as possible.

"All I want to do is talk, Mr. Lessard," the highway cop said. "You are not under arrest, you are not even detained. You may leave anytime you wish."

Now Key was interested. "All right. I'll stay."

"I know you are Key Lessard. You kill for money."

"I *fight* for money, patrolman. I have never taken a contract on another person's life."

The cop did not change expression. "Why are you here, Mr. Lessard? And you don't have to answer that if you don't wish to."

"I'm here because my dad sent for me. I was not aware of my mother's death until a few weeks ago."

"Your mother died six or seven months ago!"

"I could not be reached at the time. State your business, patrolman. I'm getting tired of this roust."

"It isn't a roust. I told you, if you wish to leave, take off."

"Would you like to search my car?"

"I do not have a search warrant, Mr. Lessard."

"And absolutely no probable cause for pulling me over, either."

"That is correct."

"*Will* you get to the *point* of all this!"

The young highway cop hesitated. "Jesus," he muttered. "I should have known the call was bullshit."

"What call?"

The cop sighed. "I got a call last night. Guy said he was from Lincoln. He said you were running weapons in for the TFL."

"The *what?*"

"The TFL."

"What does TFL mean?"

"I haven't the vaguest notion."

"Would you object if I got the keys out of the ignition and opened the trunk?"

"I didn't ask you to do that."

"Trooper, just get out of the way and let me open the goddamned trunk. This is getting ridiculous."

The cop stepped back and motioned Key forward.

The trunk open, Key, over the objections of the young highway cop, opened all his luggage. "As you can see," Key said, "there is nothing out of the ordinary back here except for that stupid-looking spare tire."

The highway cop smiled. "They are funny-looking, aren't they?"

"I don't understand the point of that little tire."

"I don't either. Mr. Lessard, I . . . I'm sorry about all this."

Key shrugged it off. "No harm done."

"I live in Lewiston. I knew your mother. I'm sorry."

"Thank you. What about this TFL?"

"Mr. Lessard, think real hard. Are you *sure* you've never run across those initials?"

"Never."

"Shit!" the cop said softly.

Key did not wish to appear too curious about it. The only difference in cops worldwide was the code of ethics they operated under.

Key looked at the young cop. Twenty-one at the most. His nametag read Cosgrove. "Been a highway cop long?"

"Just got off my probationary period."

"Well, Trooper Cosgrove, if you were to look under that newspaper on the front seat, you'd find a Browning nine millimeter. Cocked and locked. Full. One in the chamber, thirteen in the mag."

"You didn't have to tell me that!"

"But I did."

Cosgrove nodded. "Is the weapon registered?"

Key laughed. "Are you serious?"

A boyish grin spread over the cop's face. "I only

34

have one that's registered myself." He patted the butt of his sidearm. A .357 it looked like. "This one." He held out his hand and Key took it. "Ben Cosgrove. I graduated from high school in Lewiston. You probably knew my brother. I know you did; he told me about you."

I'll keep that in mind, Key thought. "Sure. Ned Cosgrove. Ned farming, I suppose?"

"Not anymore, sir. He lost his farm . . . let's see, last year."

"I'm sorry to hear that. Is there much of that in this part of the state?"

"Yes, sir. A whole bunch of it." He paused, then seemed to make up his mind about something. "That, and a lot of people arming themselves, quite heavily."

"Arming themselves? Against *what*?"

"We don't know. Lots of so-called gun clubs cropping up, too. Well . . ." He retracted that. "Not a *lot* of them. Just enough of the . . . well, wrong element to give law-abiding gun owners a bad name. You know how the national press feels about handguns."

"I've heard," Key said dryly.

"There is just a lot of . . . *weird* groups springing up."

"Weird? Like the TFL?"

"Yes, sir."

"And you thought I might be a part of one of these groups?"

"Yes, sir. You'll have to admit, you're pretty right-wing."

"I sure won't deny that. And I'm sure you heard about that, ah, little incident outside my motel last evening."

Ben smiled. "I might have. Pity you couldn't have killed the little fuckers."

"I would have, if the setting had been right."

"I heard that."

"All right. If I'm approached by one of these weird groups, what's the drill?"

"Join, and then call me. I'm in the book."

"Done. These groups, they're right-wing?"

"Yes, sir. We think they're Nazis."

Chapter 3

"Nazis," Key muttered. "In Lewiston, Nebraska? What in the hell would a bunch of neo-fascists be doing in this part of the country?"

But the rushing winds coming through the open windows of the car did not reply to his question.

Key had shaken hands with the young trooper and driven on, toward Lewiston. Toward home. Ben Cosgrove was young but solid. Short, stocky, and built like a bull. Key got the impression that it would take a very tough man to move the young trooper.

As Key approached Lewiston, the butterflies once more began circling in his stomach. The complex of buildings and land that made up the Lessard's forty-five hundred acres was located to the north of Lewiston. A huge farming operation that included dairy cows. Or at least it had at one time, Key corrected. His dad hadn't mentioned the dairy cows in quite a long time. Maybe they'd gone strictly to farming.

Key's oldest brother, David, and his wife, Martha, farmed fifteen hundred acres of the complex. His other brother, Rolf, and his wife, Jenny, farmed a thousand acres. Key's sister, Claire, and her idiot

37

husband, Lester, farmed another thousand acres. Key owned the last block of a thousand acres. Their father, Taylor Lessard, had retired from active farming.

Key glanced out the open window at the fields of wheat growing under the Nebraska sun. His mind raced backward in time. Back to when he used to spend hours on a tractor or combine. Two more months and it'll be ready for combining.

Then he was at the outskirts of Lewiston. His eyes widened in mild shock. He had expected the town to be larger, but not this much. Fast food places lined the highway. A brand spanking new motel sat by the newly four-laned highway. Over there, his eyes searched, was a new industrial complex holding several large factories. Key wondered what they manufactured. A new shopping center, housing a dozen or more stores loomed up in front of him.

Damn highway had been altered. Christ! He'd better pull over and get his bearings.

Parking on the shoulder of the highway, Key looked around him. "What the hell happened to Lehi Creek?" he muttered.

Then he found the banks of the wandering little creek. He smiled as memories flooded him. He recalled fond recollections of the old Lehi. Right over there; his eyes found the spot, approximate, under that clump of willows, where he'd lost his virginity when he was thirteen. The girl was sixteen. What was her name? Christ! He couldn't remember. All he could remember was that she'd been the daughter of a wheat cutter.

But Key had never forgotten that sweet/hot, sex-filled afternoon.

He slipped the Grand Prix into drive and eased back out on the four-lane. Patrolman Cosgrove passed him. He did not look at Key.

Then Key got turned around at a new intersection. Cursing under his breath, he pulled into a service station to gas up. The man coming out of the station looked familiar to him. But he couldn't put a name to the face.

The man served another customer in the full service lane and then walked over to Key.

"Whatever happened to Blue Valley Road?" Key asked. "I'm turned around."

The man's eyes were unfriendly. Oddly so, Key thought. He watched as the man put a grin on his face. But his eyes remained cold and ugly. "Been gone a long time, ain't you, Key?"

"A good many years." Key stuck out his hand and the man shook it.

"Don't remember me, do you, Key?"

"Yes, I do. Your face. But not your name."

"Zack Moore."

"Sure! How have you been?"

"Good. I own this place. What brings you back to Lewiston?"

"Just coming home, Mr. Moore."

The man's eyes softened. "Taylor and Ira done a good job of raisin' you kids. All of you always did have good manners. Sorry about your mother, Key."

"Thank you. I would have been home sooner, but I was out of pocket."

Zack nodded. His eyes changed, becoming unreadable. "Might talk to you 'bout that sometime, Key.

You get your bearin's and meet old friends for a time. You'll find folks have changed. Test the wind around these parts. Then come back and see me. That'll be twelve dollars and a dime, Key."

Key paid him. "Blue Valley Road?"

"Hang a right at that corner." He pointed. "That's a new street. Little dog leg come up quick. Stay with it. 'Bout a half mile you hang another right. Put you right on it."

"Thanks."

"Don't be a stranger, now, Key."

"I'll be back."

Fifteen minutes later he was approaching the southern edge of the Lessard holdings. Lester and Claire's land. For a little while longer, that is.

God! The land looked good. Clean and white fenced. Fences looked as though they ran forever. Key remembered painting them. Back then he could have sworn they did run forever. He pulled in the drive at the first house. A new house. Expensive. Very. As he was getting out of the car, a voice stopped him cold.

"That's far enough, mister. You bloodsuckers don't get this land till Monday week."

Key carefully closed the car door and looked into an angry young face. The boy held a shotgun in his hands. "I'm not a bloodsucker, boy."

"I got other words that'll suit you just as well."

"You don't even know me." Key looked around him. He saw a new pickup truck, an expensive van — one of those customized jobs — a late model Lincoln, a motorcycle, two three-wheelers, and a kids' sports car, Chevy, he thought. Now what in the hell did one family want or need with all this?

"State your business!" the boy snapped.

"If you're Lester and Claire's kid, then that makes me your uncle. For better or worse," he added dryly.

"You're a liar!" the boy popped off.

Key was just a heartbeat away from taking the weapon from the boy and wrapping it around his neck. He could see the shotgun was on safety, and only two steps separated them.

"Les!" a woman's voice called sharply, hurled from the porch. Key looked up. "Put down that damned gun!" She rushed from the porch into Key's arms.

"Hi, sis," Key said.

Her joy-tears wet his shoulders.

Key's father and two brothers were gone for the morning; gone to an auction down south in the county. Lester had gone with them. Key and Claire stood on the front porch of the expensive home, chatting.

"Come on in, Key."

Inside the home, Key stood in awe for a moment, looking around him. The furniture in the living room alone must have cost ten thousand dollars, minimum. It made Key uncomfortable. He was wary of sitting on any of it. There was a television set with a screen that looked like it had been taken from a drive-in theater. One of the most complicated-looking VCRs Key had ever seen. He had noticed a satellite dish in the side yard. The stereo looked like something straight out of NASA. Key was conscious of his sister's looking at him. Was that embarrassment on her face? He thought so.

41

"Very lovely, sis."

The boy had wandered off somewhere. Very unfriendly little punk. Key had taken an immediate dislike to him.

People pointing guns at him usually tended to cloud the first impression.

"Come on in the kitchen, Key. I *hate* this room."

Over coffee and apple pie, Key looked around the kitchen. He had never seen so many gadgets in his life.

"You use all this stuff, sis?"

"Believe it or not, yes."

"Impressive. You want to explain why you hate the living room? It's beautiful."

She sat down, wearily, heavily, the table between them. "We had three years of bumper crops, Key. Fair prices. Not great, but enabling us to make a profit. Lester went wild. He built this new house. We were living down the road. He bought and spent and tossed money around like he owned a money machine. I didn't want this, Key. We had a nice house. Not fancy, but nice. He, Lester, said he was doing all this," she said and waved her hand, "for me. We had . . . well, we'd had our problems. I'd left him several times. I guess he thought this would impress me so much I'd forget all our problems. I tried, Dad and Mom tried, Rolf and David tried, to tell him to slow down, put some money back, stop borrowing. He wouldn't listen. I'd like to be able to show you his gun collection. Key, he owns fifteen *thousand* dollars' worth of guns."

"I'd like to see them."

"I don't know where they are. About six months

42

ago, when it finally dawned on him that he was going to really lose this place, he took his guns away. I don't know where. Key, he's been acting, well, *weird*, for the last year."

Second time today I've heard that word, Key thought. Weird. Weird was it, all right. "How do you mean weird, sis? Lester has always been a big blowhard."

She smiled at her brother. "You never did like Lester, did you, Key?"

He shook his head. "Can't say I ever have, sis."

"God, you look great, Key. You look, don't take this the wrong way—*hard*."

"Hard life I chose, sis. Back to weird . . ."

"What I meant by it? Well, Lester belongs to some sort of . . . club, I guess you'd call it. He says it's a poker club. But he's lying. I know he is. He's lied so much I can read him like a good book. Let me tell you some of the people in this so-called poker club. You'll remember most of them. Ted Gilbert—he's the sheriff of Alton County now."

"Ted is the *sheriff*? Dear God, help us all."

This time she openly laughed. "Zack Moore, Niles Becker, Dexter Frank, Chris Litton, Wynn Carter, Ernie Hansen. That's just a few that you'll remember."

"Sis." Key took her hands. "Do you realize that you just named some of the biggest assholes in Alton County?"

She giggled; felt good to laugh. "Yes, I do."

"And those are Lester's friends?"

"Some of them."

The back door slammed. Young Les came stalking

through the kitchen. Arrogant was the word that immediately came to Key's mind. And ill-concealed anger. But about what? The farm? Sure, but he felt there was more.

"You want some pie, Les?" Claire asked him.

"No!" the boy snapped at her.

He walked on out of the kitchen. Key resisted an impulse to get up, spin the kid around, and slap the insolence out of him.

Instead, he sat quietly and looked at his coffee cup, keeping his mouth shut.

"Les is not taking all this well," Claire said.

"Yeah. Well, he's young," Key said, rather lamely, he thought. What the hell else could he say?

"Reading between the lines, you'd like to get up and slap the piss out of him," she said. It was not said with any bitterness. Sounded to Key like she'd like to see it. Claire always had spoken her mind.

Key sighed. "Yeah. That's about it, sis."

"Well, come on. I'll ride with you up to the house. Jenny and Martha and me fixed up your old room."

It was like stepping back twenty years in time. The room had not been changed. His high school banner was still on the wall. Go Lions. All the trophies he'd won in football and baseball. His yearbooks were stacked neatly on the bookshelves, along with his volumes of Service and Kipling and Poe and London. The writers who had influenced his young life. Hanging up his clothes, the ladies commenting on his good taste and how they wished they could get their husbands out of boots and jeans once in a while, Key noticed his old high school jacket was still hanging in the closet, along with all his uniforms; his fatigues were starched and pressed. Good, that meant he wouldn't have to buy any knock-around and work clothes. He knew he could still get into them.

And there, right there, hanging far to the side in the closet, was his white sport coat and black trousers he'd worn to the senior prom. *Jesus!* His mother had saved them over all these years.

He put his head against the closet door and closed his eyes for a moment.

"What's wrong, Key?" Jenny asked. "Don't you feel well?"

Key opened his eyes; sort of misty in the room. He blinked a couple of times. "Oh, yeah. Yeah, I feel okay. Just a little tired is all."

"Sure," Martha said. "You must be tired. Why don't you take a nap? It'll make you feel better."

And suddenly, Key was very tired. "That's a good idea."

His sister and sisters-in-law left him. The house in which he was raised became very quiet. He stretched out on the bed and was soon asleep. His dreams returned. Every experienced combat vet has them. If they say they don't occasionally dream about The War, they're either lying, have the soul of a clam, or never saw much combat.

As for Key, he had seen years of combat. Years of suffering and death. His dreams could shift from country to country, heavy brush to desert, jungle to rice paddy, city to farmland, rain to wind to heat to cold. And he dreamed in Technicolor. The blood was real, the screaming was real, the hate and passion and

45

fear and sweat-stink was real. Sometimes when he awakened, he could not be sure exactly where he was. Occasionally, for a few seconds, if his dreaming was too graphic, it took him a few seconds to adjust.

When he awakened this afternoon, he knew some-body was in the room with him. Without opening his eyes, he could sense a presence.

He came off the bed in a roll, going off on the opposite side on his feet. He spun to face the person who had invaded his room.

His father.

Standing in faded jeans and a faded denim work shirt. All seventy-odd years of hard, wang-leather toughness. Big callused hands by his side. There was a twinkle in the faded gray eyes.

"Whoo, boy! I remembered how cat-quick you used to be. You even quicker and meaner lookin' now. And touchy. That's why I just stood for a time and watched you sleep. Not grabbin' at you to wake you. You gonna hit me or shake my hand?"

Key put his arms around the old man.

The warrior was home.

Chapter 4

It was almost like old home week at the old Lessard house. The big two story frame farmhouse. Almost. But underlying the laughter and jokes and heaping plates and platters and dishes of home-cooked food, there was an undercurrent of tension. It seemed to be directed toward Lester and young Les. And no matter how they all tried, the tension remained.

None of the other young people seemed to want anything to do with Les. He mostly stayed by his father's side. And Key knew when kids don't like other kids, especially their own kin; something was bad wrong.

Lester Kidd excused himself early, mumbling about some meeting he had to attend; just couldn't get out of it.

Claire caught Key's eyes. There was a bleak look in her eyes. Key nodded his understanding.

Young Les left with his father.

The tension eased.

"Asshole!" Key's brother, Rolf, muttered.

Key still had not seen Lester and Claire's daughter, Betty. He asked Rolf about her.

"Damn good question," Rolf said. "That kid is wild as the wind. Fourteen last week. I hate to say it about my own blood kin, but Betty runs with some rough company."

Key decided this was not the time to pursue that. He was still having difficulty sorting out and putting names to the faces of his nieces and nephews who were present.

David and Martha had three kids: Glen, Rae, and Walt; twenty, eighteen, fifteen. Rolf and Jenny had three kids: Eddie, Cassie, and Peter; nineteen, seventeen, fourteen. Lester and Claire had two kids: Les and Betty; sixteen and fourteen.

"You'll get 'em sorted out eventually, son," Key's dad said. "Hell, I still get 'em mixed up."

"What's the odds of all of us going together and buying Lester's land at auction come Monday?" Key asked.

"You got two million bucks, brother?" David asked.

"Two *million*?" Key blurted.

"Actually," Jenny said, "it's a bit more than that." She taught school at Lewiston High. A small, very pretty lady in her early forties. "Two point three million."

Key shook his head in disbelief. "How in the hell could he have gotten that far in the hole?"

"When you're a fool, it's easy," Claire said.

"Now, daughter," her father cautioned.

Claire walked out of the room, her back stiff.

"I think when she leaves him this go-around, she'll be done with him," David said.

"Nobody answered my question," Key said.

"Oh, it's easy, Uncle Key," Glen said. Key noticed the young man did not refer to Claire's husband as uncle when he said, "Lester went land crazy and equipment crazy and *things* crazy. He wasn't by himself, though. Lot of people around here did the same. Although a good many hard-working, sensible farmers are losing their farms through no fault of their own.

"You see, Uncle Key, ten, twelve years ago, this land was selling for . . . well, let's just say fifteen hundred dollars an acre to average it out. Lester borrowed against his and Claire's place to buy nine hundred acres about five miles up the road. That cost him a million four. Then the bottom dropped out of land prices. The land he bought and the land he owns and mortgaged is now worth about eight hundred and fifty bucks an acre. He took a half million dollar soaking on the land he bought. Just the interest on the loan is enough to break your back. And Lester wasn't content to share equipment. He went out and bought all new equipment. Well, that sunk him deeper into debt; about another half million or so. Then the bottom dropped out on land prices and wheat and corn. It's just simple arithmetic, Uncle Key. Lester is down the toilet, that's all."

" 'Down the toilet,' " his mother said sarcastically. "Is that what they're teaching you down at Hastings?"

"Lester's output went sky-high," the young man said with a grin. "And his income went poot!"

"Wonderful analysis," his mother said. She walked off to join Claire in the kitchen, shaking her head.

"Mother thinks that because I'm a junior in college I should be speaking like a professor," Glen said, not

49

losing his good-natured grin.

Martha was also a teacher. Key looked at the kids gathered around. Good, solid kids, they appeared. No punk haircuts; the boys weren't wearing earrings; faded jeans and work shirts—boys and girls. The girls were just as tanned as the boys, and while it appeared their hands were not as callused, the girls looked as though they were accustomed to hard farm work.

"We pass inspection, Uncle Key?" Rae said with a lovely smile.

"You sure do." Key returned the smile.

"It's all in how a person is raised, Uncle Key," Eddie said. "Love, understanding, and a firm hand at the reins. I'm a sophomore down at Hastings, and I'm just as different from most of those kids as daylight is dark."

"How'd you kids resist all the dope that's floating around?" Key asked.

"Most of us didn't," Cassie admitted. "I tried it. But you see, Uncle Key, the difference is that I . . . we . . . could come home and talk it out with our parents. We knew we weren't going to get backhanded across the room or screamed at. We could just sit down and talk it out."

Key nodded. "And why do you think that is?"

"Old-fashioned values," fifteen-year-old Walt said quickly. "There is nothing for us to rebel about. Oh," he said and grinned, "maybe music, sometimes."

The other young people laughed.

Key looked around; Claire was still out of the room. "And Betty and Les?"

"One parent can't do it alone," Cassie said. "Aunt Claire tried awful hard. But Lester is a hypocrite.

Don't do as I do, do as I say. You know what I mean, Uncle Key?"

"Only too well."

"I think parents have to be honest with their kids," Glen said. "Parents can't go out and booze it up and then tell the kids they can't do it. Parents can't go out and have affairs with other people and tell their kids sex is wrong. Young people know what's going on around them. Believe it."

Key did. He shifted away from the topic. "Anything in the wind about who is going to buy the land?"

"Oh, we know who's gonna buy it," Dad Lessard said. "Big corporation from back East. Farmin' is big business now, son. I seen this comin' years ago. These folks tryin' to hold onto and farm and make a livin' out of three, four hundred acres aren't doin' nothin' but pissin' in the wind. Way the economy is now— and goin' to be for some time to come—the little family farm is dead. Someone just forgot to kick the dirt over it and bury it. Whole entire families stayin' on the land and everybody makin' a livin' out of it is over . . . for the time being, that is."

Everybody, including Claire, was now seated in the large living room of the original Lessard house, built before the turn of the century by Key's great-grandfather.

"Let's pursue that last bit, Dad," Key said. "What did you mean, 'for the time being'?"

Taylor Lessard waited until Cassie had refilled his coffee cup and placed a couple of sugar cookies on the arm table beside his chair. And everybody knew it was *his chair*. He said, "Everybody here that don't like a bit of cussin' had better head for different parts, 'cause I'm about to let the hammer down." No one left the room.

The patriarch of the Lessard clan said, "I may be an old man; a farmer with dirt under my fingernails and axle grease imbedded in my skin. But I'm no fool. I listen and look and keep my mouth shut. I see things. I see farmers movin' toward violence. Hate groups poppin' up.

"I remember the Depression. Hard times, kids. And we'll have another one. Bet on it. When the bottom drops out, it's gonna be rough as a cob."

He sipped his coffee and ate a cookie. "It pleasures me to know that everything we had for dinner tonight, except the coffee, was raised on Lessard land. Everything. And that's the way it should be. But I know some farmers who don't even have gardens. That's a shame. But then a lot of things goin' on in this world is a shame. Like the price of wheat. Last year, Key, we got the same price for wheat that I got back in 1947. But the cost to farm the same land that I farmed back then has gone up ten times.

"Lester showed me a letter he got from the government, tellin' him he was a bad manager and he'd been followin' bad financial practices. I told him that in his case, that was the gospel truth."

Everyone, included Claire, laughed.

The old man spoke his mind.

"But," Taylor said, "what the government ain't sayin' is that a lot of farmers overextended themselves on advice from the government. The government hollered about large-scale efficient farmin'. Plant fence row to fence row. Some big national magazine said Get Big or Get Out. Well, the farmers got big—now they're gettin' out. Farm writers recommended additional land purchases, sayin' we were gonna have a prosperous decade. Farmers expanded. The Land Bank was fallin' all over themselves handing out money. Other folks just handed out rotten advice.

"You don't know this, Key, but here in the States, back in the '70s, inflation was wild. Farmers had a cost squeeze on them that was forcin' farmers to get more efficient, to farm more land so's they could spread the costs over more acres. But the low commodities are only low to us. Not to the rest of the world. The farmer is not responsible for that.

"We, the farmers, geared up to feed a hungry world back then. We're still plantin', the food is rottin' in storage, and the world is still hungry.

"I ain't never asked the government for nothin'. When we had good years, we laid some back for the bad years we knew was sure to come. A lot of farmers didn't do that.

"A lot of farmers had it pretty good for a number of years. Folks who don't farm thought we had it better than we did; but we still had it pretty good. None of you kids ever wanted for a damned thing that was essential.

"I ain't faultin' anybody for wantin' to better themselves; buy things they didn't have as kids. That's human nature, I suppose. But used to be, a farmer didn't even care who the Joneses was, much less try to keep up with them. Farmers was pretty damned select breed. They didn't just work the land. They *loved* it. I've seen my daddy walk out into a plowed field many times and just stick his hands down in the dirt. He loved the land that much.

"But it's big business now . . . and gonna get worse before it levels off."

David had warned Key that the old man was becoming very vocal on the subject of farming. And, Rolf had added, Pop was losing some friends because of his hardline stance and opinions. But Jenny said that people were reading the old man wrong. Dad Lessard wasn't blaming the majority of farmers for their recent troubles; just the ones who helped bring it on themselves by greed and mismanagement.

"Used to be," Taylor said wistfully, "a farmer raised damn near everything that went on his table. Wife and girls canned and put it up. Family ate off it all winter; had some left over to give to those less fortunate. And the whole family worked. Hard work. The kids worked before school and after school. Saturdays. Sometimes Sundays. Those days were hard days, but they were good days, too."

"Priorities," Key dared interrupt his father.

Faded old eyes locked onto Key's gaze. "That's part of it, Key. Sure is. Like I said, farming is big business now. A piss-poor business, but still big business. Those that come out of this struggle will be, I hope, a lot wiser. But we're all sittin' on a powder keg. And the fuse is lit. City folks don't know what tough and mean is till a farmer gets his back up and starts reachin' for guns. Well, the American farmer's got his back up against the wall. And it scares me."

The old man sighed. "I'm babblin', and I'm tired. I watched a lifelong friend lose it all today. Bank took it. And for all my high and mighty talk this evenin', ol' Roy was just like me, 'ceptin' he had a string of bad luck where I didn't. Now I got a friend who is sixty-nine years old . . . and he ain't got nothin'. The damn bank didn't even leave him the house he was born in. They took *everything*. It ain't morally right, but the lawyers say it's legal, and you know, kids, not bein' right but being legal seems contradictory to me." He stood up abruptly. "I'm goin' to bed. 'Night."

No one said anything for several minutes. Finally, Rolf said, "Let's all adjourn to our house," after first looking at and receiving a nod of approval from his wife.

Chapter 5

Sitting out in the cool night air of the front yard, while a couple of the younger kids watched TV, Key said, "Pop sure got on a tear back there, didn't he?"

"Yes," David said. "But he's not a hundred percent correct."

"You wanna tell him that?" Rolf said with a laugh.

"Lord, no! But he's right to a degree. A lot of farmers haven't managed well. Just like Lester. But the cost of machinery has skyrocketed while crop prices and land value have dropped. I just don't know the answer to it all."

Key leaned forward in his chair. "All right, some of you answer me this: Given today's market and economy, is there even a place for small farmers? I mean, two or three hundred acre farms?"

"No," Glen answered quickly.

"That's college professor talk, boy," his father said, almost harshly.

"You're defending a dream, Dad. A heritage. I don't mean to be uppity with you, but would you like to try making it on two hundred and fifty acres?"

The father shook his head. "No. Sorry I popped

off, boy. You're right. Not unless the man farming that little place had a town job, too."

Nobody seemed to want to continue with the depressing topic.

The faint sounds of gunfire drifted on the wind. Key's head came up. "That's automatic weapons' fire."

"Gun club practicing," Rolf said.

Key looked at his watch. "At nine-thirty at night?" His eyes probed the darkness for muzzle flashes he could not see.

Nobody replied. *Weird*, Key thought. And again, the frequency of that adjective came to him.

What in the hell is going on around Lewiston?

Jenny looked at him and smiled. "I saw Rosanna Gerris today. Still an awfully pretty woman."

Key kept his mouth shut. He sure as hell didn't want to pursue *that* subject.

"Skip is about to lose his place, too," David said. "Run right, that'd be a good place."

"Yeah, with built-in help waiting," Rolf said, laughing.

"You watch your mouth," his wife cautioned him.

As Key realized none of them was going to drop the subject of old girlfriends, he said, "I assume Skip is Rosanna's husband?"

"More or less," Martha said, but did not elaborate.

The lights of a fast-approaching car bobbed on the road. The car slid to a halt in the driveway. Alton County Sheriff's Department. The driver's side door opened and closed.

"Ted Gilbert," Rolf said. "What the hell does he want out here this time of night?"

"Key Lessard!" Ted's voice boomed across the dewy yard. "Get out here!" The voice was heavy and authoritative.

And it irritated the hell out of Key. Ted Gilbert had always been a loudmouthed bully, and like most bullies, underneath all the bluff and bluster, a coward.

Key brought all conversation to a halt when he raised his voice and said, "Fuck you, Ted!"

"Key Lessard is back in town," Zack Moore said, in the meeting room of a hunting lodge used often by the TFL. "Talked to him personal."

"Heard that he was. Heard that Lester ain't none too thrilled about it, neither."

"Lester is a fool," Wynn Carter said, after draining a can of beer. "Man like Key could teach us all a lot."

"If he wasn't sent in here by the government," Ernie Hansen stated conspiratorially, his eyes narrowing.

"Key isn't working for the government," Zack said. "And don't try to look like James Bond, Ernie. You look more like Gabby Hayes."

Ernie mumbled under his breath and went off in search of another beer.

"Speaking of a fool," Chris Litton remarked, when Ernie had left the den of the lodge.

"He's that," Zack agreed. "But he's all right as long as he don't know too much about what we're really doing. And besides, he's a hard worker and as loyal as a dog."

"And about as smart," Niles Becker observed aloud.

Dexter Frank chuckled. "Now you're doing a disservice to the canine kingdom."

"We made a bad mistake letting Ernie get in this deep," another said. "But I don't know how to get him out."

"Leave Ernie alone," Zack said. "Well, we can't discuss anything of importance tonight. Not with Ernie around. So let's join hands, praise the Lord that made white people superior, and get out of here."

Ted Gilbert stood for a few seconds by his patrol car, shocked into silence. A big, solid, meaty man, he was very strong, with a square face and little piggy eyes. He had bullied his way through life, softening his real attitude toward most people with a jolly-good-ol'-boy front. But Ted was dangerous; he enjoyed nothing more than slapping prisoners around. Prisoners he knew he could bully into silence. And Ted's secret, thus far hidden to most people, sexual desires were as twisted as a nest of snakes. Many a young male hitchhiker had discovered the darkness that lurked behind Ted's eyes. And an occasional female hitchhiker.

Ted liked to inflict pain; liked to hear his victims scream.

His face flushed with anger, Ted balled his fists and walked toward the group of people sitting on the front lawn of the farmhouse.

"By God, Lessard, you can't speak to me like that," Ted said.

"Seems like I just did, Ted," Key replied calmly.

"Now what do you want?"

"I want to know what a damn mercenary is doing in my county!"

"Sitting here talking with my family. Is that against the law?"

"It might be."

"You're just as big a fool now as you were twenty years ago, Ted," Key told him.

"Boy, don't you know who I am?" Ted shouted.

"I know who I am. And I've got security clearance from the FBI, the State Department, ATF of the Treasury Department, the Central Intelligence Agency, and a half a dozen other federal agencies I doubt you've ever heard of. Now if you've got something to say to me, you put a civil tone in your voice and treat me as an equal. You understand all that, Ted?"

"By God, Key! I'm the *sheriff* of this county!" he shouted.

"I don't care who you are." Key rose from his chair. Big and solid and hard and mean looking, he faced the man. "You have a warrant for my arrest, Ted?"

"Ah . . . no."

"You have any kind of warrant for me or for any member of the Lessard family?"

"Ah . . . no."

"Then what in the hell makes you think you have the right to come out here in the middle of the night, racing up the road and shouting orders? That type of police tactics went out in America twenty years ago. And this isn't Russia."

"Take it easy," Rolf said, standing up. "Both of you." He turned to look at Sheriff Gilbert in the dim light from the front porch. "What's the matter with you, Ted? Or if you don't want to answer that, perhaps you'd like me to call Ms. Monnet and have her come out here to mediate this hassle?"

"Who?" Key asked.

"Catherine Monnet. Cat for short. She's our attorney," Jenny spoke. "She's made a fool out of Ted about two dozen times in court. I guess it's about time for her to do it again."

Ted choked back a very obscene word. He wheeled around and began walking back to his car. Key's voice stopped him, turning him around.

"I don't think you told me what you really wanted to see me about, Ted. You want to take a seat and talk about it? I can offer you some coffee."

"Big shot, right, Key?" Ted spat the words at him, hate filled. "Medal of Honor and them funny lookin' hats you special troops wear. Think you're hot stuff, right, boy? Well let me tell you this: You ain't nothing but a goddamn Jew-lovin', nigger-lovin' mercenary. And that's all you are."

He slammed the car door and roared away into the night, speeding up Blue Valley Road, taking the long way back to Lewiston, kicking up dust as he headed out the opposite direction from which he'd come.

Key turned to face his family. Questions in his eyes and irritation in his stance. "All right, gang. What's going on around here? As the young people used to say: I'm getting a lot of awfully bad vibes."

But before anyone could, or would, answer his question, more car headlights swept the road. Whoever was behind the wheel was either a very bad driver, or drunk. The answer to that was soon obvious as the car weaved and bucked and slid to a stop. A car door clunked. Young drunken laughter filled the night. A young girl staggered out and tried to walk up the driveway. She giggled as she lost her balance and fell into the ditch. The car, twin glass-packed mufflers growling, took off, abandoning the girl to whatever parental fate awaited her.

Key, still standing, said, "Let me guess the identity of our visitor. Betty."

"You are so right, brother," Claire said, disgust in her voice. She stood up. "Would you help me with her, please?"

"Put her in the bedroom off the kitchen in our house," Rolf said. "No point in trying to carry her all the way to Claire's."

"Rolf . . ." Claire said.

"You're all going to be scattered among us come Monday anyway," Jenny said. "It isn't any imposition, Claire. All right?"

The woman nodded her head. But Key could tell she didn't like it. Charity cut against the grain. "All right, Jenny."

Key walked to the now unconscious girl. She moaned softly as he picked her up. She weighed maybe ninety pounds. And she stunk like shit. She had vomited down the front of her shirt; the whiskey smell was raw. Mixed with another odor. Sex. Key lifted his eyes to Claire.

"I know," his sister said. "God, do I know. I have only one option left me, Key, and that is to chain her to a post."

"You sound like you've given up on her."

"No. I just don't know what else to do."

"She's going to have to have a change of clothing."

"She can wear some of the clothing Cassie's outgrown. We've done it before," she added.

After Key had placed the girl on the bed, he rejoined the men outside. The woman had all gone into the house.

"Anybody want to answer my question?" Key asked.

From the wall of silence that greeted him, Key gathered that no one did.

"When you're ready," he said. "I think I'll walk back up to the house and go to bed. See you all in the morning."

Key got up before dawn. He had slept well and felt refreshed. But it should have been dawn according to Key's inner clock. Then he remembered his father's telling him about daylight savings time. Few farmers liked the system, and Key certainly agreed with that. It was like a great many things the government got their hands on; screwed up.

Hell, it was *dark* outside.

His father was already up and had coffee made. He laid more strips of bacon into the pan and more potatoes to fry in another pan.

Key poured a cup of coffee. "Should be daylight out," he bitched.

"Gives the town folks more time to play," Taylor said. "Grown-ups have to have their playtime, you know."

Key could tell his father was not in a real peachy mood this morning.

Leaning against the counter, sipping his coffee, Key told his father about the gunfire he'd heard the night before. Or the hours past. It was still night. He told him about Sheriff Gilbert's visit and the things Ted had said.

His father busied himself frying eggs. He did not reply.

Key did not understand his father's silence. "Hell, I can't even get a straight answer from my own *father*!"

Without looking up from the pan of eggs, Taylor said, "Butter the toast, boy."

Over a breakfast of bacon and eggs and fried potatoes, homemade preserves and toast, Taylor said, "You work for the government, boy?"

"I have in the past."

"That don't answer my question. CIA?"

"I have worked for them. I'm not working for any government agency or anyone else for that matter. Not now. I don't know what I'm going to do. Why?"

"Well, probably a lot of folks around here think you are working for the government. Don't matter to me. Just remember, you got a pretty checkered past, boy."

"Checkered in the minds of the majority, I suppose. I won't deny that. But I still feel that something very . . . weird is going on in this county."

That word again.

"Betty come in all drunk and doped up again last night?"

"Drunk. I can't say about the dope part. Don't change the subject, Dad."

"Thought she probably would. Girl's got a problem. Claire's gonna have to put her in one of them

64

homes, I reckon. And I'll change the subject if I want to."

Key smiled. The old man hadn't changed a bit.

"Boy, you go prowl around town some. Listen more than you ask. You'll find the answers to your questions. But you watch that damn Ted Gilbert. His elevator don't go all the way to the top. Never has. He don't like you and he can make things hard for you. He ain't got one deputy working for him that's worth a shit for anything. Mean bunch. But they do their meanness on the sly. If you know what I mean."

Key knew. A roust is nothing new to a mercenary. But mercs have their own way of handling being unfairly rousted by bad cops.

And it can get downright unpleasant.

Key wanted to make some phone calls, but he'd hold off on that until he had a few more facts. And he'd do it from a pay phone.

Key left the house at eight. CDST. He drove into Lewiston, once more familiarizing himself with the town he once knew so well. A deputy sheriff's car followed him wherever he drove, staying a block behind him. After about fifteen minutes of driving aimlessly, Key had all he could take of it. He pulled over to the curb and got out. He thought he knew what Ted had in mind—but Ted never had been too smart.

Key wondered how in the hell the man ever got elected sheriff.

Even though Key had not lived in Nebraska for years, he still had a valid Nebraska driver's license and a permanent address at the farm.

He leaned against the car, waiting, his driver's

license and car registration in hand.

When the deputy, a very unfriendly-looking young man, maybe twenty-five, pulled in behind him, Key took the offensive. He walked to the patrol car and held out the papers. "You want to see these, officer?"

The deputy cut his eyes and nodded. He radioed in the driver's license number and car registration. Key stood patiently, his cold eyes never leaving the deputy's face. It began to make the young cop nervous.

"Ah . . . mister, you wanna go stand away from this car?"

"No."

Cops are not accustomed to being disobeyed. "Huh?" he said.

"I said no."

Before the deputy could respond to that, dispatch called him. Nebraska DMV was swift. No wants, no warrants, valid driver's license, car tags applied for.

The deputy silently cursed. Sheriff Ted had been wrong. Now what? Hassling folks could get very iffy. Especially some mean-lookin' son of a bitch like this Key Lessard.

The deputy handed the papers back to Key.

"Anything else, officer?"

Key knew from the expression on the cop's face that he had made a lasting enemy. There is a surprising number of ex-lawmen in the mercenary field, and a lot of police knowledge rubs off if one will just listen. Key knew that, for the most part, the old cop days were gone forever, and he personally thought it a good thing. He knew, again from listening to cops talk, that many supreme court decisions had irritated most cops. He also knew, again from listening to ex-cops — now that they were *ex*-cops, and standing on the other side of the line — most of those decisions made sense. Not all, but many of them. It goes back to that old saying that reads, Don't judge another man until you've walked a mile in his boots.

"Officer, look at me," Key said.

The deputy's eyes shifted. Mean eyes.

"As soon as I get to a phone, I am going to place a call to the FBI, the CIA, and the Treasury Department. I am going to ask them to teletype to your sheriff, their reports clearing me of *any* criminal activities or charges. Deputy, for six of the last twelve years, I *worked* for various overseas departments of the U.S. Government. I worked in countries where people of your ilk would not last ten minutes. Now, deputy, when that is done, your entire department will know that my driver's license is valid, the car is paid for and in my name; you will know that I am a legal, taxpaying, property-owning resident of the state of Nebraska. Sometime today, I am going to see a Ms. Catherine Monnet. I am going to tell her that the Sheriff's Department of this county is hassling me. I want that on record. If I am hassled again, I am going to sue Ted Gilbert's department on so many harassment and civil rights' violations you are going to think the Wailing Wall fell on you. Is that clear?"

The deputy grimaced, his brow wrinkling. "What kind of wall?"

He then stuffed his mouth full of chewing tobacco.

Key looked at him. "You are a *dumb* son of a bitch!"

The deputy almost choked on his chaw. He managed to keep from swallowing the cud and shifted it around in his mouth with all the grace of a cow. "If I wasn't wearin' this badge, Lessard, I'd whip your ass."

"Then take it off and name the spot." Key knew he was making a mistake. Knew that with people like this deputy, there was no hope. He was pure redneck. But Key hated rednecks; always had. Key could not now and never had been able to tolerate ignorance. Not when people wore it like a badge of honor.

The deputy spat. "You know where the Carson Pond is, boy?"

"Shore do, boy," Key mush-mouthed the mimicry, enjoying the red flush that crept up the redneck's neck.

"I'll meet you there in about twenty minutes."

"I'll be there."

Both men walked to their cars and drove off, toward the old swimming hole.

Key found the place without trouble. He waited, wondering if the deputy was going to bring reinforcements with him. Somehow, he doubted it. For one thing, the deputy wouldn't want Ted to know about it.

But on the other hand, the deputy might want people around him when he whipped Key's ass. And the deputy was sure, Key felt, he was going to do just that.

The deputy was in for a very rude awakening.

Key watched the patrol car pull up to the spring-fed pond. The deputy was alone. The man removed his Sam Browne equipment and took off his shirt. Well-muscled young man.

The deputy hitched at his trousers and walked

halfway to Key's position. "Well, come on, Lessard. I ain't got all day to fuck around with you."

"You that anxious to get our bones broken, deputy?"

"Get out and fight!" he yelled. "I'll teach you some respect for the law."

Key shrugged and moved away from his car. "If that's the way you want it."

Key moved swiftly. With a practiced and combat-tested maneuver, he kicked the deputy on the kneecap. The man yelled in pain, his hands instinctively grabbing for the hurt knee. Key chopped him on the side of the face with the edge of his hand. The man grunted in pain and stumbled backward. Key spun, his left foot catching the man on the other side of his face. The deputy went to one knee, his face bloody. Spinning, Key kicked him in the kidney, the blow bringing a howl of pain.

Then, very uncharacteristic for Key, he stepped back, allowing the man some recovery time.

The deputy looked up at Key, his eyes mirroring his disbelief at what was taking place. For all his life, as long as he could remember, people had told him how bad he was. His football coach, his girlfriends, all his friends. Something was really wrong here.

"Fight fair, you fucker!" the deputy yelled.

"Come on," Key told him. "You going to squat down there in the dirt all morning?"

The man lunged to his feet and charged Key, trying to bull him to the ground.

Key tripped him, sending the man sprawling, face first in the dirt.

Key laughed at him.

The deputy began crying in his total rage. He cursed Key as he rose to his feet. He swung a looping roundhouse right at Key's face. Key grabbed the man's wrist, turned, put his hip toward the man, and used the deputy's forward motion to aid in returning the man to the ground. The deputy hit the dirt hard, the air whooshing out of him.

"I'm really getting very weary of all this," Key told him. "I wish to hell you'd fight and stop assing around."

The deputy finally got it through his thick skull. He snorted into the dirt as the realization struck home that if he continued with this, Key Lessard was really going to hurt him.

Key Lessard was *playing* with him.

"Next time I'll bring some of my buddies," the deputy said.

"Yes, I expect you will. But keep this in mind: The next time, I'll kill you. And I'll do it with my bare hands, and do it so quickly you will not know what happened until your Maker pokes you in the ribs."

He left the deputy still sprawled on the ground. Key got in his car and drove off. He simply did not like to be hassled.

Back in town, he stopped at a pay phone and after consulting a small pocket address book, dialed a number just outside Washington, D.C.

"Key?" the man's voice said, after assuring him his request would be honored. "You just might be up to your ass in a snake pit out there."

"Run it down for me, Jeff."

"It's sketchy, Key. We just stumbled on it ourselves. It's some sort of survivalist/hate group/white supremacy/KKK/Posse Comitatus thing. Key, the company can't technically get involved. Just consider yourself back on the payroll."

Jeff hung up.

"Crap!" Key muttered. But he knew the rules: A favor asked and granted was a favor requested and followed through.

All right.

He drove past his old high school. It was being torn down. A lot of memories being destroyed. He drove on. Found a brand new, very modern high school. On impulse, he pulled in the drive and parked amid several dozen cars. Summer school was in session.

He walked into the air-conditioned building and looked into the glass-enclosed office to the left of the hallway. He smiled as a short, stocky man looked up and met his eyes. The older man's face wrinkled with a grin. He waved Key inside.

The two men shook hands. "Key! It's so good to see you. How in the world are you?"

"Fine, Mr. Warner. I was wondering if you'd still be coaching."

"No. I hung that up ten years ago. I'm principal now. Key, you look in fabulous shape."

"Thank you, Mr. Warner."

"Can that crap. I'm Ken and you're Key. Let's get some coffee."

The former coach and former linebacker chattered of old times and old friends and old games for half an hour. But Key could tell the older man was worried about something. Maybe he'd get to it.

"How's your homecoming thus far, Key?"

"The homecoming was fine. I just whipped the shit

71

out of one of Ted's deputies, though."

Ken looked at him. "Are you serious?"

"Yeah."

"Who was he?"

"Hell, I don't know."

Did the older man pale? Key thought so. "No big deal, Ken. Something is nagging at me, coach. Maybe you can clear it up?"

"You whipped a deputy! God, Key!"

Key noticed the man's hands were trembling. This was not the Coach Warner Key remembered. "Forget it, coach. It's either over, or it isn't. About the other thing? . . ."

Warner sighed. "Well, let's hear it."

"What's going on in and around Lewiston?"

Did the eyes of the man grow wary? Key thought so. Again that word popped into his mind: Weird.

"Key . . . you've been gone a long time. A lot of things have changed around this part of the country. You've noticed the number of small factories in town?"

Key nodded.

"Lewiston is rapidly becoming a small industrial area."

Key waited.

"That isn't what you wanted to hear, is it, Key?"

"That's probably part of it. But there has to be more."

The man stared deeply into Key's unblinking eyes. "Yeah," he whispered. Key had to strain to hear. "We'll keep our voices low."

"All right," Key whispered. He felt like a fool. Christ! What was going on?

72

"Might as well level with you," Ken whispered. "You're probably working for the FBI."

"Ken," he said, lowly and patiently. "I have never worked for the bureau. I did work for the agency—the CIA—and I've worked for various other spook groups; all of it overseas. I've run guns into places you've probably never heard of, and probably don't want to hear of. I am a highly paid mercenary. I have never denied it. I've worked as a weapons' expert and guerrilla warfare expert all over the world. But I am not employed by the FBI—okay?"

Ken sighed heavily, almost painfully. "What do you want to know, Key?"

"For openers, why is Ted Gilbert and his department putting the hassle on me?"

Ken stood up, glanced suspiciously around him. "Let's go for a walk outside. I'll show you the new football stadium."

The man is absolutely, totally paranoid, Key thought. Does he think his office is bugged? Maybe. "Ken, you're behaving as if you're afraid of something."

The man's eyes looked almost wild. "I am, Key. I'm scared to death!"

Chapter 6

The Fear

"Of what, Ken?" They were outside, walking in the warm air of summer in Nebraska.

"Where to start? Well, what does your family have to say about it? Your sensing of something being wrong?"

"Nothing. After a couple of tries, I gave it up. I feel like I'm talking to a brick wall. I heard automatic weapons' fire last night. Submachine guns in Alton County. I thought I'd left all that behind me. Gun club, the family said. Ted Gilbert tried to hassle me last night. And so did one of his deputies this morning. Ken, it doesn't take a genius to figure out that something is wrong around here."

"They think you're working for the government, Key."

"Well, what if I was?" Key challenged. "What is going on that would make the citizens so afraid?"

The men climbed into the stadium and sat down. Key's eyes picked up a flash of sunlight reflecting off glass. Without appearing to do so, Key's eyes searched the street north of the stadium. An unmarked car with a whip antenna was parked on the street. Key kept that knowledge to himself.

"The Truth, The Faith, The Lord," Ken said, the words rushing out of his mouth as though they contained a bad taste.

Key suspected they did. TFL. He kept his face bland. "What in the world is that, Ken?"

Ken sighed. "Gone this far; might as well jump on in. I'll break it down into three parts. The Truth: Jesus was not a Jew. He was a blond-haired Aryan, theoretically of British, Germanic, and Scandinavian peoples. The Jews rewrote the Bible casting themselves as the Chosen People. Writing pure Aryans out.

"This is *their* philosophy, Key — not mine.

"The Faith: All nonwhites will be destroyed in a final war — the Bible's Armageddon — and true believers will build and live in the new Israel. *All* nonwhites, Key. Destroyed.

"More of the so-called Faith: Jews and blacks are behind all the farmers' troubles. The Jews in America control the money; the Jews have always been sympathetic to the black cause. The Jews are taking the land away from whites to eventually give to the Blacks. All nonwhites are evil."

Key could not believe what he was hearing from this intelligent, highly educated man. He sat very still, listening.

"They believe that Jews, blacks, and other minorities have sprung from Satan and are subhuman. They believe the Federal Reserve System is controlled by a cabal of Zionist bankers. The IRS is illegal. The TFL is utterly ruthless, Key.

"You'll find out more; I'm just hitting the high

places. Or the low, depending on your point of view. "The Lord: Believe in the Lord—the fair-skinned Lord—and whites will very soon rise up to fight and kill all nonbelievers and reclaim what is rightfully theirs.

"Kill all people not of the white race, Key!"

Key sat and stared at the man. Finally, he blurted, "Are you fucking serious?"

"Yes. Unfortunately. But there is so much more about the TFL that I don't know, Key. You drive through town some this morning, Key?"

"Yes, quite a bit."

"Other than the new streets and buildings, did you notice anything different?"

Key thought back. Something had nagged at the back of his mind, but he never could bring the elusive *it* into clarity. "Well, yes. But I don't know what."

"Steinbergs is gone."

Yeah, Key thought. So it was. Steinbergs Department Store had been a landmark of Lewiston's main street. Old Mr. Steinberg, the great-grandfather, had been one of the founding fathers of Lewiston. Back before the turn of the century.

"What happened to the store?"

"It was remodeled and then it burned down one night. I don't know all the details, but the banks here in town—so the story goes—refused to loan Scott Steinberg any money. I don't know the reason. Scott just took his family and moved east. St. Louis, I think."

"Was it arson?"

"The fire marshal says it wasn't. But if I was a betting person, I'd bet he belongs to the TFL."

"It's that widespread?"

"I think so. See any blacks in town, Key?"

He had not.

And he really didn't want to ask what happened to them. But he did.

"Well, Key, there never was many blacks in Lewiston. But we never had any patience with prejudice, as you can remember. Nobody ever thought anything about color around here. Not until, oh, four or five years ago, that is. That's when the TFL first stuck its ugly slimy head out of the ground. It's scary, Key. The TFL remained silent, unseen, and powerful for almost three years before the state patrol got wind of them. Even now, the patrol really doesn't know who is part of it and who isn't. Not really; not enough to do much about it."

"You didn't tell me what happened to our small population of blacks, Ken."

"They left. Some lost their jobs; some were bought out—that's speculation; others suddenly received very lucrative job offers in larger cities. There isn't a single black person left in the county, Key. And not many left in the surrounding counties."

"Hispanics, Indians?"

"Damn few. And those remaining keep a very low profile. They leave if they get a chance. They're staying scared. And quiet."

Key shook his head. "Ken, excuse me, but if it was as serious as you claim, the FBI's civil rights people would be on here in force, checking it out."

"No, Key. You're wrong. No one has been hurt. At least no one that will talk about it. I've heard that blacks have been relocated around the nation—free

77

of charge. Key, if a store closes and people lose their jobs, no one's rights have been violated. After . . . well, *certain* people leave the area, the store reopens, under a different name. I know some subtle threats have been used. Very subtle threats. Finance companies don't *have* to loan money to people. Not if collateral is shaky. A bad credit report can ruin a person, and has, several times, right here in this county. And the banks can do the same thing."

Key cut his eyes. The unmarked car was still parked across the street. He wondered if they had a telescope microphone. He hoped not. "Banks. Banks. The biggest bank in town belongs to Whit Lockley, right?"

"That's right."

Key waited. Finally he said, "And you're not going to say anything more about Whit, right, Ken?"

Silence greeted the question. No doubt about it, Ken was scared.

"You owe Whit's bank money, Ken?"

"I put a new roof on my house, added a room and had to buy a lot of expensive home-care products for my wife a few years ago. Whit keeps me going."

Ken wanted to pursue that 'home-care' bit. He felt Ken would get around to it without being pushed. But Key was getting the message of quiet pressure. And fear. Ken stank of fear. "How big is the TFL, Ken?"

Ken shrugged. "No one really knows. How big is the KKK, the Posse Comitatus, the Aryan Nation, the Cross, the Sword, and Covenant — all the others? There are those who think they're all intertwined; same group but with different names to throw off the authorities. It's big, Key. Big and scary and getting bigger."

"The industries, Ken?"

"What do you mean?"

"Who owns them?"

"I don't know, Key. And that's the truth. Various people, I guess. They're not stock companies. They're privately owned. I'm sure that none of them are listed on the stock exchange."

"Interesting. Just little, privately owned companies making their little products and attracting no attention. By the way, what *do* they make?"

He looked blank for a moment. "Why . . . well, one of them makes furniture. Office furniture, I think. Another one makes some sort of gizmo for the army." He paused, looking thoughtful for a moment. "Come to think of it, I think they *all* have government contracts."

That was what Key had hoped Ken would not say. But it came as no surprise. But if it went any deeper, it would sure complicate matters.

After Key did some prompting, Ken opened up, the words coming in a rush. And Key believed the man was telling the truth. Ken was very frightened. He told Key that although he had never actually been threatened in any tangible manner, Ted Gilbert had come to see him one afternoon, late. The sheriff smiled a lot. Very friendly; good-ol'-boy manner. Wanted to know how the school system was running now that all the niggers and Jews and spics were gone. Ken had said fine. He didn't know how to take the question. Ted had said that whites had to stick together; it was too late for some communities, but not for Alton County. He had told Ted *they* had been watching him for some time.

They?

He didn't elaborate, Ted said. Just said that *they* knew everything that went on in the county. And that *they* knew who was against them and who was on their side.

At that point, Ken had looked at Key with tears in his eyes. "I'm sixty-two years old, Key. Not the man I used to be. Kathy, you remember my wife, Kathy? She's bedridden; has been for a long time. Shortly after Ted's visit, I went home one evening, and the regular nurse who had looked after Kathy for three years was gone. I asked where she was. The woman smiled and said from now on *they* would see to my wife's needs and well-being. She said *they* take care of their own. It was at that point I really got the message, Key."

Insidious, Key thought. Cancerous. "What have they demanded of you, Ken?"

"That's the odd part, Key. Nothing tangible. Nothing I could take to court. Last year, when we had to hire some new teachers, Ted came to see me. Said he probably didn't need to tell me this, but he just wanted to remind me to pick my new teachers very carefully."

"Carefully. That could be taken in ten different directions."

"Sure."

"But he didn't specifically tell you not to hire minorities?"

"Oh, no."

"Slick. Ted's smarter than I gave him credit for being."

"No, he isn't. Not really. I had both of you in class,

remember? Ted is ignorant. What's worse is he's proud of that ignorance. Someone is behind Ted. Ted is not the leader of this . . . cell of the TFL."

"And you have no idea who that person might be?"

"Not . . . really."

Key didn't push it. "I'm staying out with Dad, Ken. Anybody, *anybody* starts leaning on you, you call me, and I'll do some ass-kicking."

Ken smiled. His eyes had lost some of their haunted look. "I will, I promise. Key, please don't say you heard any of this from me."

"You know I won't. But just to make it look good, coach, how about getting a football and tossing me a few passes?" Key laughed at Ken's laughter, and the men stood up. He said nothing about the unmarked car.

That was still there. Mute and silent.

"LC nine to LC one."

"Go one."

"On tach."

"On tach. Go."

"Two subjects talked for a time, then started laughing. They're out in the middle of the football field, tossing a football around and acting like kids."

"Ten-four. Go on back to patrol. The old man didn't say anything. He's too scared. LC one out."

Sheriff Gilbert turned to the man sitting in the seat beside him. "Everything is just as fine as wine." He grinned.

"Don't be too sure," the man cautioned. "Key is anything but a fool. You keep an eye on Warner. He's soft and breaking. And tell your goddamned stupid deputies to stay away from Key. After what happened this morning, they should realize Key is an expert in fighting. How is your deputy?"

"Bruised and banged up some. Hurt ego. Said Key handled him like a baby. That won't happen with Stan, though. Stan can take Key."

"I doubt it. Just keep him away from Key."

"Yes, sir. Oh, that stuff Key told my deputy he was gonna have teletyped in? From them government agencies?"

"Yes."

"It come in. Key's clean as a whistle with most agencies, but a bad boy with some others. But nothing to arrest him on."

"That's what I expected. Key doesn't know how well connected we are in Washington. But don't hassle him. Leave him alone. We don't want any government people in here. I think Key is all right. I think he just wants to farm."

"Yes, sir. I reckon I'd better try to explain why I done what I did last night."

"You were drinking. You lost your head. Stupid. Just don't let it happen again. Keep your hatred for Key under control."

"Yes, sir."

The man got out of the patrol car and walked to his own car. He drove off.

Ted Gilbert shot silent hot daggers of hate toward the moving car. "It ain't just Key I hate, you son of a bitch! I hate your guts, too. I'll kill you someday. Bet on it."

He started the unmarked patrol car, floorboarding

the pedal, digging out in his hot rage.

Long after Key had left the football stadium Ken Warner sat in the stands. His thoughts were many — and frightened. He didn't think Key had noticed the unmarked sheriff's car across the way. But Ken had. And it frightened him. He didn't know how much more he could take. He hated himself for his fear. He had always been a strong man, mentally and physically.

Until this TFL thing had reared up, like some ugly, silent, rabid beast, infecting all their lives. And what was so bad was that he knew he was virtually powerless to combat it.

And Kathy knew something was wrong. Very wrong. She was bedridden but not stupid. She knew, and his fear was touching her, as well.

He couldn't permit that to happen. He *would not* permit that to happen.

There was a way out. Yes. There certainly was.

But he wondered if he had the courage to do it.

Key drove the back roads, wandering, getting more feel of the country, remembering times and places past. He pulled off the county road onto what had once been — and probably still was — lovers' lane. He parked his car under the shade of a huge old tree and got out, squatting down. Willows concealed car and man from any traffic that might be coming from the north.

Something evil was taking place in Alton County.

Something evil and ugly and very profane.

Key toyed with the idea of just saying to hell with it and getting out.

He glanced up at the sounds of a car driving slowly south. Whit Lockley, behind the wheel of a big Cadillac. He had a serious look on his face.

"Now what in the hell would *he* be doing way out here?" Key muttered.

Key waited. About two minutes later, an Alton County Sheriff's Department car came driving south, Ted Gilbert behind the wheel. His face looked tight with anger. Neither man had noticed Key or Key's car.

"Whit and Ted," Key spoke to the sighing winds of summer. "Now isn't that interesting."

84

Chapter 7

Key gave it several minutes and then drove back to Lewiston, taking a different route from the one taken by Whit and Ted. While he had waited, he thought about and rejected his idea of taking off. He could not leave his father and brothers and sisters to face this horror.

That was the best word he could come up with to describe it.

Other than -- *weird*.

On the outskirts of Lewiston, at a service station, Key called a friend of his down in Georgia. He inquired about price, haggled for a few moments, then instructed the man to ship him an M-16, half a dozen extra mags, and a couple of thousand rounds of ammo. Not the new type of 16, but the older, fully automatic model.

Anything else?

Yeah. You got a case of grenades handy?

Sure. You want me to mix them up?

Yeah. Incendiary, frag, HE. Stick it all on UPS and mark it camping supplies. Rush it.

Day after tomorrow okay?

Fine.

Key smiled. It's easy to buy arms in almost any country in the world — especially the communist bloc nations — if you know who to call and they know you.

He consulted the phone book and found the address of one Catherine Monnet, Attorney at Law. He punched out the numbers, identified himself, and asked if he could stop by and see her.

She was just leaving for lunch.

Well . . . might he buy her lunch?

A short pause. Very well, if he could be there in five minutes.

He could, since he had just found the street marker and discovered he was right down the block from her offices.

Cat Monnet was one of those truly astonishingly beautiful women. Classic beauty. The type of woman that has a tendency to make most men nervous. Hair the color of golden wheat, deep blue eyes. Perhaps five-six. As the little fellow put it: a ten. She cast an exterior coolness that Key felt was a defense field, that, because of her beauty, she had been forced to erect over the years. Early to mid-thirties.

She likewise appraised Key, concluding he was everything — and probably more — she had heard about him from his family. She detected a solid barrier around the man.

"Do you like pizza?" she asked.

"I used to," he said with a grin. The smile softened his features, chipping away some of the hardness. "But it's been a long time since I've tried it."

"Leave your car here. One of the deputies is sure to see it and report back to that nitwit of a sheriff."

Key laughed. He immediately liked this lady.

"Why are you laughing?" she asked.

"Because I think we share the same opinion of Ted Gilbert."

"I rather doubt your opinion of the man is as low as mine."

"Don't bet on it. I've known him all my life. Ted hates me."

"Let's pursue why Sheriff Gilbert hates you," she said, after they had ordered lunch.

The pizza place was a chain, but nice. A family place where two people could be seated for an adequate degree of privacy.

"Why Ted hates me? Ted is a bully. Always has been. He tried to bully me when we were young boys. Eight or nine years old. I whipped him. We were in the same class all the way through school. In high school, Ted was—" He chuckled. "*Sweet* on Rosanna Emerson. Her name is Gerris now. Seems like I beat him out of everything he ever wanted. But I didn't do it intentionally. I didn't plan it; it just worked out that way. I beat him out of a first team linebacker slot and then started going steady with Rosanna. He despises me. Swore back then that someday he'd 'get me.' "

"He is now in an excellent position to do just that," she reminded him.

"Oh, he's already begun. That's one of the reasons I wanted to speak with you. To get it on record."

He doesn't talk like a mercenary, Cat thought. Oh, sure! Now you're an expert on mercenaries, huh? How many mercenaries have you spoken with? None. That you were aware of, that is. "How so?"

Key explained.

87

She smiled when he told of asking various government agencies to teletype his record to the Alton County Sheriff's Office. "Will they do that for you?"

"Some of them will, I'm sure of that. I don't want any trouble with Ted or his people, but if it comes my way, I'll handle it."

Cat felt a slight tingle of excitement as she looked at the man and listened to his words. She did not need a guru to know how Key Lessard would 'handle it.' As an attorney, she felt compelled to warn him. "Don't go off half cocked, Mr. Lessard."

"Full cock, Ms. Monnet. Cocked and locked. Always." He smiled. "And my name is Key."

"Cat."

"Fine. Here comes the food. Lord, look at the size of that pizza."

They talked over lunch; vocally feeling each other out, testing the waters. Both were conscious of a spark leaping about, touching first one, then the other.

She was from the Midwest — Chicago. Practiced law in Chicago for a few years. Made a solid name for herself. She came to Lewiston five years ago, doing research on a case. She liked the small-town pace and decided to stay.

Was she related to the Chicago Monnets?

Yes. Daughter.

Key arched an eyebrow. He had heard of them all his life. That made Cat a very wealthy woman.

That would explain the invisible field around her.

The conversation shifted to his family and what he planned to do.

Farm.

She smiled at that. "You've been a combat soldier for all of your adult life, Key. Can you just turn it off that quickly?"

"I can sure try."

They were aware of eyes on them, even in the relatively private section of the restaurant. They were seated out of earshot, but not out of line of sight.

Over coffee, Key said, "I suppose we'll soon be the talk of the town."

"I'm sure. Small town. You mind?"

"Not at all. You are the Lessard family attorney, right?"

"That is correct."

"I'd like to have you on retainer."

"Fine."

"What's going to happen to my sister after Monday week?"

"Financially?"

"Yes."

"She isn't in that bad a shape. When I set up practice here, she came to see me. That was during one of her separations from Lester. At that time she held several pieces of land. I arranged the sale of them and placed the monies into good solid ventures. She's going to have to watch her finances; not going to be able to take cruises or extended vacations in Paris. But she'll be all right."

She looked at him strangely.

"Are you wondering why my family didn't discuss this with me?"

"It crossed my mind."

"I've only been home about twenty-four hours. It's been hectic. And . . ." Should he level with her? She studied his face as he paused. Was this beautiful successful woman a part of the TFL? He didn't think so; but he could not be sure. He'd already gotten his boots wet. Might as well wade on in up to his knees. "To tell you the truth, Cat, I'm having a difficult time getting straight answers to questions from nearly everyone in my family. And I don't understand it."

"Perhaps they don't know what side you're really on," she said.

"I keep hearing that. Are we choosing up sides? What game is going on around here?"

She glanced at a diamond-encrusted watch. "I've got an appointment in a few minutes. We'll have to head back. Lunch is on me."

Another one who doesn't answer questions. All right. He'd play it her way. "It's only fair to reciprocate. What are you doing for dinner?"

She glanced at him. Suspicion in her eyes.

Is everybody in this damn town paranoid? Key wondered.

"Nothing," she replied.

"Would you have dinner with me?"

"Why?"

The question took him by surprise. He didn't quite know how to respond. He opened his mouth to say something—he didn't know what.

"Yes. I think I'd like that," he heard her saying. "One oh four Willow Lane. Where are you planning on taking me?"

"I haven't the vaguest idea."

"I thought not. Well, perhaps we'd best plan on eating at my place. If that's all right with you?"

It was.

"Oh, by the way," Key said. "I just beat hell out of one of Ted's deputies this morning. Thought you might like to know that."

She blinked. "Which one and why?"

"I don't know his name. Nothing will come of it. Why? He didn't like me and I didn't like him."

"You do like to live dangerously, don't you?"

"It seems to go with the territory."

She dropped him off at his car and drove away. He wondered whom she had an appointment with.

Promised to be, he hoped, an interesting night.

It was going to be all of that. And a lot more.

"What have you been doing today, Key?" Claire asked.

"Oh, getting the feel of things. Seeing some people. A whole lot of nothing, really."

His sister smiled at him. "You and Cat have a nice lunch?"

Key returned the smile as he marveled at the small town intelligence network. If a major power could ever perfect the system, it would be world ruling and Orwellian in scope.

"Surprisingly delicious pizza and some good conversation. I'm having dinner with her this evening."

"You always were a quick mover, Key. We all like Cat." She cut her eyes at him. "But she has made some powerful enemies in this county. Keep that in mind."

"Uh-huh. I keep hoping some member of my family will volunteer some information about the goings-on in Alton County."

91

Claire was cleaning up Dad Lessard's house and doing the weekly washing and ironing. Their dad was roaming around somewhere in the county, bouncing around in a fifteen-year-old pickup truck. Taylor Lessard did not believe in buying anything new until whatever he chose to replace had been broken so badly it could not be repaired or was economically unfeasible to fix. Whether it be a toaster or a tractor.

Up until his retirement from farming, he had kept mules on the place. Never knew when some piece of equipment would break down. Besides, mules could do a lot on a farm. And Taylor could grow their feed; damn sure couldn't grow gasoline.

Key watched his sister's face. Did her eyes narrow slightly at his remark? He thought so. He wondered if any of his family had been threatened. He decided not to ask. Not yet.

"Where is Lester?"

Claire did not look up from folding clothes. "Who knows? Who cares?" Her remarks were black bordered with bitterness and near hatred.

"Betty?"

"She staggered out of bed about ten o'clock. She and Les have gone off somewhere."

"Don't you know where, sis?"

She looked at him. "No, brother. I don't know where. If I order them to their rooms, they laugh at me and do as they damn well please. I grabbed Les one time, a few months ago, after he laughed at me. He hit me."

"I hope the little shithead never does that around me."

Her smile was filled with rancor. "Times have

92

changed, Key. You've been gone a long time. Turn on the radio sometimes, Key, and tune it into a rock station. Listen to songs about screwing and losing one's virginity and how it feels the first time."

"Are you serious?"

"Damn right, I'm serious. If a parent attempted to discipline kids today the way Pop did us, that parent might well be charged with child abuse. In the eyes of the law, Les and Betty are still juveniles. And brother, don't you ever think the kids today don't know it . . . and know enough law to stand up to you. If they want to. I tried to raise Les and Betty morally. Lester always stepped in and took the kids' side against me. I couldn't do it by myself, Key. I just couldn't. If I had divorced him, the land would have been torn apart. Now," she said, shrugging, "it doesn't make any difference."

There were tears in Claire's eyes. She walked out of the room.

Child abuse! Key shook his head. Since when was a good old-fashioned belt to the ass child abuse?

Key remembered the time his father had blistered his butt. Key must have been fifteen. He had looked his dad straight in the eye and balled his fists. Key woke up on the living room floor, wiser, sorrier, and with a sore jaw. Taylor Lessard had been a Nebraska state champion middleweight and had fought professionally for several years.

There never had been any toleration of bullshit with Pop. You did as you were told.

Child abuse?

No. Just a slight attitude adjustment, that was all. Key found the gun cabinet, took out his old double-barrel twelve gauge shotgun and inspected it. Still in fine condition. He walked out to the large well-equipped workshop, found a tape, measured the barrel to federal limits, then allowed himself a quarter inch more for safety's sake. He marked it, locked the weapon in a vise, found a hacksaw, and cut off the barrels.

Conscious of eyes on him, Key turned around. His brother, Rolf, was standing in the wide, double doors of the drive-in workshop, watching him.

"Are you thinkin' a load of trouble is goin' to come at you, brother?" Rolf asked.

Key sanded down the burrs on the twin muzzles and hefted the extremely lethal and stubby weapon. "Should I be expecting trouble, Rolf?"

"Whatever comes your way, Key, I expect you'll be able to handle it." He walked away.

"Double-talk," Key muttered. He watched as Rolf fired up a tractor and sputtered off, heading for the fields. "Bullshit from my family. I feel like I'm fumbling around in a dark mine field."

He found a box of shells and buckshot, and loaded the shotgun, placing shells and shotgun on the back seat of his Grand Prix, tossing a jacket over them. Claire was gone when he reentered the old house. Looking out the kitchen window, Key could see his brothers and the kids working in the fields.

The house was silent except for the normal sounds of wood expanding and contracting. House talk.

Key made a pot of coffee and drank a cup, sitting at the old kitchen table.

"Well, I hate to do this," Key muttered. "But I am going to find out what is going on around here. One way or the other."

He went prowling.

He searched for one hour and could not fine one scrap of paper with any threatening or intimidating words on it. He found his dad's bank statements and a rubber band-bound bundle of deeds. He was startled to learn that his father was a wealthy man. The old man owned a hell of a lot of land, houses, and buildings, which Key had known nothing about. It put his wealth into the millions of dollars. Key found a copy of his dad's will. Everything was spelled out to the letter; all the t's crossed and the i's dotted.

Catherine Monnet might be the family's attorney. But she had not handled this will.

Key wondered why.

Nothing was owed on any Lessard land. It was all clear except for what Lester had pissed off. Rolf and David were still paying for their homes, but the payments were not astronomical. Key figured the boys had done much of the work themselves, cutting the building costs by a large percentage.

Then he found a three-year-old copy of the *Alton County Sentinel*. The headline read: Fear And Disgust In Alton County.

Key wondered what happened to Loathing?

The accompanying article dealt with the resurgence of hate groups within the area. Neo-Nazism was mentioned more than once. Hillbilly and vigilante justice was touched upon — without detailing it. Bigotry and fanaticism were mentioned several times. Twisted religious values and false gods were attacked. Hatred and racism and the KKK.

Key had many friends who had been born and

reared in the Deep South. He knew from listening to them talk that many southerners — and northerners and westerners and easterners, too — would probably join some off the wall group if it would bring some relief from the so-called "black problem." They would do it as a last resort only, but many would join.

Was that occurring here in this part of Nebraska?

Key reread the article, trying to make some sense of it. What vigilante justice? No names, dates, or places were mentioned. What happened to who, what, where, and why? Key could understand the bigotry part, recalling Ken's words. And the twisted religious values; he could understand that, or at least as far as the article took it. He looked at the byline: Henry Randolph.

He put the paper back where he'd found it and walked into the kitchen. He thumbed through the phone book, finding the number of the *Sentinel* and dialing it.

"Henry Randolph, please."

There was a short pause and a sharp intake of breath. "Is this some sort of ugly, sick joke?" the woman's voice asked.

"No," Key said, recovering quickly. "But it is long distance," he lied. Sick, ugly joke? Now what in the hell was going on?

"That remains to be seen, I suppose. Were you a friend of his?"

Were? "Yes. A long time ago. In school. We've been out of touch for a long time."

"I see. Well, I suppose I owe an apology, Mr? . . ."

"Martin. Dave Martin."

"Very well, Mr. Martin." Key got the impression she

didn't believe that was his name. "Henry Randolph was killed three years ago. Almost, Mr. Martin, to the date."

"I see. I am really very sorry. Was it an accident?"

Again that short pause. "Some people claim it was."

She hung up.

Key replaced the buzzing receiver. "What in the hell is going on around here?" he muttered.

"Dave Martin?" Key's father spoke from behind him. "How many names you got, boy?"

Chapter 8

Key noticed his father had stopped a respectable distance from him before he spoke. He met his dad's eyes. "Just as many names as it takes, Pop."

"I don't even want to hear about that side of your life, boy. You had to have been snoopin' to hear about Henry Randolph."

"I will certainly admit to that." Key did not elaborate as to the *where* of his snooping.

"You can get hurt snoopin' around in this county, boy," the old man warned.

"Dad, if you're not careful, you can get hurt crossing the street."

"Don't sass me, boy. Older you are the lippier you get."

"You want a cup of coffee?"

"You make it?"

"I did."

"Don't like Claire's coffee. She slips that damned decaf in on me. Tastes like bull piss smells." He grimaced. "Says it's good for me."

Key laughed at his father's expression. "This isn't decaf."

"Fine. Well, hell, don't just stand there! Pour me a cup and tell me about your first day back in town."

Father and son sat with the table and thirty-five years between them. Key tried to stare his father down. Impossible.

"You got something on your mind, boy?"

"I got a lot of blanks spaces that need filling in."

"You always did ask more questions than normal folks had answers to."

"How do you learn unless you ask questions?"

"What do you want to know, son?"

"Everything you know about what is happening in Alton County; this part of the state, I suppose."

"Grain prices ain't worth a shit. Folks is losin' their homes. Kids ain't got nearabouts the respect for elders they used to. People—"

"Cut the bullshit, Dad!"

Taylor sat staring at his son. But not in anger. He sighed, dropped his eyes, and looked into the steamy darkness of his coffee.

Key softened his tone. "The TFL . . . have they ever threatened you?"

The old man lifted his eyes. "You have been beatin' the bushes, ain't you, Key?"

"You going to answer my question?"

"You're one man, what do you think you could do?"

Key slowly smiled, the smile changing as it grew. It reminded the father of a snarling tiger he'd seen one day in a zoo. His son's eyes were bleak and void of feeling.

Taylor suppressed a shudder. "I get the picture, boy. Son, you've been gone a long time. Times and people change. Attitudes toward life change. A lot of people are in a bind, and they've got to have somebody to blame for the squeeze. But they never want to look at themselves." He sipped his coffee and grew silent.

"Dad, you're right, I have been gone a long time. I haven't kept up with what's been happening here in the States. When I came back from 'Nam, all I could see was a bunch of hairy punks burning the flag and shouting obscenities at me. One of those fags out in Frisco spat on me and called me a baby-killer. I got out, Dad. As far away as I could get before I killed one of those so-called 'peace people.' "

"Me and your mother, we wondered why you didn't come home."

"Now you know. Dad, what in the hell is the Posse Comitatus?"

Taylor met his son's eyes. "All right, all right. You're goin' to wart me till I tell you. Near as I can learn, it was started some years back by a fellow name of Henry Beach. I think he was from up in Oregon. Yeah. The Posse is headquartered now up in Wisconsin, I think. They believe that the sheriff is the highest elected official in the county. What he says is law. Period. Like the KKK and the Aryan Nations, they got all sorts of, well, *weird* . . . ." That word again. ". . . ideas about Christ and being Christian. And they don't believe in payin' taxes. That's just one of the things they don't believe in. You ever heard of a fellow named Gordan Kahl?"

"No."

"Well, he died in a shoot-out with lawmen down in Arkansas a couple years back. He's a Posse hero. A martyr. Not too far from where we're sittin' there was a farmer killed fightin' the state patrol a few months back. I don't know whether that man was a member of the Posse, or not. Some says he was. What I'm gettin' at, boy, is some folks believe all those groups, includin' the TFL, is all bound together. Loosely, tightly." He shrugged. "I don't know. Some folks say all these groups have a following of less than five thousand. Son, I'd put it at closer to twenty-five thousand."

"Are you serious, Dad? That many?"

"Yeah. Maybe ten thousand of them is hard core; rest is hanger-ons and sympathizers. The government claims their numbers is shrinkin'. Don't you believe it. That's government malarkey. Propaganda. The government don't want the public to know just how strong and how much support these groups really have. Everytime some guy loses his farm or his business or goes bankrupt for whatever reason, or the IRS falls on them and damn near ruins them, or folks read about millionaires not payin' *any* taxes — well, you got more candidates for some right-wing group. There's all sorts of reasons why people join these groups. But the TFL, boy, it's said, whispered is a better word, to be the enforcement arm. They recruit some and they enforce. And they kill."

"Did the TFL kill Henry Randolph?"

"You're askin' for a personal opinion, now?"

"Yes."

"I think they did. If you're goin' to snoop, you'd better know something about Henry. He was a good reporter; had he lived he would have made it very big, I'm thinkin.' He was, oh, maybe twenty-five when he was killed. He was gettin' real close to the top men in the TFL. You probably been snoopin' around the house. You didn't get his name from nobody in Lewiston. So I reckon you found that newspaper in my desk."

"That's right."

"Twenty years ago I'd have whipped your ass for that." He looked his son up and down across the table. "But I'd sure hate to be the one try that now. You look like you eat Jeeps for breakfast."

"Dad, I've eaten things for breakfast, and all the other meals, too, that would make a buzzard vomit. Matter of fact, I ate a buzzard once.

"I don't doubt it a bit. Can you kill with your hands?"

"Yes."

"Have you?"

"Yes."

That news didn't faze the old man. Before the law turned in favor of criminals, Taylor Lessard had shot more than one man for trying to steal from his farm. "What else you wanna know, son?"

"Anything and everything else you know about the TFL."

"I don't have no proof."

"Probably not. But for all your butchering of the English language, you're a well-educated man, and you know how to listen and retain. You still get the Sunday *New York Times*?"

Taylor smiled. He did.

"Still do the crossword puzzle in ink?"

"Stop dancin' around it, boy. Get to the point."

"Have you, or any member of this family, ever been threatened by any right-wing group?"

102

"No, we haven't. And I think David and Rolf would have told me if they had been."

"But you do know people who have been threatened?"

"Yeah. At least they've hinted to me that they have. People in these parts are scared, Key. There are Posse, TLF, KKK sympathizers in a lot of the sheriff's departments throughout the state. A fellow just doesn't know who to trust."

"That's the best way I know of to gain total control. How about Ted Gilbert?"

"Solid TFL. And every member of his department is, too."

"But he's not the head honcho?"

"Oh, hell, no!" Taylor spat out the words. "Ted is the epitome of a redneck. Whatever he can't understand—which is damn near everything—he belittles, hates, scorns. Ted calls himself a Christian; but he's anything but that. Next you're gonna ask me who is the head of the TFL, right? Well, I don't know. I don't even have a clue. Hell, boy, it could be one of a dozen men. Might not even be anyone from around here. I just don't know."

"Or a woman?"

"Doubtful. The TFL, from what I can gather, don't allow women in the top ranks. If a person is hardcore Posse—not TFL—he drops out of the system. Don't have a driver's license; gets rid of birth certificate and marriage license. You close out your bank account. You refuse to pay taxes. Silver is the common man's metal; you use that. Go back to a system of barter. And you learn how to steal without, hopefully, getting caught. You keep a lot of guns, and a hell of a lot of ammo. Lots of food and water cached."

"So they're primarily survivalists?"

"Yes and no. Some are more in to that than others. I personally think they're a bunch of nuts. But dangerous nuts. Their primary goal is to get rid of the state, to rear a generation of children that can't be traced. That is, kids with no birth certificates, who don't go to school and who are raised and grow up as true sovereigns of God and Constitution."

"Then they want the destruction of the nation?"

"Looks that way. Anarchy. Key, you be careful. The TFL plays dirty."

Again, that tiger's smile. "Dad, I'm considered a worldwide expert in playing dirty."

"Yeah, I expect you are. But you fought for the Jews overseas, didn't you?"

"Where did you hear that?"

"Rumors."

Key shook his head. When he was working as a gun for the Israeli government, against the PLO, he was under very tight contract to the agency. If news of that was out, that could only mean the agency had a leak—or someone with access to top secret files was working for the TFL. The latter, probably. Christ! How big was this group of fruitcakes?

"What's wrong, boy?"

"This group, or groups, may be bigger than everybody thinks."

"Oh, they are. And gettin' bigger. They're heroes to a lot of people with their backs to the wall. The TFL plays religion up big. Bible in one hand, a Mini-fourteen in the other."

"That's a good weapon."

"What? The Bible or the fourteen?"

Key looked up to see if his dad were joking. The man was smiling at his son.

"Very funny, Dad."

"Who's who and who's Jew?"

"I beg your pardon?"

"Favorite sayin' of the TFL. Jews are considered nonwhites; they're devils. Enemies of white people. You see, boy, the TFL is, or has become, a symbol of strength against the state, the banks. Its members really think they're patriots. Outlaws in their own country. They talk tough and they are tough. Very heavily armed and well organized; dug in deep. A very good intelligence system. Very expensive computer system. Newsletters. The whole bit. You are either one hundred percent for the TFL, or you're a child of Satan. Their sworn enemy. Good for only one thing: to be killed."

"Sounds like a delightful group of people."

"Just peachy," the old man said dryly.

Telling his father where he would be that evening — at least part of the evening — Key dressed casually and drove into town. His mind refused to believe that something as large, as dangerous, as the TFL could have existed this long, grown as big as his dad claimed them to be, without the government's discovering them and their intentions.

But obviously, they had managed to do so.

Unless — someone high in government held the reins of the TFL.

Was that a possibility?

Yes. Nothing could be discounted.

He pulled in at Zack's and gassed up, chatting for a moment with the man. He asked directions to Willow Lane.

"Oh, it ain't hard to find. Rich, snooty part of town. Bankers and lawyers and such live over there. Bloodsuckers, ever' one of them."

"Bank been giving you a hard time, Zack?"

"Banks give ever'body a hard time, Key. Things have changed in the years you been gone. You'll see with your own eyes, I'm sure. I heard you was datin' that uppity lawyer. Lots of folks 'round here don't like that woman."

"I don't even know her very well, Zack. What seems to be the problem with her?"

"Got Jew blood in her for one thing." He studied Key's face for a moment. "So I hear. From way back. Might be part nigger, for all I know. She thinks she's better than the common folk. But mainly, Key, she's on the wrong side."

Zack turned and walked away.

The man looked at his sleeping wife. She'd been in considerable pain, and he'd given her a shot about an hour back. Now she was sleeping peacefully.

She's still beautiful, he thought. After all these years, she's beautiful.

Memories flooded him. And flooded his eyes with a mixture of joy and pain. They had been married for forty years.

Today was their anniversary.

He wondered if she had remembered it. He didn't know. Her pain might have dulled that memory. Just as well. For he didn't have a very nice anniversary present for her.

Or did he?

He had left his job early, dark thoughts in his frightened mind. He did not want to spend the rest of his life being a servant to the TFL. That would be intolerable. Just the thought sickened him.

He *owed* the TFL, and the TFL felt they *owned* him.

And, he thought, sighing, in a way they did.

He sat for a moment longer, looking at his sleeping wife, lost in thoughts precious only to them. So many good years between them.

He got up and went to his gun cabinet, pulling out a pistol and checking the loads. Full. He walked back into his wife's bedroom.

"I'm sorry, Kathy," he said. "I am so very, very sorry. I just don't know what else to do."

Chapter 9

"He won't be the only person to tell you that, I'm sure," Cat said.

"Care to elaborate?" Key asked. He sipped his martini very carefully and very slowly, allowing the ice to soften it. The lady made a very wicked drink. Many of these and he wouldn't be able to find his ass with both hands. And he knew he could not afford to get stopped with liquor on his breath. He felt if he was ever put in Gilbert's jail, he would never leave there alive.

"On the Jewish bit? I don't know. I don't think so. The Monnets came over from France a couple of centuries ago. I was raised a Catholic. I used to date a Jewish boy . . . back in high school. Maybe that's where it came from. Would it have made any difference to you if it were true?"

Key laughed. "No. The rumor probably got started because of the Monnet connection with big banks and big business."

"Well, maybe. I think part of it is because I was friends with Henry Randolph."

She dropped that in Key's lap, all the while watching his face for some reaction. Key kept his expression unflavored. At least he hoped he did. If she were friends with Henry Randolph, that would sure account for some hard feelings. If Zack were a member of the TFL. And Key felt sure he was. No doubt about it, the man was a black hater.

"Who is Henry Randolph?"

Her eyes searched his face. Her smile, when it came, was tainted and curved with a hint of sarcasm. "You must think me a fool, Key. Don't. For I assure you, I am not."

Key placed his drink on a coaster. He stood up, facing her. "I do not think you a fool, Cat. I don't know what to think. My family is acting very, well, *weird*." God*damn*, he couldn't get away from that word. "The sheriff and at least one of his men have tried to hassle me. I don't really know why. I think it's more than a high school grudge. I'm hearing gunfire in the night. I spoke with an old friend this morning—who shall, for the time being, remain nameless—and he is frightened half out of his mind. And we were being watched by somebody in an unmarked car while we talked. I'm told there is some sort of ultra right-wing group, or groups, working in this area—that no one, or only a few, will talk about. Now I hear that you're not the right person for me to see, socially, because you're on the 'wrong side.' The wrong side of what, Cat?"

"You're working for the government, Key. You may claim you're not, and maybe you didn't come here working for them. But in the past thirty-six hours, you've contacted them. I'd bet a thousand dollars on

109

that."

Key said nothing.

The faint sounds of sirens cut the night, penetrating the brick walls of the lovely home in a very respectable and well-groomed part of town. Both of them listened to the wailing until it died away.

"Not too far away from here," Cat finally broke the silence.

"Is that odd?"

"Yes, very. The Sheriff's Department almost never uses sirens in this part of town. Maintaining decorum, and all that, you know."

The phone rang. She moved gracefully across the thickly carpeted den and answered it. "Oh, my God!" she said. She listened for a few seconds more. "That's horrible. Yes, of course. Yes, we'll both be here."

She hung up and faced Key. "I'm your attorney, Key," she reminded him. "Whatever you say to me must remain confidential." He nodded, knowing now the call was official. "That person you spoke with today—the one you said was frightened? What is his name?"

"What's happened?"

"His name, Key."

"Ken Warner."

"Oh, God, I was afraid of that. Ken just killed his wife and then turned the gun on himself. That call was from the Sheriff's Department. A murder/suicide."

Key sighed and shook his head. "Damn! You keep saying the Sheriff's Department, Cat. What happened to the Lewiston Police?"

110

"We have no city police. The Sheriff's Department is under contract to handle both city and county matters. A number of communities are doing that. Sheriff Gilbert will be here any minute. Along with his bodyguard, I'm sure. A simpleminded thug name Stan Tabor. He is, of all things, the county's chief deputy."

Key nodded, recalling his father's word: *The sheriff is the highest elected official.* A pattern was developing, for sure. "Let Ted come on. I have nothing to hide or fear."

It was still daylight out, thanks to daylight savings time. More time for adults to play games. And harder on country kids waiting for buses when school was in session.

Key could not envision conditions so bad that his old coach would kill himself. He had seen that the man was scared, badly scared. But —

Cat broke into his thoughts. "Keep your answers simple, Key. Don't elaborate unless you are asked to do so."

"Like I said, Cat: I have nothing to hide or fear."

A knocking on the front door. Not a friendly knock. More an authoritative, demanding, arrogant banging on the door. Both Key and Cat grimaced at the sound. It reminded Key of secret police in some of the less-than-democratic countries he'd worked. Cat opened the door and admitted Gilbert and another man. The second man was introduced as Chief Deputy Stan Tabor.

Key took an immediate dislike to the deputy. Big and solid but with the beginnings of a beer belly, the man's stance indicated arrogance, and his broad face and thick lips were stamped with a touch of cruelty. Ted's enforcer, Key thought.

"Lessard," Ted said, giving the name a greasy sound.

"Good evening, Fatty," Key replied, addressing the man by his grade school nickname.

The sheriff flushed, and the deputy balled his big fists, taking a step forward. "Easy, Stan," Ted cautioned.

"Let him come on," Key said. He was standing, facing the men, about six feet separating them. He looked at Tabor. "In front of my attorney, without any provocation from me, I'd like for you to get hostile with me."

"You're pushing, Key," Ted said, a touch of uncertainty on his face. "Back off, man."

"No," Key corrected. *"I'm* not doing the pushing. I just don't like to be hassled. I've seen far too many overbearing cops in developing nations, that's all. I thought America had outgrown that. You pound on the front door like you're raiding a whorehouse. You hung enough grease on my last name to crank my car out there. And you know it. You want to talk to me, sheriff—fine. You make it Key, Mr. Lessard, ol' buddy, or any other friendly term. All right?"

Ted suddenly clicked on the charm that rednecks can turn off and on like a light bulb, hiding the dangerous ignorance they all wear so proudly. "We all knew and loved Coach Warner, Key. Sorry if we came on hard."

"Fine." Key stepped forward and stuck out his right hand, toward the deputy, forcing the man to take it or

112

make his true intentions known. Tabor took the hand — reluctantly. Ted shook Key's hand, but both lawmen — so-called — could not hide the open dislike in their eyes.

Dropping Key's hand, Ted asked, "Did you speak with Coach Warner today, Key?"

"You know I did, sheriff. One of your unmarked units was parked across from the football field."

Ted's smile held grudging respect. "Yeah, so it was, Key. But the stakeout had nothing to do with you. What did you talk about?"

Lying son of a bitch! Key thought. "Oh, we talked about old times, old games played, old friends. Rehashing years past. He told me about his wife being sick, bedridden. He talked about how expensive it was putting a new roof on his house. Buying home-care products for his wife. He spoke of Lewiston becoming a small industrial town. We talked about what a tough time the farmers were having. Let's see . . . I guess that's about it."

Ted made some notes in a small notepad. "Did he seemed depressed to you, Key?"

"Yes, he did." Only a half lie. "His hands were trembling, and sometimes he seemed on the verge of tears." Forgive me, coach. "I just didn't know how to pursue it."

Now a very sorrowful expression crossed Ted's face. The basset-hound personality surfaced. "I wouldn't have known either, Key. Terrible, terrible thing. Whole town will be just sick about it. Key, you and me, we got off on the wrong foot the other night. I'm sorry about that. Hell, we're both growed-up men; no

113

point in carryin' silly grade-school grudges. From this point on, we'll just start all over. How about it?''

"That's fine with me, sheriff."

"Oh, heck, Key." Ted shuffled his cowboy-booted feet and plopped his ten gallon hat back on his head. "Call me Ted."

"You don't believe any of that good-old-boy crap, do you, Key?" Cat asked.

Cat had prepared the salad and baked potatoes while Key looked after the thick rib eyes on the outside gas grill. Both liked their steaks rare, garlic dressing on the green salad, and butter *and* sour cream on the potatoes. Cat had planned cherries jubilee to be served with kirschwasser.

Key chewed for a moment. The steak was as tender as he'd ever tasted. "No. I know Ted too well. He's clumsy and obvious, but he can fit in almost any rural society. Chewing tobacco, hunting clubs, slap you on the back, and pickup trucks. And shotguns hanging from a rear window rack when the season is still six months off. I'm not putting down rural people, Cat. I came back to join them. It's just that I know there are other ways to live. The country life used to be simple and good. Now I'm not so sure."

"Not so simple anymore, Key. And not as good. It isn't as hectic as big city life, but many of the same pressures now apply in the country. Television enlightenment has arrived. Both the good and the bad of it."

"Cat, you know I lied to Ted about what all Ken said to me, don't you?"

114

"Well, I don't *know,* but I certainly suspect."

Key decided to plunge all the way in with Cat. "You remember I told you he was scared?"

She nodded.

"He told me about the TLF."

Cat's fork clattered to the table. She stared at him.

Ted Gilbert faced the man in the gathering gloom of that period between dusk and full night. The deceptive shadows of gray and black distorted the man's face. "What did Key tell you?"

"I think he leveled with me. Warner seemed depressed to him. Voice shaky and hands tremblin'. Key got his back up for a minute; I come on a little hard, I reckon. But we got it squared away. We're ol' buddies again." He grinned hugely.

The man is a fool! the other thought. But a useful fool. "If you believe that, you'll believe anything. Key does not like you now and never has. Keep that in mind. Key is very smart." Unlike you. "But I agree with your assessment of their conversation. I don't think Ken told Key anything of substance. But that will remain to be seen as time goes by. Ted, I warn you now: Key will never take part in the TFL. Never. I've kept up with him over the years, as best I could. Key is tired of war and guns. He is back home to farm; and that's all. He is not a joiner and never will be. He's a loner. And you and your men leave him alone. We'll work around him. And we'll do it for another reason: He might get bored before the summer is over and start looking for some action. We have to be sure he doesn't find it here. I don't want him hassled in any way. Is that clear?"

"Yes, sir. He won't be. I'll put the word out to handle him with kid gloves. But there's a hitch: Stan's got his stinger out for Key. He might try him sometime."

"He'll be a damn fool if he does. But if he does, you put the word on Stan that he'd better not do it while in uniform."

Ted's reply was peevish. "I done told him that twice."

"Tell him again. If Stan screws up, his job's on the line. Is that clear?"

"Yes, sir."

The man wheeled around and walked to his car. He drove off.

Ted waited until the taillights had vanished from sight before muttering, "No-good, smart-aleck bastard!"

The sheriff got his own car and sat for a moment, calming down. He intently disliked the leader of his cell of the TFL. But he knew better than to cross him. Ted was getting tired and impatient with all this secret, slipping around business. He knew it was essential, but he was still tired of it.

Bunch of damned heathens! Ought to just start wipin' 'em all out. Right now. But he knew he must wait until the Man said to move.

Ted also did not share the Man's opinion of Key Lessard's toughness. Oh, Key was a big ol' boy; not much doubt about that. But he was just one man. Ted didn't believe in all that hand-to-hand fighting stuff a

116

feller sees on the TV and in the movies. None of that fancy oriental gook shit was for real. All that hooin' and hawin' and jumpin' around. Ted figured that he, himself, could take Key in a stand-up fight. And he knew Stan could damn well take him. Stan played pro football for three years. No goddamn soldier boy was gonna whip Stan.

Ted, like so many people, had a lot to learn about certain soldier boys. And Ted, like so many other people, was going to learn it quite painfully.

Cat quickly recovered her composure. She picked up her fork and laid it across her plate. She stared at Key.

"What did Ken Warner tell you, Key?"

Key resumed his eating, chewing slowly, savoring each bite. Like so many men who have spent their lives in the field, Key knew to eat when he was hungry, drink when he was thirsty, and sleep when he was tired, if one had the time to do all these things. As he ate, he told Cat everything that Ken had said.

"That poor, frightened man," she said.

"Not anymore," Key summed it up.

"What do you plan on doing now, Key?"

He looked up. "Have dessert."

Key left the home of Catherine Monnet at nine-thirty. They exchanged a very simple good-night kiss at the door and left any further personal matters for time to take care of. Key said he would stop by her office for lunch the following day, if that was all right with her.

It was.

He had tested the waters in his mind and believed Cat was not involved in any TFL doings. She knew about them — as much as anyone outside the organization did — and she strengthened Key's personal thoughts that the majority of farmers in the area had no direct involvement and wanted no direct involvement with the TFL. But a quiet campaign of subtle terror had been waged by those in the TFL. A lot of people were scared. The TFL was using the same tactics as the night-riding KKK of a century past.

Or Hitler's Gestapo.

Key drove the now quiet streets of the town, very much aware that a car was following him. It had been a long time since Key had spent any time in America, but he remembered his own youth in this very town. The streets were not this quiet twenty years ago. And Key found that very odd.

Twenty years back, maybe two out of ten kids had their own cars. He felt sure that percentage had been drastically upped. If so, where were the kids? He drove past several drive-ins. Only a few cars were parked around them.

And that car was still following him.

He circled back through town and drove past the theater. Empty appearing, except for the personnel checking up for the night, preparing to close.

Strange, came to Key's mind, momentarily, he thought, smiling, replacing weird. Where the hell was everybody?

118

He glanced into his rearview. Those headlights were still back there. But staying a full block away. He pulled into a drive-in cafe and parked. The car that had been following him drove on past, a woman at the wheel. Even at this distance there was no mistaking who it was.

Rosanna.

Key waved the young carhop (he guessed they were still called that) away, and pulled out, following the car. Just outside of town, she pulled over. Key got out and walked up to the car, driver's side.

"Rosanna, nice to see you. What I can see of you, that is."

She smiled, wondering if his words contained a double meaning. She could hope. "Key. I heard you were back. Could I talk to you, Key?"

Key studied the woman's face in the dim lights from the dash. She had aged, naturally, but was still a very lovely lady. Her high school beauty had matured and deepened with age. Time had treated her very well.

"Of course. You want to talk here?"

"Follow me, Key. We'll talk over at the point."

Key chuckled. The point. Christ, he'd forgotten all about that place. The point overlooked a small river just west of Lewiston.

She shared his laugh. "Yes, it's still there. But the kids don't use it anymore. Not for what we . . . used to. I own a cabin there."

He smiled at the "used to." Hot young screwing. Words of passion/endearment that were spoken to be forever meaning. In many cases they lasted about a week and a half. "All right. Lead on, ma'am."

She smiled again. He knew what she was smiling about. That night they almost got caught.

Jesus, Rosanna, here comes a car!

Help me find my panties!

Their knees banging on the dash, the steering wheel, and anything else they could hit, the teenagers managed to get dressed before the sheriff pulled up alongside and told them to hit the trail.

Key's father had found Rosanna's panties. When he opened the glove box the next day. On the way to church.

The road to the point had been dirt and gravel back in Key's youth. Now it was blacktop. Rosanna's "cabin" was a large, very expensive-looking lodge structure, set several hundred yards off the road, thick timber concealing it from snooping eyes. He pulled into the drive and followed Rosanna up the sidewalk and into the house. She clicked on the lights and stepped inside, motioning Key inside. Rosanna was dressed in tight-fitting jeans and a blouse she looked like she might bust out of any moment. Key remembered those breasts. Intimately. He stepped into the lodge, wondering what he might be getting into. Both emotionally and physically.

He turned to speak to her and closed his mouth as a huge banner greeted his eyes. The banner, or flag, whatever, was secured to the north wall of the lodge. Under the flag, on a stand, was a Bible. On either side of the Bible sat a brass cross. The flag was white, snow white, with five light blue stripes, running in a silent slant from top to bottom. A blue cross was on the top corner, left side, and on the bottom, right side, as Key faced it. The letters KC were centered on the flag.

"Do I salute, or what?" Key said, without taking his eyes from the flag. "Pray, maybe?" he said in a kidding tone.

When Rosanna did not reply, Key turned to face her.

"Welcome home, Key," she said.

Key sighed.

Rosanna had a pistol in her right hand, the muzzle pointing at him.

Chapter 10

Key stood very still, his hands at his side. Thinking very chauvinistically, Key knew that a revolver in the hands of a woman was bad enough, but a semiautomatic pistol was very bad news. His eyes remained fixed on her face. She smiled and held out the pistol, an old, well-cared for Colt .380, 1903 model, Key guessed. A very dependable semiautomatic pistol that fired a respectable round.

Key breathed easier as she dropped the muzzle. "Skip gave this to me some time ago. I remembered it last week, when we split the sheets for good. I don't know a thing about guns."

Oh, Jesus, Rosanna! Don't you remember all the weekends we used to take pistols down along this very river and shoot tin cans and turtles and snakes? Goddammit, stop lying to me. You were a damn good pistol shot. He said nothing about that.

His trained eyes had noted how expertly she had held the .380, not at all like a person who knew nothing about firearms. He took the pistol from her and ejected the clip. Fat round-noses gleamed their brass at him. He worked the slide. The weapon had not held a round in the chamber. And he felt she knew that all along.

"Nighttime is no time for pistol training, Rosanna. But I'll be happy to check you out during the day."

"I'll take you up on that, Key. How about tomorrow afternoon?"

"Fine." He remembered his luncheon date with Cat. "Three o'clock. We'll have plenty of daylight, I'm sure," he added very dryly.

She smiled. "Sounds good. And I don't like daylight savings time, either."

The high school homecoming king and queen of twenty years past stood for a moment looking at each other. In the bright light of the lodge, Key could see that time had indeed treated Rosanna well. She looked twenty-seven instead of thirty-seven. He could detect no sign of gray in the dark hair spilling around her face. Dark eyes with that familiar heat smoldering behind them. She looked as though she had not gained one ounce since the last time he'd seen her: Nineteen years ago. In front of Greene's Drug Store. Key mentally reviewed his recent driving of Main Street. Greene's Drugs was gone. Like Steinberg's Department Store. Gone.

"You bring me out here to point guns at me, Rosanna?"

Her laughter had not changed much, either. "No. I just wanted to talk with you, see you. It's been a long time, Key."

"Almost twenty years." He had to say, "You

123

haven't changed, Rosanna."

"You . . . have," she replied honestly. That much Key knew was true. "I mean, I would still know you anywhere. But you've changed."

"Yes, I know."

"Watch out for Skip, Key. He's not the same Skip you knew in high school."

Another one to watch out for. A fellow could easily become paranoid around here. "Most of us change, Rosanna. Why should I watch out for Skip?"

"Our last, well, troubles, started when I heard you were coming home. I mentioned to Skip that I would like to see you. That maybe we could all get together and have some sort of informal class reunion. You know, Ted and Whit and Linda and Merci and Al and Louise and Ned and June—all the old bunch. Boy, after I said that, it went downhill in a hurry. He's always been kind of jealous of you. He ranted and raved and said he'd kick your ass. And then, as I knew would happen, he hit me. That was the last straw. He's hit me a lot over the years, and I always forgave him. But no more. The papers have been filed."

Key assumed she meant the divorce papers. Rosanna's words had come in a rush, as if the faster she spoke the better she would feel. Maybe she had to tell somebody.

"This lodge belong to Skip?"

"Oh, no. This is mine. Dad built it just before he retired. When he died several years ago, it was willed to me."

Key pointed to the blue and white banner. "What is

124

that flag supposed to mean?"

"I don't really know. It belongs to Jerry. I thought he'd have gotten it by now."

"Jerry?"

"My oldest child. Jerry is seventeen, Paul is fifteen, Mary is twelve. Jerry and Paul belong to . . . some sort of club. A youth group. That is their banner."

Key looked at the crosses on the banner. "Is it some sort of religious group?"

"I think so. Jerry and Paul never talk about it."

Well, goddammit, woman, ask them! "Don't you ever question them about it?"

"Not really. It wouldn't do any good. They'd just tell me to get out of their face."

Key simply could not imagine a child of his—if he had any, that is—telling him to "get out of his face." He hated to think what he might do should that unlikely event ever occur.

Rosanna laughed at the expression on Key's face. "It's a brand new ball game out there, now, Key. I believe I've got a chance with Mary, but the boys . . ." She shrugged. "I don't know. They walked out with their father. Has Claire spoken with you about Betty?"

"She didn't have to. I personally witnessed it the other night." He did not feel he had to elaborate.

"Yes. Betty dates Jerry."

Wonderful. "Does he drive a car with loud mufflers?"

"Yes."

Enough said.

The time-worn king turned warrior and the still

125

lovely queen stood in their rustic court and looked at each other. For a moment they had run out of things to say.

Rosanna glanced at her wristwatch. "I guess I'd better be getting on back. Take the sitter home. I've been looking for you all night." She smiled. "That's not really true. I've been waiting for you to leave Cat's house."

Interesting. "You and Cat get along?"

"Oh, yes. She's a nice person. She just . . ." She closed her mouth.

"She just . . . *what*, Rosanna?" Goddammit, Key wished somebody would finish a sentence.

"Oh, nothing. Forget it. See you at three?"

"Right."

Key slept late, for him, getting out of bed at eight the next morning. He could sense the farmhouse was empty. He showered and shaved and dressed in jeans and western shirt and boots. He fixed breakfast and took a second cup of coffee out on the porch to sit and sip as he looked around the peaceful farm scene.

Why then did he not feel peaceful?

He knew the answer to that: All his battle-tested senses were working overtime. He was up, alert, anticipating an attack.

But where were the battle lines? Where would the attack originate?

Questions he had no answers for.

The day had begun with a gray overcast, the clouds fat and gray and wet. It would rain before noon.

Key wondered where his father was. What he did, how he spent his time now that he was retired. Probably visited old friends; maybe down at Benson's Feed and Seed. Playing checkers and gin rummy and talking.

Key put a change of clothing into a small overnight bag and tossed it in the back seat of his Grand Prix. He left a short note telling his dad he probably would not be back until the next day and for him not to worry.

He drove into Lewiston and parked in the bank's side lot, carefully locking the car and pocketing the keys.

Whit spotted him just as he entered the building and waved him over. Key was aware of eyes on him as he walked with Whit. Some friendly, some just curious. He ignored them. Over coffee in Whit's office, Key arranged to have a checking account opened as well as a savings account. He arranged to have funds transferred from his bank in New York City. Whit did not seem at all surprised at the amount of money Key moved. Key always had believed bankers knew more about the private lives of citizens than they had a right to know.

Computers.

Business taken care of, Whit leaned back in his plush, padded executive chair and said, "So, Key, what do you think about Coach Warner?"

"A tragedy that should not have happened. I spoke with him only hours before he killed himself."

"So I heard."

News gets around quickly. What else did you hear,

Whit? Let's find out. "Whit, what do you know about the TFL?"

The banker blinked, losing some composure. He recovered quickly and smiled tightly. He shook his head. "Boy, it didn't take you long to find a stick and stir up the waters, did it?"

Key shrugged. "That doesn't answer my question."

Whit waved his hand; a curt, impatient gesture. "They're a bunch of nuts! A very, very small group of people attempting to stir up the folks with a lot of lies and a few half-truths. My God, Key, have they contacted you?"

"No. I don't know who *they* are. But I heard the name a time or two. The group sounds awfully poisonous to me."

"They are. So I hear," he quickly added. Too quickly? Maybe. "We've received some letters from them here at the bank. They were threatening to do this or that. Nothing ever happened. Obviously."

Did you really, Whit? "What did you do with the letters? I'd like to read them."

Whit pursed his lips and shook his head. At that moment, he looked like a big frog. "Oh, I tossed them into the garbage."

Lying, Key thought. My old friend is lying through his teeth. No banker would brush something of that nature aside. The FBI would be called in faster than a guy could spit. So why would Whit lie about it?

Whit was smiling at him. "Don't worry about the TFL, Key. They're a bunch of harmless nuts, that's all."

"If he could talk, I wonder if Henry Randolph

would agree with that assessment?"

Whit lost his smile. Did his eyes turn mean, wary? Key couldn't be sure. "Randolph was a smart-assed, cocky young reporter, Key. He made half the people in this county angry. But he wasn't murdered. The state police issued that report. He had a wreck. Where are you getting all this information, ol' buddy?"

"Just listening to people talk. I didn't say he was murdered, Whit."

Whit stuck out his hand. "Glad to welcome you to our bank, Key. Glad you're home. Hope you stay with us a long, long time."

Key knew a dismissal when he heard one. He shook the hand and walked out.

He cut his eyes just as he reached the door. Whit was punching out some number on his phone. Key wondered who he might be calling.

And why?

Flat out lying to me, Key thought as he drove out of the bank parking lot. Whit just looked me right in the eyes and lied. Is Whit part of this TFL crap? Or is he so naive as to really believe the TFL is a group of harmless nuts?

One or the other.

He checked his watch. Ten o'clock. He stopped at a newsrack and picked up a newspaper. He parked his car and walked into the small park opposite the courthouse. The sky had darkened somewhat, but the rain was still holding off. He spent the next fifteen minutes reading several articles about the nation's farmers. No doubt about it, many of the farmers

129

were in bad trouble.

Key came to the conclusion that a lot of the farmers' problems had to do with the government mixing foreign policy with agri exports, restricting markets for U.S. farmers' goods and withholding lines of credit for large customers—like Russia. They—the government—want to use agriculture as a foreign policy and political carrot, so to speak, but the government doesn't want to pay the farmer for it.

Key leaned back on the bench. Maybe some of the nation's farmers had tried to live too high and wide; practicing shortsightedness instead of putting money back for a rainy day. But by and large, the fault did not lie with the majority of farmers.

He turned to the markets page and looked at the price of wheat.

He couldn't believe it.

Two dollars and fifty-eight cents a bushel.

Christ, it should have been four dollars and a half, at least.

He checked milo, corn, soybeans. All low. Foolishly, ridiculously low. There was no excuse for those low prices, not with a hungry world to feed.

With wheat at two dollars and fifty eight cents a bushel, a farmer couldn't break even.

Key was beginning to understand why come people would lean toward groups like the TFL. Misguided, but forced to grab at straws. Or guns.

In many cases, the man who drove the bread truck was making more money than the farmer who grew the grain to make the bread.

Key felt that every worker should earn a fair living,

but a line was going to have to be drawn somewhere.

He heard a familiar rumble of mufflers. A gaggle of teenagers tumbled out of two cars that rolled to a stop by the curb. Key's niece, Betty, among them.

"Just loafin', Uncle Key?" she asked.

"Just loafing, Betty."

Betty was really quite a shapely, pretty girl—now that she didn't have puke running off her chin and didn't smell like a goat in rut.

Key looked at the kids. "Introduce me to your friends, Betty."

"Oh, sure, Uncle Key." The names meant nothing to Key until she introduced Jerry and Paul Gerris. Key kept his smile in place and nodded at the girls and shook the boys' hands.

The kids all had several things in common: They had pouty mouths, not much in the way of manners, and affected a sullen air about them. And Key could sense something else: They were, to a person, wary of him.

"Well," Betty said. "I guess we'll see you around, Uncle Key."

"All right, Betty." Key watched them pile back into the cars and rumble away. He heard one of the boys say, "He's a big, rough-lookin' bastard, ain't he?"

The kids growled away, off to do only God knew what.

The sky began to send down a light mist. Key drove the town one more time, spending forty-five minutes firmly implanting the lay of the town back into his mind. Twice he saw Stan Tabor and twice he lifted his hand in greeting. The deputy did not return the greeting, only scowling.

Key felt it amusing, in a dark sort of way.

Tabor was several years younger then Key, and as Key drove through the steadily increasing rain, he pulled on old memory banks and brought what he knew about Tabor to light.

Key had consumed, page by page, any magazine or newspaper he could find while overseas, especially those few stories about Nebraskans. Tabor would be about thirty-three or four. A star football player in high school, Tabor had gone on to college and played two years before busting out because of bad grades. He played pro ball for a couple more years, but he just wasn't good enough to stay with it. The problem was Stan Tabor was just too stupid.

And stupid people in positions of authority can be very dangerous.

He pulled into the small parking area in front of Cat's office and went in. Her secretary smiled at him when he introduced himself.

"Ms. Monnet's been trying to reach you all morning, Mr. Lessard. She had to go to Omaha on a case. She'll be back about noon tomorrow."

In one way, Key felt relieved. He had a growing case of Rosanna-on-the-mind.

He located the chamber of commerce office and got a county map before driving out into the county. As he drove, he smiled, hoping his dad would not get too inquisitive and open up the boxes coming that day by UPS. His father might well drop his upper plate upon sighting the contents.

Key braked suddenly and pulled over as far as he could get on the narrow shoulder of the county road. He stared at a complex of buildings set well back from the road. He couldn't be sure from this distance, but one particular building looked very much like a church. And one of the buildings resembled a barracks. All that sure hadn't been here when Key was growing up.

The complex seemed, looked, innocuous enough, but something about it set off an alarm deep within the man. Key stared through the rain at the buildings, trying to understand what had caused him to stop; what had brought on the feelings of alarm.

He could not pinpoint the reason for it.

He looked at the chain-link fence around the complex of buildings. A four-strand chain-weld fence was around the fields in front, back, and on both sides of the complex. But why another fence around the complex itself?

Security, sure. But why that much security? What did they have to hide? Or what did they have inside they didn't want to get out?

"Hey, you!" The shout brought Key out of his musings.

Key looked up. Two men stood in camouflaged rain gear by the gate. Where in the hell did *they* come from? he wondered.

Key cracked a window, passenger side. "Yeah?"

"Move along. No one is allowed to stop here."

Key tried. He really tried to keep the lid on his temper. But he just couldn't. Or wouldn't. Whatever.

All he originally wanted to do was just come home. Live peacefully. Farm the land. Instead, he was meeting mystery, hostility, hassle, and horseshit.

Key got out of the car. "Do you people own this road?"

"No. It's a county road. But that don't make no difference. You move if we tell you to move."

"Why should I?"

One of the men produced a silver badge. Key knew that, in the past, a gold badge meant a working, full-time deputy sheriff. Silver meant a special deputy. Appointed by the local sheriff for posse work, crowd control, things of that nature.

"Is that special deputy's badge supposed to impress me?" Key asked.

"Carry your ass, boy!"

"Fuck you," Key said with a smile. "This is a public road, that is a public shoulder, and that is a public ditch." He pointed them all out, as if dealing with a couple of retarded people. Which, he thought, he might very well be.

The men smiled. "You from around here, boy?" one asked.

"No," Key said, only a half lie.

The second man said, "What do you think?"

His partner said, "Why not? Ain't nobody comin' from either direction."

Key did not understand any of it. But he got the impression the men had something unpleasant in mind for him. He walked swiftly toward the pair. He watched as one fumbled under his cammie rain gear.

"You freeze, goddammit!" the second man yelled.

Key jumped, his booted feet catching the fumbling man in the chest, knocking him sprawling. A .45 caliber semiautomatic pistol fell from under the rain suit. Key drove his fist into the second man's crotch. The man doubled over and began puking on the side of the road. The first man was getting to his feet just as Key's boot caught him under the chin. Blood and bits of teeth splattered on the rain-slick shoulder of the road. For insurance, Key kicked the gagging man in the mouth, turning out, temporarily, his lights.

"I'm really getting tired of this," Key muttered, walking back to his car. "They're going to keep on with this shit and I'm going to get mad and hurt somebody."

He pulled out, leaving the men where they had fallen. He took another look at the complex. Far back, behind the complex, there was a thick stand of timber, maybe seventy-five or a hundred acres of timber. Even that seemed odd to Key. It appeared to be—

Yes.

A training area.

Now why would he think that? A church with a combat training area behind it?

And why would he think it was a training area? Didn't make sense.

And why were those men back there preparing to draw down on him with guns?

That didn't make any sense either.

But then, very little he had encountered since returning home had made any sense.

He shook his head and pushed what he had just

seen and done far back into his mind and drove away.

But he could not push away the feeling that he was being watched as he left.

By very hostile eyes.

Chapter 11

It was raining heavily when he pulled into the curving drive of Rosanna's lodge on the river. Her car was under the double carport. Key pulled his Gran Prix in beside hers. As he was getting out, the side door opened and Rosanna stepped out.

Was that a touch of sadness on her face? Key thought so.

"I didn't know whether you'd show up, Key."

"I never thought about not coming out. Oh, I met your boys in town about an hour and a half ago."

"Oh?"

"Yes. Betty was with them. Along with some other kids. I don't recall their names."

"Little thugs and hamburger whores, I'm sure."

"Hamburger whores?"

"Yes. They put out for a hamburger. Come on in, Key."

The huge banner was still in place. For some reason Key could not understand, the banner was disturbing to him.

Hamburger whores? That was a new one on Key.

"Did you bring a change of clothing with you, Key?"

"Yes, as a matter of fact, I did."

She met him look for look, then smiled. The sadness did not leave her face or eyes. "Planning on spending the night?"

"I don't know. Is that an invitation?"

She shook her head. "No. Just a question, that's all."

Key turned his head slightly. Was that gunfire? He thought it was. In the rain? He cut his eyes to Rosanna. "Did you hear anything just then?"

"Probably gunshots. There are several gun clubs with shooting ranges out here. As a matter of fact, I come out here often to practice my shooting. Nobody pays any attention to it."

"I see. You told me yesterday you didn't know anything about guns."

"You knew I was lying."

"Yes, I did. We used to come out here as kids and shoot pistols. Remember?"

"Vividly."

Key sat down with a sigh. He leaned back on the couch. "Rosanna, would *you* please tell me what in the hell is going on in this county?"

"Why stress 'you'?"

"Are you going to tell me?"

She shrugged her shoulders. Key watched the rise and fall of her breasts with the gesture.

"Does that mean you don't know or you aren't going to tell me?"

"How about some coffee, Key?"

He exhaled slowly. Hell, play it her way. Do I have a choice? "Fine."

"Black, one sugar?"

"You have a good memory."

"Unfortunately."

She did not elaborate on that.

Coffee mug steaming on the low table in front of Key, Rosanna sat in a chair opposite him, facing him. "You want me to tell you the truth, Key?"

"It would be nice if somebody did."

She dropped her eyes. "I don't know, really, what is going on." Lying—she's lying. "I can tell you what happened to me and to a few of my friends. Then you add it up." Look me in the eyes, Rosanna. Stop lying. "One day Lewiston was a nice place to live. Very nice. The next day—no, that's a slight exaggeration of time—the town, no, the *people*, seemed to change."

"How so?" Look at me, goddammit, look at me.

She didn't. "Fear. That's the best word I can come up with. No, there is another word: Distrust. It just seems like people don't want to talk about . . . well, whatever it is that's wrong."

My old high school sweetheart is lying through her capped teeth, Key thought. "The TFL?"

Rosanna paled. Her hands trembled. "Old boyfriend of mine, don't even *think* those initials, much less say them aloud."

Key sipped his coffee and stared at her. "Will you please tell me, if you can, or will, how a bunch of right-wing, neo-fascists, probably very few in number, could, or have, whatever, buffalo an entire town into fear and silence?"

139

She rose abruptly and paced the room. Outside, the ever-increasing storm lashed its winds and rain against the lodge. Lightning lanced its fury, and thunder rumbled. Rosanna turned to face Key. Raising her arm, pointing at the banner, she said, "The kids will tell you, if you ask them, those letters stand for the name of a boy who was killed a few years ago. Kevin Compton. And maybe they do, but they have another meaning: Kill for Christ."

Key blinked. "I beg your pardon, Rosanna?"

"Kill for Christ. You know anything about Hitler's youth movement of the 1930s and '40s, Key?"

"Well, yeah. As much as the next guy, I suppose. Why?"

"The KCs are the TFL's youth organization. Their slogan is Kill for Christ."

"Rosanna, are you serious?"

"You're damn right I'm serious. Key, I could be killed for just telling you this. Like Mr. Warner."

"You think the coach was killed?"

"I think he was driven to kill his wife and then himself, yes."

"I'll buy that. Go on."

"Both the TFL and the KCs are paramilitary groups. They have drills twice a month. They use real guns and real bullets."

"Now wait a minute. How do you know all this?"

"I was cleaning up Jerry's room one afternoon, last year. I found all sorts of literature. I spent the rest of that day reading about the groups. I got so scared my hands were shaking."

"Do you have the literature?"

"No. The next day, while Jerry was at school, I

140

went back into his room. The pamphlets were gone. I was afraid to ask anybody about it. So I started snooping, listening more carefully to Skip and the boys talk. Pretending not to, but really listening. It didn't take long for me to discover all that crap I'd read about was what the boys were practicing. It's frightening, Key."

"Calm down, Rosanna. Every off-the-wall group of nuts and kooks and banana cream pies have their so-called youth movements. It's all part of the lunatic fringe. You still haven't told me how the TFL have managed to buffalo this entire town." Or what you're really up to this stormy afternoon. 'Cause Rosanna-darlin', I just flat out don't trust you."

"Files."

"Eh?"

"Files. Dossiers. Key, this group is big, very big. Thousands of members. It's nationwide. Bigger than that. It's all over the *world*. In every white nation — Aryan nation, the TFL calls it. From what I have learned, which isn't much — women aren't allowed much authority in the TFL."

Then how do you know this much, ex-high school sweetheart?

"They have computers hooked up, plugged in, or whatever it is that computers do, into other computers, like banks and S and Ls and government computers and credit bureaus and . . . hell, Key, just name something. The TFL has their slimy fingers in it."

Right-wing, racist, lunatic computer hackers. This mess just keeps getting stickier and dirtier and more complicated. "Have you ever been contacted by any member of the TFL or the KCs or any of their offshoots, threatening you in any way?"

She sighed. "Key, you know I have. Or suspect it, at least. And . . . several of my friends have. Sort of."

Sort of? Jesus Christ! "Rosanna, what do you mean, 'sort of'? Either they have, or they haven't. Which one is it?"

"Key, you don't understand. If . . . *they* learn I've told you anything, they'll . . ." She closed her mouth.

"Kill you?"

"She shook her head.

"Your name will never be mentioned in connection with this, Rosanna. I promise you that."

"You remember Merci Hebert?"

"Sure. We all graduated together."

"She never married. Lives here in Lewiston. She had a lesbian affair a long time ago. Back in college. Somehow, the TFL found out about it. That's how deep they go, Key. They have people in all walks of life. Anyway, they confronted her with it. Then they showed her files, photocopies, taken from a hospital where she'd had an abortion back during high school. *Twenty years back*. They threatened to expose her past. To the Catholic church, the town. She said she would never go along with them on anything. Then Stan Tabor arrested her one night on some trumped-up charge. I can't prove this; it's only hearsay, rumor. She was taken out into the country to some home. Some complex of buildings behind fences."

Bingo!

"Merci was forced into some . . . well, unnatural sex acts while some men filmed it. Then when it was over, she was shown films of other local women.

142

Some of them very prominent in Lewiston society. It's rumored that the sex acts were . . . well, very deviant in nature. But the camera didn't show the women being forced. It only showed them enjoying it, doing it voluntarily."

"Go on."

"That's a sample of the more obvious things the TFL have done. Usually, I'd guess, they'd just compile a file of people and confront them with it. You see what I'm getting at?"

"Everybody has dirt, right?"

"That's what I'd guess."

"What do they have on you, Rosanna?"

She walked to the rain-drenched window and stared out at the stormy afternoon. Without turning around, her breath clouding the pane, she said, "A man came to see me one afternoon. I will not now, or ever, tell you his name. He showed me pictures of child pornography. He told me, asked me, how I'd like to see my Mary in one of those pictures. He told me, in great detail, what would happen to her. It was awful, disgusting. After he left, I made it to the bathroom before I threw up. What do they ask of me?

"Really, very little. A contribution to, as they put it, 'God's work,' every now and then. A pledge to remain silent about them. And . . ." She sighed. "I might be asked to help out once in a while."

Like you're doing now? Key wondered. "Did you tell your husband about this man who came to see you?"

"No, but he knows about it. I can't prove that, but he does."

143

"His own daughter?"

She shrugged.

"The TFL professes to do God's work, right? But they rape and coerce and blackmail to get their way. How do they justify it?"

"They claim the end will justify the means. They say they have to fight fire with fire."

"Bullshit!"

She turned from the window with a start, her eyes wide as if she'd seen something that frightened her. "If you repeat any of what I just said, Key, I'll deny it."

"Relax. It's between us. Who fronts the local . . . well, cell, of the TFL?"

"I don't know. And that's the truth. I don't want to know."

"How many people that you know have been contacted, threatened, blackmailed by the TFL?"

"I told you. Most won't talk about it. But all my close friends have been contacted in some way."

"No town has that much dirt, Rosanna. It's impossible. There has to be more to it."

"Yes. But I think perhaps the majority of people in town, those who don't have something to hide, who aren't in the Jesus Files—"

"The what kind of files?"

"The Jesus Files. That's what I'm told the dossiers are called. Those people who are clean, well, I think they're just scared. It's contagious, Key. And to tell you the truth, as I see it, is this: I believe that a majority of people around here support what the TFL is doing. Maybe not entirely, but to a degree."

"That is very difficult for me to believe, Rosanna. I

144

don't remember the people around here being racist."

She was silent for a time. When she spoke, her words were touched with bitterness. "It isn't all racist. People who aren't racist can support a part of the TFL."

"How?"

"You've never had your farm seized, Key. Losing it through absolutely no fault of your own. You've never seen your entire life's work flushed right down the toilet. You've been gone for all of your adult life, Key. Out of the country. America, I mean. I doubt you're aware of the changes that have taken place in the U.S. For twenty years this nation went liberal. Murderers turned loose, scot-free, by liberal judges. Plea bargaining by thugs and punks and dopers and rapists and armed robbers and killers. Morals and ethics and standards of living eroded, rotted by . . ."

Key waited for her to finish. When she did not, he asked, "Eroded by . . . whom, Rosanna?"

"I'm not a racist, Key. You know that. Jimmy Brown was our best friend in high school—yours and mine. He ran with us. Jimmy and Lila. It never made any difference that they were black. Did it?"

"No. Where is Jimmy?"

"I don't know. Chicago, I think. His parents died a long time ago. He left after graduating from college and never came back."

"Lila?"

"She teaches in Lincoln. We still correspond a few times each year."

"What were you going to say, Rosanna?"

"Key, this is supposed to be a nation of free speech, right? Anyone should be able to speak the truth, as they see it, without fear of reprisal, right? It's changed, Key. Unless you're a so-called minority, you'd better keep your mouth shut. You'll see, if you stay back in America. God knows I despise the TFL and everything they stand for. But they make a few valid points, Key. They can take a half-truth and turn it just this much." She made a gesture with a small hand. "And have desperate people joining them. There is going to be a race war in this country, Key. I really believe that. And Key, I'm going to be on the winning side. I might not like the methods or many of the people I'll be associating with. But I'll worry about that and them after the smoke clears."

Key wasn't sure exactly what Rosanna was talking about. Or where she stood. She kept evading issues; speaking in semi-riddles. Was she a willing participant in the TFL? Or just where in the hell did she stand?

"Rosanna, are you telling me, after what the TFL did to you and your friends, you *support* them?"

She turned away, once more looking out at the stormy afternoon. Key waited. When she again turned to face him, she had tears in her eyes. "We're in a war around here, Key. I think you're sensing that. Have sensed it. Some of us have to do things we really don't want to do. Keep that in mind. You remember the story about the man riding the tiger — afraid to stay on and afraid to get off?"

Key nodded his head, his coffee forgotten and cooling on the table. The thunder rumbled as he looked at her. He knew where she was coming from now. "Who is Kevin Compton, Rosanna?"

A wicked licking of lightning ripped the sky. Thun-

146

der slammed, rattling the windows. The lights went out just a half second before the back door burst open.

Rosanna began screaming.

Chapter 12

Key hit the floor, rolling and twisting as he fell. He could see the shapes of men, three, no, four of them, leaping into the room from off the carport. The men wore battle dress, their faces shrouded by ski masks.

They had weapons in their hands.

Rolling, Key came up just as one of the hooded men swung the muzzle of a Mini-14 in his direction. Key ducked just as the man fired; he could feel the heat of the slug as it passed him. Something stung the side of his neck.

Key drove his balled fist into the V of another man's legs, smashing the man's balls. The man squalled in agony and dropped to the floor, crawling toward the door. Key grabbed up the man's pistol, a Colt .45, cocked and locked, and thumbed off the safety, triggering off a round.

But the recoil was more that of a .22 caliber. Odd.

Even the subdued booming of the .45 was enormous in the house. A split second after Key fired, a man screamed, dropping his Mini-14 and stumbling backward.

A man screamed something at Key. But Key could

not make out the words. The attacker screamed at Rosanna, then pointed an AR-15 at her.

Key shot him in the stomach. But instead of the impacting slug knocking the man spinning — and Key knew he had a true shot — the man simply turned and ran out the side door.

"Hit the floor, Rosanna!" Key yelled.

The sky deepened to the pitch of midnight, plunging the already murky den into near total darkness. The hooded men ran from the room. Key held his fire, believing he had a pistol with bad ammo. He heard the sounds of engines cranking up, followed by the slick sounds of tires spinning. The motor noises faded.

"You okay, Rosanna?"

"Yes."

Key eased the hammer down and laid the .45 on a table. "See if the phone works. Call the sheriff's department."

The lights popped back on as she was fumbling for the phone, lifting it to her ear with shaking hands. "It works. I'm calling them."

Key looked out the side door. The man he had shot in the gut was gone. There was no sign of blood on the concrete of the carport.

No way, Key thought. Just no way that was possible.

What the hell was going on?

"And you have no idea who they were, Rosanna?" Ted Gilbert asked. The .45 Key had used was sealed in a plastic evidence bag.

"None whatsoever, Ted. We were just talking—I was standing there and Key was sitting on the couch—when the lights went out and the side door burst open. It was crazy. They just started screaming and firing. Neither one of us could make out the words. But one bullet hit the window here." She pointed to the shattered windowpane. Oddly shattered. Key had never seen a window shattered in that manner by a single slug.

Key picked it up, conscious of State Patrolman Cosgrove's eyes on him. "I drove my fist into the balls of the man closest to me and grabbed up his forty-five. That one." He pointed to the pistol in the evidence bag. "I fired and knocked the Mini-fourteen out of another guy's hands. There." He pointed to the semiautomatic rifle. The rifle was oddly intact. A .45 slug would have shattered the stock. "I spun around in time to see a man pointing an AR-15 at Rosanna. I shot him in the stomach. He dropped his weapon and ran out the door. That's his weapon there. I yelled for Rosanna to hit the floor. The men ran out the side door. I elected not to follow them. That's it, sheriff."

"Well, Key," Ted said. "You done what you had to do. No question about that. Stan, you take pictures and gather up all the guns. I'll tell you what I think, Key. I think after we get through lookin' at them guns, we're gonna find 'em loaded with blanks. I'd bet a month's pay on that."

So would Key. He recalled that strange stinging on his neck after the man fired at him. He would bet he

150

had been hit with wadding. The men had been firing blanks. But why? And who were they? What point was all this?

He put that into words.

Ted said, "I think they were some good ol' boys from around here, Key. I think they took a chance and wanted to see if you was as tough as your reputation made you out to be. That's my opinion."

"Ted, I make no secret of the fact that I carry a nine millimeter pistol in my car. The state patrol knows it. What if I had used that weapon?"

"Then I reckon there'd be bodies all over this place, Key."

Key sure agreed with that.

"Folks," Ted said. "Let's not talk about this for a time, huh? We like to keep what happens in our county in our county, you know? We don't want the national press in here, 'cause they distort what they report."

"I sure agree with that," Key said, but not agreeing with Ted's motives for keeping them out.

Ted's eyes lit up, his expression changing. He looked at Key with new interest. Was that a victory smile on the man's face. Key thought so. But what victory had he won or witnessed? "You do, Key?"

"I certainly do." Key watched the man's face change. Might as well play the game, he thought. Let's see where it goes. "I have nothing but contempt for most of the national press."

"You don't say? I reckon all that knockin' around the world you done brought you in contact with a lot of press-types, huh?"

"Too many of them." In truth, Key had never been interviewed by any member of the press in his entire life.

Ted cut his eyes toward Patrolman Cosgrove. "Thanks for the assist, Ben. We can handle it from here on."

A dismissal.

The young highway cop nodded his head and left the house. Ted waited until the sounds of his car faded before speaking.

"What do you think about niggers, Key?"

Careful, Key silently warned himself. Play it Ted's way. "I try to avoid them. I always fought on the white side in Africa." Most uninformed Americans believe there are only two factions fighting in Africa: White and Black. That is a deadly misconception. With the exception of South Africa, most of the conflict is between communist black guerrillas and blacks seeking a more democratic form of government.

"You don't say? Most folks had you figured wrong, Key," Ted said. "How 'bout Jews, Key?"

"I don't like them." He said it flatly.

"Well, I be goddamned." Ted hitched his ass up on a table and looked at Key. "I can't figure you, Key. Word come back here that you was fightin' for the Jews."

"I was. But if you had a choice, with big money offered, between fighting for the Jews or the Arabs, which side would you take?"

Ted slowly nodded his head. "Yeah. I see your point. Key, you been gone a long time, ol' buddy. The

152

United States has changed a lot during that time."

Ted looked at Rosanna. "Rosanna-baby, how's about fixin' us some coffee?"

"Of course, sheriff." She walked out of the den, into the kitchen.

"Let's sit and talk some, Key." Ted waved a hand toward a chair. "Hell, we got all that silly high school grudge-crap behind us now."

Seated, Key said, "You were saying something about the nation changing?"

"For the worst, ol' buddy. The U.S. of A. has hit the pits. It's bad. Cops' hands is tied when it comes to dealin' with street slime. Taxpayer money is bein' used to feed lazy-assed jungle-bunnies. Their lack of morals is spillin' over to white kids. We can't take much more of it, Key. You know where I'm comin' from?"

Key knew. "Yes, I do, Ted. But I don't know what can be done to correct it."

"Ahh, but there is a solution to the problem. You see, Key. Jews control the banks, the money supply. Big business. The TV networks and the newspapers. A person ain't never gonna hear the truth about niggers 'cause the Jews won't let it be spoken on the airwaves or printed in newspapers or books. It's all one-sided. The niggers is always right, the white people is always wrong."

Key was beginning to understand a little more of how the TFL worked; how they played on the passions of people.

"Hell, Key, some Jews even *marry* them sambos." Ted shook his head. "You know what I mean?"

"Oh, yeah." It was as if the attack on the lodge

153

were secondary to Ted. Key now felt no effort would be made to find the attackers. In fact, Key felt the sheriff knew who the men were; might have even had something to do with the attack. But damned if he knew why.

Key bent down to pick up his coffee mug off the carpet. Knocked off during the brief—whatever in the hell it had been. Placing the mug on the coffee table, Key leaned back, meeting Ted's eyes. Stan Tabor had gone into the kitchen. Key could hear his voice, speaking to Rosanna. He could not make out the words.

"The truth is bein' kept from the American public, Key," Ted said. "The Jews know if the taxpayin' public finds out the truth, they'll revolt."

What truth and who will revolt?

"The white people have to be shown that Jews and niggers is the enemy. We can handle the communists; we know their strength and true intentions—they make it plain. But those others, Key, they sneaky."

Key nodded in agreement. "Well, Ted, it's like you said: I've been gone a long time. I know, in the time I've been back, that the farmers are in trouble. But whose fault is that?"

"Jews, Key. The Jews control the banks. The Jews is keepin' the price of grain and other farm goods down, forcin' farmers into bankruptcy. It fits, Key. Think about it."

Yeah, it all fits if a very persuasive speaker is in front of a lot of desperate people, all looking for someone to blame for their troubles. "I noticed Steinbergs and Greenes were no longer in business."

Ted grinned. "Yeah. We got . . . ah . . . they left. Look, Key, we're gonna have a meeting tomorrow night, out at my place. You 'member the old place? Sure. 'Bout seven. You be there?"

"I'll be there, Ted."

Over coffee, Stan took a few more notes while Ted asked a few more questions about the attack. By now, Key knew it was all a sham. But what was the point of the attack? A test? For what? Key felt he might never find out.

The sheriff and his chief deputy left a few minutes later. Key and Rosanna sat in the den, looking at each other.

"What did Stan have to say, Rosanna?"

Her features hardened. "He said, quoting, 'You done a good job, baby. When you gonna shake loose with some of that pussy?' I *despise* that man."

"Understandably so. So your having me out here was a setup?"

"I didn't have a choice, Key. I felt you would understand. But I swear to you, I didn't know what was going to happen. It scared the hell out of me."

"I noticed."

The phone rang. Rosanna picked it up and listened for a moment. "Fine, baby. I'll be home in a little bit." She hung up and turned to Key. "My daughter, Mary. The TFL just returned her to my house. She said she had fun on the picnic. Do I have to say more?"

"They had her to make sure you'd go through with this?"

"Yes."

"How about your husband?"

"He didn't know. It wouldn't have made any difference. He would have obeyed orders."

"But that's his *daughter!*"

Her gaze was very bleak. "Believe me when I say, Key, he would have obeyed orders."

She said it with such hardness that Key knew then he was dealing with, or about to deal with, an organization that was as ruthless as any he'd ever faced. "I wonder why the sudden turnaround where I'm concerned?"

She shrugged. "I think the TFL desperately needs men of your experience."

"I wonder if the order came from the top."

"I'm just a little, very unwilling cog in a great big wheel, Key. I don't know."

"I can't believe you'd pull something like this!" the man screamed the words. "You goddamned, ignorant bastard."

"It worked, didn't it?" Ted defended his actions.

"Maybe. But how in the hell did the state patrol get involved in it?"

"He was sittin' in the office when Rosanna called. Just bad timin'."

The man paced the floor of the warehouse, his shoes squeaking as he walked. The cuffs of his suit pants were wet from the recent rain. He whirled to face the sheriff. "You are aware that if I reported this to the top, they'd kill you?"

"I know. Look, it worked. You was wrong about

Key and I was right. Okay, okay I went out of line some. But I played my hunches and they proved out. Look, wouldn't you rather have him with us than against us? Dammit, we *need* his experience. We got to have it. Link said Key was like a goddamned tiger back there."

The man paced for a few seconds more. "Maybe you're right. One thing for sure. We can keep a better eye on him this way. But goddamn you, Ted, if you ever mention my name to Key, you're a dead man. You understand that?"

"I understand. No one will mention your name. That's a promise."

The man, still angry, spun around and stalked out of the warehouse.

Key and Rosanna stood in the den in silence. Both knew that anything that might have been developing between them was gone. At least for the moment.

"I'm unwillingly committed to this, Key," she said. "And I hope you know why. I despise my husband and the TFL, but I will not allow my daughter to be hurt."

Key nodded his head. "Tell me about this Kevin Compton you mentioned."

"Key, get out of this county. Go . . . somewhere. But get out. Please. Don't become involved in this."

"You can't seem to make up your mind what side you're on, can you?"

"You're a fool, Key!"

"Kevin Compton?"

"It happened about . . . I don't know . . . five or six years ago. In a town not far from here. He was sixteen, I think. He was attacked by a gang of young black toughs. They tried to mug him—hit him with a tire iron, I think it was. Kevin died. The blacks got off without doing any prison time. They claimed Kevin made some racial slurs toward them. Provoking the attack. They claimed, of all things, that it was self-defense."

"How many were there?"

"Five."

"Did Kevin provoke the attack?"

"No one seems to think so. He wasn't that type of boy. Kevin was really a pretty nice kid. But the case kept dragging on and got blown out of proportion."

"Then there was injustice done?"

"I really, personally, believe so. But, on the other side of the coin, how much injustice has been done against black people?"

"That's not the point. That kind of thinking feeds hate groups. What is done and past is over. If justice is not administered fairly and equally, it's a sham. I wish to hell people would understand that."

"Now which side are you on, Key?"

"Neither one, Rosanna."

"You can't have that attitude in this county, Key."

"Wanna bet?"

"I'm telling you, Key: Get out of here."

He shook his head. "I'm back home to stay, Rosanna. No one is going to run me out. I'll listen to what Ted has to say, then I'll politely decline any offer to join and go my own way."

"They won't let you do that, Key. Believe me, I know. And if you try to fight them, they'll kill you."

"A lot of people have tried that over the years. I'm still alive and well."

"You've always fought a known enemy, Key. With the TFL and all the other groups aligned with them, you're fighting—or will be fighting—an unknown. Key, these people, almost all of them, are shadow people. And you're standing right in the middle of their territory."

"We'll see."

She sighed, shaking her head in frustration and defeat. "You'd better go, Key."

"All right. How about that broken window?"

"I'll tape something over it. One thing about the TFL being in this county: We don't have much in the way of crime. I'm sorry about this, Key."

"We all do what we have to do, Rosanna. Why don't you take your child and get the hell out of this part of the country?"

Her look and answer was filled with sadness. "And go where, Key? I inherited a lot of rent property when my parents died. I own farmland I lease out. I own the farm equipment it's worked with. Do you know what would happen to my property if I were to leave?"

Slick, he thought. The TFL is mighty slick. Their main weapon is fear and intimidation. "I could probably guess."

"And you'd probably be right. That's what keeps a lot of people staying."

"I . . . see."

"So nothing else has to be said about my leaving, right?"

"I guess not."

"It's been nice seeing you again, Key. Maybe we'll see each other again."

"Under better circumstances, I hope."

"Not around here, lover. Not for a long, long time."

Key nodded and walked out the door without looking back.

As he backed out of the drive he thought: All in all, it was shaping up into one hell of a homecoming.

Chapter 13

Key did not feel like returning to the farm. He did not feel like doing much of anything except knocking the crap out of somebody.

Problem was he didn't know who that somebody might be.

On impulse, he cut down to Highway 34, turned west, and drove the miles to Grand Island, checking into the first decent motel he came to. He called his old (or was it his present) employer outside Washington, D.C. and asked to speak to Jeff.

Gone home.

Key thanked the man and hung up. He had Jeff's home phone number and dialed it.

"Jeff, what in the hell have you got me into now?"

A couple of thousand miles away, Jeff laughed. "Same ol' Key. Come right to the point. No 'how you doing?' No 'how's the wife and kids?' Just . . . *bang!*"

"I repeat: What is going on out here?"

"That's what we want you to find out. Same

arrangements as before. Five hundred a day plus expenses. So far you've earned a couple thousand taxpayer dollars. What can you report?"

Key started to bring the company man up to date. But his inner warning light began silently flashing. He had worked for the company many times, but had never fully trusted it. "Fifty thousand dollars, Jeff, placed in my overseas account. You have the number and the means."

"Don't you trust me, ol' buddy?"

"No."

Jeff laughed. "I'll have it done tonight."

"I'll check it first thing in the morning."

"I know that."

"You ever heard of the TFL?"

"I've heard of the PTL. My wife is hooked on it."

"Very funny, Jeff. Hysterical. You missed your calling."

"Have you had a bad day, Key?" Jeff asked blandly. "You're very testy."

"You might say that."

"Have you picked up your gear you had shipped express?"

That didn't surprise Key. The company knew damn near everything that was going on. Especially who was buying what sort of arms from whom. Sometimes they let it go through, sometimes they blocked it.

It all depends upon who is doing the buying and for what.

"Not yet. Did it arrive?"

"As far as we know, yes."

Key hit the high points of the past two days, leaving a lot out.

"Join them, Key."

"I haven't been asked. Jeff, I cannot believe an organization of this much power and secrecy would approach me this fast with an offer to join. Not when you consider the government has not, as yet, as far as I know, been able to penetrate them."

"The gold badge boys have penetrated some groups; this is a new one. New to us. But they're all tied together. Bet on it."

There was a knock on the door. "Gotta go, Jeff." Key hung up and swung off the bed, answering the door. State Patrolman Ben Cosgrove faced him.

Ben was dressed in civilian clothes. Key waved him inside and shut the door as his eyes swept the young man. Was he wearing a wire? Key couldn't tell.

"You follow me, Ben?"

"Yes, I did. I have to talk with you, Mr. Lessard. It's very important that I speak with someone I feel I can trust."

"Ben, you don't know that you can trust me. You don't know anything about me."

"I know more than you think. I've checked you out pretty thoroughly—doing it very quietly. I . . . well, you've got a checkered past; no one could deny that. But from what all I can find out about you, you're not a racist or a radical; you have no desire to overthrow the government—"

"What would I do with it?" Key interrupted with a

grin.

The grin was not infectious. "And oddly enough, even though you worked as a mercenary, you paid taxes on the monies you earned. I find that incredible."

"I paid taxes on *some* of the monies I earned," Key corrected.

"No matter." The patrolman brushed that aside. "I have to play my hunches, and my hunches say you're straight."

"Thanks for the trust. But how can I trust you? You might be wearing a wire."

The patrolman took off his shirt, his jeans, and his boots. All he kept on was his jockey shorts. He was not wearing a wire. Not unless his dick was the size of pencil. A very small one.

"Put your clothes back on, Ben. You're not my type."

The highway cop managed a grin. "That's a relief."

As Ben dressed, Key ordered coffee and sandwiches sent to the room. Sitting down, looking at Ben, Key asked, "Okay, trooper, what's the problem?"

"Mr. Lessard, I think the patrol has been compromised."

Upon closer and careful questioning, Key learned that Ben believed two or three state patrolmen might have some direct ties with the TFL. Several more that Ben knew of might have sympathies toward the TFL.

It was about what Key had expected to hear.

"Ben, a half dozen people out of a force of several hundred does not mean the patrol has been compromised."

The young patrolman's eyes flashed. "Maybe not," he said hotly. "But it's sure a damned disgrace."

Very idealistic young man. "Cops are human, Ben. None of you sprang directly from Camelot."

"You don't talk like a mercenary, Mr. Lessard."

Key smiled. "Have you known many mercenaries, Ben?"

"I've never known *any* mercenaries. Before you."

"What is your opinion of what took place today at Rosanna's?"

"I think it was a test, Mr. Lessard."

"My name is Key. My father is Mr. Lessard. What sort of test and why?"

"A test to see if you are as tough as your reputation makes you out to be."

"Then Ted was probably telling the truth back there."

"I think so. I also think that the sheriff set up the test."

Key leaned back in his chair. A very uncomfortable chair. Maybe Rosanna was right. Maybe Key should just pack it up and clear out of Alton County. It was certainly a tempting thought.

But Key knew he wouldn't, couldn't do that.

Key spent another hour chatting with the young state patrolman. At the end of that time, he was convinced Ben Cosgrove had no ties with the TFL. But Ben was convinced that his own brother, Ned, was involved.

Key was also sure that he had found a much needed

friend in the highway cop.

When he told Ben about being invited to a meeting at Sheriff Gilbert's home, the young man was both appalled and fascinated; and, Key thought, suspicious.

"Relax, Ben. I'm not a likely candidate for burning crosses and wearing bedsheets."

"That's not it, Key. They might be setting you up for a fall."

"That thought has crossed my mind. But I don't believe that's it. I think they need men experienced in weapons and explosives. And I think I'll be asked to join."

"Will you?"

Key didn't know; hadn't made up his mind about that. He sure as hell didn't owe the agency anything. He had given them a lot of good years and was tired of the strain. He'd made a lot of money working deep cover for the company, but he'd given them sweat and blood for his pay. He felt he owed them nothing. And the thing that puzzled him more and more, as he thought about it, was why the agency was so interested in the TFL. Why didn't they just hand it over to the bureau?

Unanswered questions on top of more unanswered questions.

But Key felt he did owe his family. He believed that would be the deciding factor.

He also had to make up his mind about Ben Cosgrove. Looking at the highway cop, Key made both decisions.

"Yes, I will join them, Ben. And whatever I learn about them, I'll be relaying that information to two parties. You'll be one of them."

"I won't even ask who the other is."

"That would be best. Then I won't have to lie to you."

"Key, have you considered that I might not be what I say I am?"

"Yes."

"Suppose I did turn out to be working for the TFL?"

Key's eyes turned cold as he looked at the highway cop. His voice brought chill bumps to Ben's flesh. "If that turns out to be true, you'll never hear the bullet that blows your fucking head off."

BOOK TWO

THE UNREST

Chapter 1

"Some boxes came for you yesterday," Dad Lessard told Key. "I put 'em in the room off the den. Didn't open none. Don't wanna know what's in 'em."

"You sure about that, Dad?"

"I'm certain. Fresh pot of coffee on the stove. You want breakfast, you know how to cook it. I'm goin' into town. You gonna be here tonight?"

"I'll be going out. I may or may not be back tonight."

The father's eyes searched the son's face. "Don't get your ass in a crack, boy," he warned. "And you know what I mean."

"I'll do my best."

The old man appeared to have something else on his mind. But whatever it was, it remained unsaid. He walked out of the house.

Key stayed close to the house that day, reading, puttering around—and thinking about the upcoming meeting that night. Something he viewed with very mixed feelings.

At noon, he called Cat's office. Her secretary informed him she had been delayed and would not be back until the next day.

Key opened his boxes and inspected his hardware. The M-16 was not new, but it was in excellent shape. And fully automatic. He spent an hour going over his ammo, checking each round for burrs; he discarded a half a dozen rounds, believing they might malfunction and jam up the weapon. He checked the grenades, one by one. It was indeed a mixed bag, including a dozen of what was probably the most lethal grenade ever manufactured: The M-512 Firefrag, produced by Accuracy Systems. The M-512 combines both fragmentation and incendiary capabilities—in large doses—but remains the size of a standard CS or smoke canister.

Then Key laughed softly as he reached the bottom of the box. A steel pot and a gas mask in a pouch. His buddy was needling him, for Key did not like gas masks; usually that's the first thing a G.I. will discard. Key started to throw the mask away, then hesitated. No, he'd keep it.

Key realized then he had known all along he was staying in Alton County. His subconscious mind had been made up all along. As a professional warrior, he knew when to run and when to stay—the discretion over valor bit. Only a fool stands and dies when there is nothing at all to be gained by it.

He filled his extra clips and stored everything in a shed behind the main house.

For some reason, unknown to Key, his brothers and sister were staying away from him.

And he wondered why?

He took a nap, something he did only rarely, then showered and dressed. He pulled into the drive of the old Gilbert home — restored and renovated — promptly at seven.

"I ain't never seen a nigger that's as smart as a white man," a middle-aged man was saying as Key walked in. He recognized the speaker as Chris Litton. Litton had never been one of Key's favorite people. But no man's racial beliefs ever played much importance as to whether Key liked or disliked him. Key believed a person was entitled to his opinion. As long as that opinion did not end with that person's fist colliding with Key's nose. Free speech was part of the price one must pay for living in a democracy.

Although there are some who would stifle that part of the Constitution, all the while practicing their own form of venomous spewing of the mouth — on both sides of the color and/or race line.

Key had learned long ago that the world was filled to capacity with closet hypocrites.

Key was surprised at the number of people in attendance at the large home. He guessed between thirty-five and forty people. All men. That jibed with what he'd been told about the membership of the TFL.

And Key knew he was right in the middle of the TFL.

Key was familiar with the names of almost every man present. He could put faces with the names of most. Their age ranged, he guessed, from the midtwenties to early sixties. And they looked fit. To a man.

There were cold drinks, coffee, and iced tea; but no

beer or hard liquor. Plates of sandwiches were on the table in the dining room.

After Key was introduced and sized up by each man present, Ted took Key's arm. "Eat up, ol' buddy. We got us a fine speaker tonight. Come over from Arkansas to be with us for a week or so. You'll meet him later on."

Key ate a sandwich and walked around the house, a glass of iced tea in his hand. He listened to fragments of a dozen separate conversations. Some extolled the virtues of this weapon over that one; they discussed the price of silver and who had what to swap and where to find it. They spoke openly of their discontent with the federal government and how they "wished to hell something could be done about it." Overthrowing it seemed the best answer.

And their solution to almost every problem they felt faced America was simple: Violence. But they never mentioned the TFL.

The pot is boiling, Key thought, moving from group to group. If several hundred of these little bands of men are meeting across the land—and he did not find that number hard to accept—the nation is truly in trouble. Deep, divisive trouble.

Key moved from group to group, listening, saying nothing.

". . . time a nigger farts a congressman's got his nose stuck up the coon's ass."

". . . goddamn lawyers is the problem."

". . . goddamn bankers is all in cahoots. I'll be glad when the economy falls apart."

". . . oughtta shoot every goddamned queer we can find."

Violence.

Hate.

Bigotry.

All wrapped up in a religious banner.

"All right, folks!" Ted shouted down the buzz of conversation. "Let's all ease out to the barn and find a seat."

The barn had not been used as such for many years. It had been completely remodeled and refurbished— on the inside. The outside still looked like a barn. But the inside had been turned into an adequate, if not fancy, meeting place, with chairs and a raised platform and rostrum. The men seated, Ted took the podium and waved the group into silence.

"In just a minute, boys, I'm going to introduce our guest speaker, John. You all know why I don't use his last name. In this the Land of the Free and the Home of the Brave, with guaranteed free speech, we have to be careful that Big Brother don't find out about these meetings. If that happens, we gonna be hassled and probably arrested. 'Course if we was colored black we wouldn't have nothin' to fear. We could cuss the white people and talk about overthrowin' the government and fuckin' white women and all that, and the government would leave us alone.

"But our time is comin', boys. With the help of the true Lord, we're gonna make it. Now before I introduce John, let's all stand for a moment of silent prayer and meditation."

John took the podium as the men were sitting back down. Key guessed him to be in his mid-forties, solidly built and very capable looking. He smiled at the group and laid a clipboard on the stand.

"I thank you all for coming out this night. What I am about to read to you is a newspaper article that was written anonymously. It is chillingly accurate, and reads as follows:

"I am living in a nightmare, whence I cannot awaken. Welcome to my nightmare.

This is the Land of the Free and the Home of the Brave. Whisper the truth in this brave, free land, and they call you a bigot. Suggest the obvious and you are a fascist. Welcome to my nightmare.

We give cash money, free medical services, food stamps, free housing, and utility subsidies to the poorest class of society, as a payment for producing welfare babies, usually illegitimate. Those who pay the taxes for these services—the workers—must first pay their taxes and then pay retail prices for goods and services. Welcome to my nightmare.

Everyone can do everything as well as anyone else, whether they can or not. If the test results prove otherwise, change the tests. We no longer value equality of opportunity, but rather equality of result. Equality of opportunity means that some will fail; therefore, boost up all those who might fail, even though now no one may succeed. We must now discriminate in favor of minority children and grandchildren, and against other children and grandchildren, in the name of justice. Welcome to my nightmare.

Lawyers and judges control every facet of our lives, public and private. No one is safe from a lawsuit, no matter how ridiculous. Policemen cannot arrest, teachers cannot teach, bureaucrats cannot administer, without fear that they soon will answer to somebody's lawyer, for some half-forgotten mistake. So, in many cases, they do nothing at all. Welcome to my nightmare.

You may speak these words privately, because everyone knows they are true. You may not speak them publicly, because then you are intolerant; you despise the poor; and you smile upon oppression. We adore freedom of speech, but do not dare use it. Use it, and we will punish you. Welcome to my nightmare.''

John paused for effect, his eyes touching every man in the huge meeting room.

Slick, Key thought. He knew, from talking with friends, that the welfare departments in America were out of control. But as any person who possessed the ability to see both sides of any issue, Key knew he could truthfully attack the whole, but not the part.

Slick. Just damned slick. And he doubted the judge meant for his remarks to be used as John was using them.

". . . We're in a war for survival, friends," John was saying. "There are many out there," he said and waved his hand, "bent on destroying this nation. And those of us who gather in small groups, attempting to find a way out of the horror, are labeled, branded Nazis, bigots, terrorists. You know all the names we're called by the left-leaning press. Just as you all know the real enemies of America.

"Let me tell you something that you might not

know. For years true Americans have tried to make English the official language of America. For years their efforts have been thwarted. I've been to certain sections of this once great nation where I thought I was in a foreign country. All the damned gibber-jabbering would make you sick. And very nervous. True Americans are rapidly becoming an endangered species—deliberately so. And we all know who is behind that movement, don't we?"

The men nodded their heads in agreement, murmuring hate-filled words about Jews and niggers and spics and slant-eyes.

Key thought: If these people ever get all their shit together, they are going to be a very awesome group, indeed.

I wonder how many groups like this are scattered around the country?

Ted Gilbert stepped up on the platform, announcing a question and answer session. He smiled at Key. Key returned the smile, making a circle of thumb and forefinger, signaling Ted he was in agreement with all he'd heard that evening. Ted's smile widened.

John answered the barrage of questions thrown at him. Guns, explosives, survival gear, how to survive a monetary failure. And he did so in that same calm voice in which he'd delivered his short speech.

And while he was knowledgeable on certain matters, Key soon realized the man was no weapons or explosives expert. And he had no knowledge of guerrilla warfare. He was an organizer, an administrator, and probably very good at his multiple jobs. But Key doubted the man had ever seen combat. John verbally painted combat as glamorous and macho.

178

Combat is anything but glamorous. Combat is dirty, gut-wrenching, mind-warping, and hideous. The smell of torn and burned and ruined flesh is quite simply a subject that cannot be related to a noncombatant. It is impossible to describe on paper on in a speech. One must experience it.

And Key knew John had never seen actual combat. But looking around the room, his eyes briefly touching each man present, Key was sure he recognized the stamp of the marine, the paratroopers, the combat vet, on several faces. Those were the ones who asked no questions of John. They didn't have to. They knew more than John did about combat.

When the question and answer session had concluded, Ted motioned for Key to join him. Key shook hands with John, knowing the man was inspecting him.

"I've heard of you, Mr. Lessard," John said. "It is indeed an honor to meet you."

"Yes, sir!" Ted said. "Me and ol' Key go way back, John. What did you think of the gatherin', Key?"

"Very interesting and very informative," Key replied. "I enjoyed it. I've been gone—out of the country—for a good many years. Since my return, I've had my eyes opened on a great many issues."

John lit his pipe and puffed for a few seconds. "Oh? How is that, Mr. Lessard?"

Steady, Key thought. Be careful. Your answers right now will probably determine whether or not you're allowed inside this group.

"The farm crisis," Key said. "The money crisis in this country. Declining morals. The nation's lack of direction. Hideous music on the radio. Filth. And,

I'll have to admit it . . . niggers."

John smiled around the stem of his pipe. "Porch monkeys. Yes, you're right. Products of a welfare state. Lay all that on that goddamned Negro-loving Roosevelt's door steps. Hitler had the right idea, of course. His only problem was that he didn't include the black race along with the Jews. The United States made a terrible error in judgement by fighting Germany back then. We should have left Hitler alone; that great and noble man would have solved a lot of problems for us. You agree with that, Mr. Lessard?"

The words burned Key's tongue even as they were forming. But he knew he had to speak them. Convincingly. "Yes, I do—now. But I'm wondering if it's too late for us to do anything about it."

John and Ted cut their eyes at each other at Key's use of 'us.' "Oh, I think not," John said. "But we don't want you to make up your mind about . . . our group for a time. Say," he said smiling, "you know what total confusion is, Mr. Lessard?"

"Well . . . no, I guess not."

John winked at Key. "Father's Day in Harlem."

John and Ted slapped each other on the back and laughed. Key joined them with a smile.

John took Key's arm. "Come, Mr. Lessard. We want to show you something. It's disgusting and vile, but worth viewing nonetheless. It graphically depicts our enemies."

"One of them," Ted said.

"Quite right, Ted," John said. "One of them."

A big screen TV was wheeled out and hooked to a video machine. Key had a hunch what he was about to see, and his hunch proved out.

A porn flick.

But more than that. Key felt he was about to view a snuff film. The men in the film were black and menacing looking; the woman was white and young and rather pretty — in a blank, doped-up sort of way. The young woman was first whipped by the black men, then raped and sodomized.

Then killed.

It was not the most disgusting thing Key had ever seen. After a lifetime of war, there was very little left that could shock Key. He had long ago learned how to turn off his mind to horror. Professional warriors must learn to do that — or lose their mind.

And Key knew who would be blamed for the porn and the killing: Blacks and Jews.

John did not disappoint him. With the lights back on, Key had to hide a smile as the men in the room wriggled and squirmed in their seats, attempting to hide the fact that all of them had a hard-on from viewing the skin and snuff film. They sat with passion-induced red faces, licking dry lips and, as subtly as possibly, pulling at themselves.

What a bunch of jerks! Key thought. No better than the stories he'd heard concerning SS and Gestapo men who got their nuts off by torture.

And these people are going to save the nation? How wonderful.

Reasonably assured that Key was, if not yet a member of the group, at least sympathetic to them, John let the verbal hammer down after the killing pornography. He banged his fists on the stand and poured out his hate, the venom spewing like raw sewage from a broken pipe.

Key sat through it, forcing himself to remain attentive and to nod his head and smile in all the right places. He felt unclean, wanting very much to take a long, hot, soapy shower.

He remained in his seat, listening.

But he felt sick to his stomach.

Chapter 2

For all of John's hatred and bigotry, he never once in his wild, sometimes screaming harangue, advocated killing. He spoke of doing "something" to the niggers and Jews. He spoke of "stopping once and for all the black savages and the Jews." But he never mentioned violence as the way to do that. He spoke of every member arming themselves, but he never mentioned using those arms in any act other than self-defense.

Slick, was the word that came to Key's mind. John is no fool.

And he wondered if John could possibly be the head of the TFL.

No, Key rejected that. Key did place John very high within the organization, but the group John was a part of might not necessarily be the TFL, since he believed the TFL to be an offshoot and part of a much bigger hate group.

The meeting closed with a prayer to the "true Jesus Christ."

Key wondered how the members could possibly believe that crap.

"Key," Ted said, approaching him after the meeting. "Betcha never thought you'd find something like this in ol' peaceful Lewiston, huh?"

Key's reply was given in all honesty. "No, I didn't, Ted. But I can see where something like this is certainly necessary, conditions being what they are."

There was a funny, odd light in Ted's eyes. He patted Key's arm. "We'll be in touch, boy. You hang loose, now."

Key looked around him. The men attending the meeting had slipped away into the night, leaving the farm four and five to a car, to cut down on the sights and sounds of traffic. Again, Key thought: Slick. They've been doing this for a long time; they've got it down pat.

Restless, tension high within him, Key drove the back roads of Alton County, not knowing where to go to unwind. Or how to unwind.

He looked down on the floorboards, passenger side. A sheet of paper lay on the mat. Pulling over, Key turned on the interior light and read the typewritten words:

Do not be confused. Race is the main issue. The time for revolution against Zog is near. Be ready.

Zog?

Key read on. ZOG, according to the letter, meant Zionist Occupation Government. The letter took the position that a consortium of Jews, mostly bankers, really ran the government of the United States by controlling all the money. Jews controlled the major TV networks and the news departments; Jews controlled the nations' newspapers and major publishing companies. If one doubted that, just watch the credits roll at the end of whatever program.

The letter was a quieter rehash of John's words. Key folded the paper and put it in the glove compartment.

State Patrolman Ben Cosgrove's words returned to him. *We think they're Nazis.*

That made more sense than anything Key had come up with thus far. The Nazi Party, under a different name, using the economic strain that many farmers were feeling, could very easily fill their membership quotas with desperate people, faced with losing their homes and farms and way of life.

Those people, dissatisfied with their government, would be looking for a place to put blame.

And that is how hate groups are formed.

Same old song, different jukebox.

So if all these off-the-wall groups were, in fact, just a front for Nazism, it stood to reason that one man headed them all. But who was he and where was he?

More unanswered questions.

Key cut off the interior light and pulled back onto the road, heading home.

Key stayed close to home until the weekend. He puttered around the shop, helping his brothers do minor equipment repairs. He fixed the back steps of the main farm house, installing a new railing on one side, replacing the rotting railing.

On a Friday afternoon, working alone with Rolf, his brother asked, "Did you enjoy the meeting at Ted's house the other night, Key?"

Key laid down his wrench and wiped sweat from his face. "How'd you hear about that, Rolf?"

"Word gets around. Be careful, Key."

"A lot of hate in this county, Rolf."

"A lot of hate in this whole country, Key. It's unhealthy."

"Have you ever felt like joining any right-wing group, Rolf?"

Rolf looked at him and walked off without answering.

Dad Lessard called to Key from the back steps. "Phone call for you, boy. A woman."

"Key?"

He recognized the voice. Cat. "Yes."

"Sorry I had to miss our luncheon date the other day, Key. But I've been very busy."

"You all caught up, now?"

"Oh, yes."

"How about dinner?"

"Fine. My place all right with you?"

"Wonderful. About seven?"

"Anytime after six, Key."

"I'll see you then."

Key turned to find his father staring at him.

"Something on your mind, Dad?"

"Yeah. You're really plannin' on stayin' around,

ain't you, boy?"

"Yes, I am."

"You thinkin' about gettin' serious with that female lawyer?"

"It's a distinct possibility."

Dad Lessard grunted. "You could do worse. You two get hitched up, both of you ought to move on out of this part of the country. Sell out and get out. Before it's too late."

"How about you and David and Rolf and Claire, Dad?"

"We'll make do." The old man turned and walked away.

"Dad!"

Taylor did not look around. He closed the door to the room he had turned into an office/study.

What was that line from Alice? Curiouser and curiouser!

Cat wore tailored slacks and a blouse that, together, probably cost more than a lot of people made in a week. Her shoes were of soft Italian leather. Several hundred bucks' worth of footwear, he guessed.

"I pass inspection?" she asked with what seemed to be a strained smile.

Key stepped into the house. "Oh, yes. Sorry if I stared."

The front door closed, shutting out the heat of the late afternoon, or early evening, depending on one's inner clock. Discounting the DST, Cat said, "If one has money, I don't believe in hoarding it. Or are you one of those people who believe in wealth redistribution?"

Might be a very defensive afternoon. Or evening. Whatever. "Not hardly. I'm not really sure I believe in paying taxes. Not the way it's set up presently, that is."

Her smile was still a bit strained around the edges. "I seem to find that philosophy somehow familiar."

"I belong to no right-wing group, Cat. None."

"Yet," she corrected.

"Word gets around, doesn't it?"

She did not reply; only stared at him. Her eyes were hot with — anger? Key wasn't sure. But he could sense a growing wall of — what? Hostility, perhaps, building between them. Something was slightly off-center. He was certain of that.

"You want to tell me what's wrong, Cat?"

"You tell me."

"All right. I went to a meeting out at Ted's place. Heard a speaker from Arkansas." He decided not to mention John's name. "It was an interesting evening, to say the least." If she wanted to hear more, she could prompt him.

Key watched her relax just a bit, losing some of her tension.

"Cat, if you are so disliked and distrusted by so many people around here, why do you stay?"

"It's a free country."

Key laughed at that.

Her face flushed, Cat said, "You don't believe that?"

188

"Why, hell, no! And neither do you. Oh, we enjoy more freedom than most other countries, but let's don't go overboard with the vocalizing of it."

She held up her hands in a gesture of surrender. "Okay, Key. Let's not quarrel anymore. I'm . . . I'll admit to being somewhat uptight. I apologize."

"You weren't uptight when you called the farm today. What's happened since then?"

She walked to a small French desk and picked up an envelope, holding it out to him. Key removed the single sheet of paper, typed single-space, and began to read.

The letter was filled with profanity, outlining in great detail what the sender, or senders, would like to do to Cat—and how he, or they, would like to do it.

"You get this today, Cat?"

"Yes."

"Somebody has a vivid imagination."

"Bullshit!" she spat. "Somebody has a garbage can for a brain."

The letter was unsigned except for the initials K.C.

Key sat down on the couch and reread the letter. There were many misspelled words, and the note was very juvenile in content, suggesting sexual activities that were, at least to Key's mind, physically impossible. Or damned uncomfortable. Kids, came to his mind. Kids wrote this.

"The KCs," Key said.

"You're familiar with those initials?"

"Kill for Christ."

"I beg your pardon." Cat sat down on the couch beside him.

"It's the youth movement of the TFL. They call themselves Kill for Christ. Young people wrote this letter. Not the adult members of the TFL."

"That's interesting, I think. How did you find out about the KCs?"

"Someone told me." He had promised Rosanna he would keep her name out of it, and he intended to keep that promise.

She nodded and decided not to pursue it. "I won't ask who. I'll fix us a drink."

After the initial tenseness and slight bickering, that delicate intimacy they had both felt during their previous encounter gradually returned, gentling them both.

All that was cracked when Key said, "Tell me what you think happened to Henry Randolph, Cat."

"I think he was murdered. Murdered by the TFL when they felt he was getting too close to revealing the top men. I—"

The doorbell donged softly, followed by the faint sounds of running feet.

Cat rose from the couch and walked to the door, pulling it open. The small circular porch was empty, except for a box sitting on the bricks.

"Key!"

Key walked swiftly to her side, his eyes finding the box. "You expecting some late delivery?"

"No."

"Don't touch it." He squatted down beside the box and looked at it. It was addressed to Miss Catherine Cunt Monnet, printed in block letters. A string was tied around the box, ending in a bow at the top.

Key cautiously slipped a finger under the bow. No trip wire was connected there. He slowly ran his finger all around the cord and under it. It was not connected in any way. He untied the bow and let the string fall. He could see a dampness seeping out of the bottom. It appeared to be blood. He looked up at Cat.

"I don't think you want to see this, Cat."

"Open the box, Key. I'm a big girl, now."

A dead cat was in the box. The poor animal had been tortured before being killed. A note lay on top of the cat: A Pussy For A Pussy.

Key heard Cat's hiss of revulsion. She paled and put a hand to her mouth. Key put the lid back on the box and retied the cord. "Get me a garbage bag, please."

He dropped the box into the bag and tied it closed.

"And I had such a nice dinner planned," Cat said.

"You can go ahead and fix it. This won't affect my appetite."

She shuddered and said, "I seem to forget that beneath that thin veneer of civilization, there beats the heart of a savage."

Key ignored that. "I'll put this in the trunk of my car; dispose of it on the way home tonight."

She pointed to the bag. "How could you eat after viewing *that*?"

"I've seen much worse, believe me. Back in a minute."

The ugliness tucked away in the trunk of his Grand Prix, Key returned to the house, closing the door. Cat had freshened their drinks. He sat back down on the couch.

"I apologize for calling you a savage, Key."

"I've been called much worse, I assure you." He sipped his drink.

"Yes, I don't doubt that."

"Are we friends again?"

She smiled at him. A hundred watt smile. "We never stopped being friends."

"And you're convinced I'm not a part of the TFL?"

"If you are, it's because you're working for the government."

He knew he would never convince her he was not. And really, was he? Key had doubts about that. Nagging doubts. "Have it your way, Cat. How did you get crossways of the TFL?"

"I asked too many questions about too many things, Key. I was friends with Henry Randolph. I defended the so-called *wrong* people too many times. Until I had my phone number unlisted, just recently, I would not get hysterical over the many obscene phone calls I received. I wouldn't run, Key."

"I seem to recall that small town hierarchy can be tough to buck."

"The elected and appointed leaders of Lewiston are merely figureheads, now, Key. It's all changed since you lived here. The TFL runs this town. Believe it."

"When are we going to eat?" he asked. "My stomach is starting to protest."

"Barbarian!" But it was not said unkindly. She touched his arm and rose to put the finishing touches on dinner.

Key followed her to the kitchen. She waved him to

one side, silently rejecting his offer to help.

"How many farmers do you think are part of the TFL?" he asked.

She replied without hesitation. "Between one and five percent of them. The rest—I'm speaking of those around here—are just scared. Not knowing where to turn."

How similar to Hitler's movement, Key thought. "Would you say the percentage is closer to one than to five?"

"Oh, yes."

Key dropped the subject of the TFL, and he and Cat engaged in small talk over a delicious and carefully prepared dinner.

She brought them back to seriousness by saying, "Are you going to the auction Monday?"

"Lester and Claire's land and equipment?"

"Yes."

"Be kind of hard for me to miss it. It's right next to the house, practically. You?"

"I'd like to be there on Claire's behalf. There are a lot of things that belong solely to her. However, it isn't really necessary. You want me there?"

"Yes."

"Then I'll be there."

"I'll keep the coffeepot hot for you."

She lifted eyes that appeared to be simmering as hotly as the promised coffee he'd mentioned. Key thought he knew the message that lay behind those eyes.

"You don't believe in moving very fast, do you, Key?"

"It's always best to reconnoiter the objective first. Cuts down the odds of getting hurt."

"A double-edged statement if I ever heard one."

"Only if you wish to take it that way."

"You finished?"

He smiled. "Or just getting started."

"The man is a veritable master of double-talk. Let's try the latter."

"I thought you'd never ask."

"You damn sure weren't going to," she said, closer to the truth than she realized.

Chapter 3

When he awakened Monday morning, the previous weekend was blurry for Key. A mixture of satin-smooth flesh, hard, erect nipples, grasping wetness, and gasping sounds of sex.

For all his rugged good looks, Key had never been a womanizer. It wasn't that he couldn't have been; it just seemed he had never had the time. Key had, since young adulthood, disliked one-night stands. Even with — that woman who still burned in his mind, he had never taken the initiative. Key was sure of himself in combat; sure of himself with weapons and explosives and nearly every other aspect of war that could be brought up. He had never been sure of himself with women.

He was not sure if the wariness was of the women or of himself. He got along well with women, always respecting them as equals; liking and treating them as he would like to be treated. And despite his chosen way of life, he was never anything but a gentleman. He disliked profanity being used around women.

Key could be accurately called a study in contrast. He was a very complicated man, although it took one time to discover that about him.

Cat had discovered it.

And Key was not at all sure of his feelings about that. He was a private man, normally an impassive one; even in combat he was cold and calculating, always mentally reviewing the odds, never rushing into the unknown.

But in the matter of Catherine Monnet — he wasn't behaving as the Key of old. And that fact disturbed him; shook him a bit. Scared him just a little.

Jesus! Was he falling in love?

Monday morning dawned clear and hot, the sun bubbling up, late, thanks to daylight savings time, screwing up everybody's inner clock — including the animals.

This time, Key was the first one up in the main house. He took a slight juvenile satisfaction in the fact he had risen ahead of his father. As near as he could remember, that event had only occurred a couple of times in his life.

He fixed coffee and carried a cup out to the porch, sitting in a straight-backed chair, propping his booted feet up on the railing. Just as he had done hundreds of times in the past, in his youth.

His youth — gone. But it was not something Key regretted or pondered often.

Key had heard his father's stirrings in the house while he was in the kitchen. Dad Lessard soon joined

196

him on the porch, sitting down in a chair beside his son.

"Don't get in the way today, son," the father warned. "Just stand back and let what's going to happen, happen."

"What are you trying to tell me, Dad?"

"You gettin' hard of hearin'? Just what I said. Everything may not be what it seems to be. You just keep that in mind."

The old man sat silently and stared out over his land. His land. No longer his, nevertheless, Dad would think of it as his until the day he died.

"Been to visit your mother's grave since you been back, boy?"

"No, sir."

"Plannin' on it?"

"Yes, sir. Soon." Key was not looking forward to that.

"I made all my arrangements, boy. Anything happens to me, you, *you*, see lawyer Nolan, Carl Nolan, over in Lincoln. I'm worth considerable. And I don't want any squabblin' between you kids, neither. You hear?"

"Yes, sir. You figuring on going deep six anytime soon?"

"When it's my time, it's my time. But no son of a bitch is gonna push me . . . into doin' nothin' I don't wanna do."

"I . . . don't know whether I'm following you, Dad."

"Things ain't always what they seem boy. What you see this day, at the auction, just might be for show.

Bear that in mind."

Dad Lessard rose from his chair and walked into the house.

Leaving Key more confused than ever.

Ned Cosgrove was the first to arrive at the auction site. He got out of his truck carrying a shotgun in his hands. Right behind him was Chris Litton, Niles Becker, and several dozen other men, all armed with shotguns. Several hundred other men and women arrived, swelling the crowd. Some were armed. When the auctioneer arrived, the crowd refused to let him out of his pickup, encircling the truck. The auctioneer rolled up the windows and sat in the cab, clearly frightened. Other men and women arrived. They were grim faced, some armed.

Key stood with Claire and his brothers and their wives by the fence separating the properties. They watched in silence.

Lester and Les, Jr. stepped out of the Kidd house, both carrying rifles. A cheer went up from the swelling crowd. The cheering died an unnatural death as sheriff's deputies began pulling up and getting out of their cars, led by Sheriff Ted Gilbert.

Key looked back at his father's house. Dad Lessard was sitting alone and quietly on the front porch, watching, waiting, but taking no part.

Whit Lockley drove up in his big Cadillac. He was allowed to get out, but the path made for him by the hundreds of men and women and kids was narrow and opened grudgingly.

"Goddamn thief!" someone yelled at Whit. "Dirty bloodsucker! Why don't you leave us alone?"

"Move to New York and kiss a Jew's ass!" a woman yelled, her face contorted and ugly with hate and anger.

Strangely, a very small smile moved across Whit's face. The banker did not appear to be the least bit frightened.

Odd, Key thought. He's surrounded by armed, angry men and women, and he isn't afraid.

Watching it all, Key recalled the day he had first seen Whit on the country road, and moments later Sheriff Gilbert driving by. Had the men been meeting in secret? Key felt those odds were strong. In cahoots? Maybe. It would certainly be a strange partnership, but one that more and more seemed logical. Whit had the brains, Ted had the power and the muscle. And Whit's being a banker would certainly be the perfect cover.

It began to slowly fit together in Key's mind.

"You son of a bitch!" a man yelled at Whit. "Why don't you move to Russia?"

Key could not see the face of the man who had yelled. He watched two vans glide to a halt in front of the Kidd property. TV people. The TV crews began filming, shoving mikes in front of what appeared to Key to be very eager-to-talk mouths.

It all seemed—engineered.

"Now, folks!" Ted yelled, his voice just barely audible over the crowd noise. "This won't do. You got to let the law run its course."

The crowd booed him.

199

"It's legal stealing, sheriff!" a man yelled, his voice hoarse. "And by God, we've had enough of it. No more. With guns and God's help, no more. We're standing firm this time."

The crowd surged forward in a circle, surrounding the sheriff and his two deputies. Stan Tabor was not among them. A group of men began rocking the auctioneer's truck. The two men inside were clearly frightened, their faces pale.

Key wondered where Cat was. She had said she was coming out.

He asked Claire.

His sister shook her head. "I don't know. I hope she doesn't come out. This could turn violent."

"Mr. Lockley!" Ted yelled.

"Get your men out of here!" Whit returned the shout. "Get the auctioneers clear and safe of this area." He raised his voice to a near scream. The crowd hushed somewhat. "You people listen to me. We're leaving. But we'll be back. Be advised that you're all breaking the law."

Hoots and catcalls and obscenities greeted Whit's words. A man yelled, "We're all through being pushed around, Lockley. Bastards like you are not going to steal any more land around here."

"We're not stealing it!" Whit called. "If you make a debt, you've got to pay it. You all know that. It's legal and fair."

The crowd began booing him, cursing the banker. Ted took the man's arm and led him safely through the crowd. With a deputy leading the way, the auctioneer, the banker, and the lawmen left the area and

200

drove away.

The crowd began cheering.

"Don't they realize Whit will be back?" Key asked. "And the next time, he'll probably bring the state patrol with him."

Neither his brothers nor his sister chose to reply directly to that.

Rolf said, "The farmers won a round, finally."

Key looked at him, not believing what he'd heard. "It's going to be a very short-lived victory, brother."

"I wouldn't say that around anyone except us," David told him. "Tempers are stretched very tight around here."

"Meaning? . . ." Key asked.

"I'd hate to think what it all might come to, Key. So far all of the Lessard family have stayed clear, with the exception of Lester. But . . ." He shrugged his shoulders, leaving the obvious unsaid.

"You mean you, all of you, are going to have to pick a side?" Key asked.

His brothers and sister walked away, leaving Key with the fence and the cheering crowd.

Cat dressed in fashion jeans, western shirt, and Italian boots. No one would mistake her for a farmer's wife, but that was somebody else's problem, not hers. She had tried wearing cowboy — or cowgirl — boots. They hurt her feet.

She was not looking forward to attending this auction. Not at all. They were usually tearful, very emotion-filled affairs. And why not? A man and woman standing by while their entire life's work is sold off, many times to strangers.

She took a final look around the den and walked to the front door. For some reason she could not quite fathom, she was uneasy. The upcoming auction? Yes, that was part of it, she was sure. Yet she wondered.

She shrugged it off and stepped outside, pulling the door shut. She did not lock the front door. She never did. She did not like locked doors. That was for big cities, not for small midwestern towns. She recalled the dead cat left on her doorstep and almost reconsidered locking the door. No, she thought. No.

She stepped off the porch into the warm summer morning and walked to the open garage, standing for a moment beside her car. Something caught her eye.

Her bicycle had been moved. Or had she done it? She could't be sure. But she knew that was not where she normally kept it. Had someone been in the garage?

"Cat," she muttered. "You're imagining things."

Then she looked down. Her car door was not fully closed.

She hesitated. She could not remember whether she had closed the door tight or not. "Oh, crap!" she said, opening the door and getting behind the wheel.

She put the key into the ignition.

Then she heard the buzzing.

She froze, not knowing what it was. Was it some sort of automotive warning device? Was her battery down or something? Cat knew very little about cars. One started the thing and drove off. If it didn't start, one called someone to fix it. That was that.

Whatever it was buzzed again. It didn't sound like anything electronic.

Something moved under the seat.

Moved?

Cat grabbed for the door handle just as that buzzing sounded again.

Buzzing? No, it was more a dry rattling kind of sound.

Then she knew what it was.

She screamed and shoved the door open, literally falling out of the car. She was half in, half out of the car.

A horrible pain struck her left ankle. Bright pin-points of light ripped through her head. Painful flashes of light. She kicked her legs; at least she kicked her right leg. She wasn't sure if her left leg was functioning.

The pain.

That sharp pain hit her again, propelling her into action. She clawed her way out of the car, falling to the concrete garage floor, scurrying and crawling away from the car. She turned and looked back at the car, the door open.

She began screaming as the young couple from across the street began running toward her.

A rattlesnake lay on the carpeted floorboard, coiled and rattling and flicking its tongue out at her.

Cat fell tumbling into painful darkness.

"Key!" Dad Lessard called. "Come quick, boy. The hospital just called. It's Miss Cat."

Key ran to the porch. "What happened, Dad?"

"She's gonna be all right. But it was some close. Somebody put a rattlesnake in her car last night. Bit her on the ankle. You better get to the hospital right now, son. She's askin' for you."

Cat's lower left leg was swollen grotesquely. Her face was gray and sweaty, her eyes shiny, reflecting the pain she was experiencing.

"I never did like to lock doors," she whispered. "Always considered it a nuisance. Guess this might change my mind."

"The doctors say you're going to be all right," Key said, and he had spoken to the doctors. They assured him she would fully recover. But had she been just five minutes later in getting help, she might well have lost her foot. Or worse, although it is rare that anyone dies from snake bite in this country. But it does happen.

"I feel like shit," she said.

"You look beautiful to me."

"God, you're such a horrible liar! What happened out at Lester's?"

Before he could tell her, the doctors shooed him out of her room. He told her he would be back the next day.

Key drove straight to the sheriff's office.

Stan looked at him with undisguised hate. Ted met him with upraised hands — both of them. "I know why you're here, Key, and by God, I don't blame you a bit, partner. Terrible, terrible cowardly thing to do.

But Key, we don't have a thing to go on. I mean nothing."

"Prints?" Key felt solving crimes of this nature with prints were rare, but he had to ask. He felt it had probably been done by the KCs young men with no fingerprint records.

"Nothing, partner. Not one other than Miss Cat's and the guys' down at the garage where she gets gas and oil changes. And we went over that car and are *still* goin' over it. Key, she's made enemies around here. God, it could have been anybody."

Key knew that telling Ted about the dead cat would accomplish less than nothing. He changed the subject. "What happens to Lester, now, Ted?"

"I don't know. Nothing like this ever happened in Alton County before." He met Key's eyes.

Lying, Key thought. Ted is lying. Hell, is that surprising?

Ted said, "Come on in the office, Key. Let's sit and talk some."

Seated, coffee poured, Key waited for the sheriff to open it.

"I'm not tryin' to make light of what happened to Miss Cat, Key, so don't misunderstand me. We'll give it all we got, and that's a promise. But for a moment, let me ask you something. What'd you think about the meeting the other night?"

"I'd like to hear more. Providing it wasn't some of those men at the meeting who did this to Cat."

Ted was genuinely startled. "Good God, Key! We're not savages. Might not none of us like Miss Cat very much, but none of us would do anything like what

205

happened to her today. Believe it, old son." Oddly, Key did believe him. He was convinced the KCs planted the rattlesnake. "Now, if she was a Jew or a nigger, well, uh, that'd be different. You know what I mean?"

Key knew. He nodded his head.

"Good, good! Lord, I don't want you to think bad of none of us. We're just tryin' to hold our own and save what we got, that's all."

It was early to do it, Key knew, but he had seen and heard enough to know the cancer that gripped this part of the state had to be cut out. And quickly. Key decided to wade on in up to his waist and to hell with the consequences.

"All right, Ted. Let me tell you something. I think you know there is a tendency in this country to lump all right-wing patriotic people together."

Ted sat up straight in his chair. "You *damn* right, boy. You so right."

"The country, the nation, has gone to shit since I left it twenty years ago."

"Sweet music to my ears, Key."

"But with your group, well, I'm going to have to do some serious thinking on it. Seems to me that you've got a bunch of guys in there that don't know their assholes from their elbows about guerrilla warfare."

Ted leaned forward, placing his elbows on the desk. "That's exactly why we need a man like you, Key. Not that we're gonna do anything really wrong, you understand," he added. "It's just that we'd like to know more about weapons and explosives and urban warfare. You know what I'm talking about?"

Key knew then only too well what the sheriff had in mind. To pick his brain but never let him fully inside the inner circle. All right. If that was as close as he could get, so be it. At least he would know the names of many of the men involved.

"What do you want me to do, Ted?"

"Stay loose. We'll be in touch. Oh, and you give Miss Cat my best, now, you hear?"

Chapter 4

Key felt helpless after leaving the sheriff's office. He wanted to strike out at someone, but didn't know who. He wanted to talk to someone, but didn't know who he could trust.

All in all, he thought, this is a real pisser.

He drove home.

As he drove past Lester's, quiet now, a group of young people were parked out front, talking to Betty. Two carloads of them. Several of the young men jerked their heads and laughed as Key drove past. One of them looked at Key and made a snaky, wriggling gesture with his hand.

There was Rosanna's son, Jerry, the seventeen-year-old dip-shit, standing by a car, laughing at Key. Key did his best to ignore them all.

Then it came to him: He had not seen Skip at the meeting at Ted's. He found that odd. Nor had he seen Lester there. Odd.

And he wondered if seventeen was considered legal

adulthood in Nebraska. He had been gone so long he couldn't remember. He hoped it was, because if Jerry had anything to do with putting that snake in Cat's car, Key was, without doubt, going to hammer his young ass into the rich earth of Nebraska.

And enjoy every second of it.

"You look like you could bite nails and spit out tacks, boy," his father said to him.

"At least that."

"How's Miss Cat?"

"She's going to make it. All right, Dad, truth time. Level with me and give me all of it. That scene at Lester's this morning; it was staged for the benefit of the press, right?"

The old man rubbed his face with a callused hand. "Yeah, I think it was."

"Now what happens?"

"Lester gets a little more time."

"And hate gets a shot in the arm, right?"

"That would appear likely."

"What good will a little more time do Lester? He's still going to lose his farm, isn't he?"

"No doubt about that. But why don't you ask him? Here he comes."

Lester and Les, Jr. were walking toward Key and Dad Lessard. Key could tell from Lester's stiff stance the man was feeling cocky and looking for trouble. Cutting his eyes, Key could see Claire on the front porch of Dad's house. Her face was tight with anger.

"Watch it, boy," Dad warned. "Lester's got his stinger out for you."

Key's smile was grim. "I'm so overcome with fear I might just faint."

209

Dad chuckled. "David and Rolf and families just joined sis on the porch. I think they're hoping for a show."

It is something that most urban dwellers do not understand. The middle class and above urban dwellers, that is. Blue collar workers understand it perfectly. People who do hard physical work tend to settle their differences outside the courtroom, if at all possible. They settle it with fists; sometimes guns or knives. Usually fists and boots. For the most part, farmers are much more worldly than urbanites give them credit for being. They think and act and vote as rationally, if not more so, than their city cousins. But insult a man out in the country, and you are highly prone to getting your jaw jacked. Lawyers and judges do not enter into it. Sometimes they might later on, but that doesn't occur often. But if it does happen, as the saying goes, The get-back is a son of a bitch!

"Lester," Key said.

"Key," the man replied. "I hear tell your Jew-lovin' girlfriend got bit by one of her relatives this mornin'."

Key slapped the man. Slapped him openhanded with a big, hard, callused hand. The blow rocked and staggered the big man, bringing a thin trickle of blood from Lester's mouth.

Les, Jr. jumped at Key. Key pushed the boy away roughly, warning, "Stay out of this, boy."

Lester recovered his balance and fought away his shock. No man likes to be slapped. That is the consummate insult to manhood.

"That remark was uncalled for, Lester," Key told him. "Don't ever let me hear you say anything like it again."

210

"Well, how about this, then?" Lester swung at Key.

Key turned and grabbed the wrist behind the balled fist. He straightened out the arm and flipped Lester. The man landed on his ass in the grass.

A hard fist stung the side of Key's head. Pivoting, he hit Les, Jr. with a left and a right, knocking the young man flat on his butt, bloodying his mouth. "Rolf!" Key called. "Keep this little craphead out of this or I'll hurt him."

Rolf and Eddie were already on the run. Father and son jerked up Les and held him.

"Fight him fair, son," Dad urged. "He don't know none of that tricky stuff like you do. I taught you to box."

"Screw a fair fight!" Key said, not taking his eyes off Lester. "There is no such thing, Pop."

Key stepped forward just as Lester was getting to his knees. Key brought his knee up under Lester's chin, smashing the knee into the man's jaw. Blood squirted, and Lester howled in pain, both hands to his bloody mouth. He rolled on the ground as Dad Lessard winced.

"Jesus, boy!" Dad said.

Key waited until Lester got to his feet — something he ordinarily would not do. He had been taught in special warfare schools and learned firsthand in actual combat that once you put the enemy on the ground — finish him.

Key buried his right fist in Lester's gut. The man doubled over, the air whistling from his lungs. Key brought a hard fist down on Lester's back, just over the kidney. Lester screamed in pain and fell to the ground.

211

The fight was over.

Key was not even breathing hard. He stood over Lester while Les, Jr. cursed him, calling him everything, none of it complimentary.

The young people who had gathered in Lester's front yard came running over. Betty fell to the ground, beside her father, crying. She lifted a tear-streaked face to Key.

"You goddamned, sorry-assed, lousy motherfucker!" she squalled.

Key resisted an urge to jerk the girl up and paddle her behind.

No adult present vocally objected to her language.

Key knew then the homecoming was over and done. There would be some obligatory and half-hearted protestations from his brothers and probably his sister—the objections from his father would be the most genuine—but for him to remain on the farm complex would only cause friction.

You Can't Go Home Again.

In more ways than one, Mr. Wolfe.

Just ask any number of Vietnam vets who served in hard-ass special units.

Rolf broke the shock-filled silence. He spoke the words that Key knew would be coming from the mouths of those people who did not understand the hard-learned lessons of combat.

"He needed a good butt-kickin', Key," Rolf said. "But not like this." His eyes were on his moaning and bleeding brother-in-law.

"Spare me, Rolf," Key said, disgust in his voice. "I don't want to hear your crap." He looked at his father. "I'll get my gear together and pull out, Dad.

Find me an apartment in town."

The father's eyes were filled with sadness. "I don't know you anymore, boy. But you don't have to leave what is rightfully yours."

"Yes, I do, Pop. And you know it. You're all looking at me like I'm a wolf among lambs. And maybe I am."

Key walked into the house. No one tried to stop him.

Key drove into Lewiston and checked into a motel. He had plenty of time to look for an apartment. Or, did he?

He wondered why he would think that. He returned to the office and paid in advance for a week. He felt—uneasy.

Back in his room, he called the hospital, checking on Cat. She was resting comfortably, the floor nurse informed him. No, she could not have visitors that day. You're welcome. No, not that night, either. You're welcome.

Key stretched out on the bed and forced himself to relax, putting his mind in neutral and gradually dropping off to sleep.

The ringing of the telephone awakened him. He looked at his watch. Five o'clock. He must have been very tired.

"Key? Ted Gilbert here. Look, man, I hate to have to do this, but Lester's sworn out a warrant for your arrest."

And my attorney is in the hospital.

"You there, Key?"

213

"Oh, yeah. I'm here." But how did you know where to find me? No one in the family even knew where he was. What the hell is going on? "What's the drill, Ted?"

"Oh, it's nothin', buddy. Just come on down to the jail and post a cash bond. Or a property bond. You just walk out. That's all."

Sounded easy enough. But, Key thought, maybe walking into the jail would be the only easy part. Getting out might be a bitch.

"All right, Ted. I'll be right down."

"Good boy! I'll be here; handle it myself."

Key walked into the lobby and used the pay phone to call Jeff at the agency. Gone for the day. He tried his home. No answer. He called another friend at another spook department. Not there.

Key didn't like the feelings he was experiencing. Not at all.

He drove to the jail and parked. Once inside the building, he knew his hunches had been correct.

Stan Tabor stood with Sheriff Gilbert, facing Key. Other deputies quickly ringed Key, blocking any escape.

All the men were smiling at him.

"Ted." Key kept his voice calm. Inwardly, he did not feel at all calm. "What do I have to sign?"

Ted laughed at him.

"You find something amusing about all this?" Key asked.

"Shore do, Key," the sheriff replied. "You almost made it inside the group, Jew-lover."

"What are you talking about, Ted?"

"Lyin', goddamned son of a bitch," Stan said.

"You know damn well what we're talkin' about."

Ted hitched his butt up on a table and looked at Key. "I'm some disappointed in you, Key. But I got to hand it to you—you're a good actor. You had me fooled. For a time."

"Assuming I know what in the hell you're talking about . . . now what?"

"We want to know what you've reported to the Feds in Washington."

Key sighed. He had been correct in thinking there was a bad leak somewhere. "Ted, I came home to farm. Nothing more."

"You're a liar, boy."

"Well, if that's what you believe, I suppose there is nothing I could say that would convince you otherwise."

"Except the truth."

Key smiled. "The truth, as you want to hear it, Ted."

Stan shifted his booted feet. "Lemmie have him, sheriff. I'm tired of all this ya-ya."

"In time, Stan," Ted said. "In time. We don't want him whipped so bad he can't talk."

Key laughed, looking at Stan. "You don't really believe this pus-gutted asshole, by himself, is going to do any damage to me, do you?"

Stan balled his fists and flushed. Ted waved him back.

"Might be a good fight at that. But not here." He looked at a deputy. "Get Lessard's car keys and move his car. Put it in the impound area. We'll say we found it abandoned." He cut his eyes to Key. "Give him your keys, boy. We can do it hard or easy. Up to you."

Key tossed the car keys to a deputy. Anything to buy a little time. "Now what, Ted?"

"We take a little ride, Key. Then ol' Stan here is gonna see how tough you are."

Chapter 5

The family, with the understandable exception of Lester and son, gathered in the old farmhouse. There were long faces and much averting of eyes.

Claire broke the silence. "I don't like Key leaving, Dad. It isn't right."

"No one said it was, girl," Taylor replied. "It was Key's choice. He knows what he is — we don't."

Rolf looked up. "What does that mean, Pop?"

The old man sighed. "Key's different, boy. He's a warrior. Been one since he became a teenager. Really, probably, longer than that. Your mom and me, we know things about that boy that don't none of you know. Key took after one of his long-dead relatives. That's who I named him after. I knew the boy was different soon as I laid eyes on him lyin' next to your ma in the clinic. Key never was one for cryin'. Just look at you. Hard eyed, even as a baby. I never knew the original Key Lessard. But from what my granddaddy told me, he was a ring-tailed tooter. Modern-day western writers would say Key rode the hoot-owl trail. He wasn't really an outlaw. But he was a bad man to fool with. He was a gunfighter. Killed twenty men; that's fact. Provable. He was a loner, just like Key. He fought to win, just like Key. And it didn't make a damn to him how he won. He wasn't a back-shooter, but he was pure smoky hell when he got stirred up.

"Your brother, now, Claire. Let's see. David, you was in the army. Rolf was in college. And you, girl, was in Council Bluffs visitin' folks when Key got into trouble. Two bums come at Key with knives. Key was down at the creek, shootin' snakes. Key, just calm as all get-out, pulled out that old single-action forty-four of mine and started shootin'. Didn't kill neither of them, but he dropped them both, hard hit. And it wasn't 'cause he didn't try to kill them. Old Sheriff Faulkner covered it up. I paid for the bums' hospital stay and then Sheriff Faulkner run them both out of the county. Law could do that back in those days. Your mother and me, we asked Key how he felt after he shot those bums. He just looked at me with those cold eyes and said, 'Why, Pop, I feel just dandy.'

"I knew then I'd named him right. 'Bout a year later, he and Rosanna was on a date over to York. Might have been a year and a half—don't remember. Two town boys jumped him in a parkin' lot of the movie house. Lord, but Key hung an ass-whippin' on them that was fierce. Both those boys stayed in the hospital, in traction, for a long time. Their parents wanted to sue me and your mother, but the lawyers told them to drop it. And there were other . . . incidents when Key was growin' up that made me realize he was different from the ordinary. It never

218

came as any shock to me or your mother when Key turned professional adventurer. He's a good man, but a hard man."

Claire went to the picture window of the house where she was raised and stared out. "I hope Key doesn't think I'm angry at him for whipping Lester. I had just never seen anyone fight like that."

Her father said, "I don't believe he thought that at all, girl."

"I hope he's all right," Rolf said. "I'm ashamed for what I said to him out in the yard."

"Your brother's been in tight places before," the father said. "Not that I'm suggesting he's in one now. But knowing Key as I do, he probably is."

It came as no surprise to Key when he was taken to the complex of buildings he had spotted that rainy day on the way out to Rosanna's lodge. Once inside, he realized that the men of the TFL had done their homework as far as security was concerned. The inside area, those buildings behind the second heavy cyclone fence, was patrolled by dobermans: huge, vicious-appearing dogs. The gate to the second fence was electrically operated, either by a lock-switch located on both sides of the gate or by a guard inside the compound.

The gate closed silently behind them.

"Gettin' your eyes full, Key?" Ted asked.

"Not much else to do," Key replied calmly.

"You're a cold one," the sheriff said, grudging respect in his voice.

Key was sitting in the cage of a squad car, the door and window handles removed. Stan was driving. Key's was, for the moment, a helpless feeling.

"How do you get by with this . . . complex?" Key asked.

Ted smiled. "It's the Alton County Sheriff's Department training area. Among other things. The sheriff's departments from Pike and Bishop Counties train here, too." Two more counties to stay clear of, Key thought. Providing I get out of here with my skin, that is. "And it isn't public property," Ted continued. "It belongs to a very rich man in . . . it belongs to him. Let's just say he believes very strongly in law and order."

"And the Nazi Party," Key said.

Ted and Stan laughed.

"And since it isn't public property," Key said, "you can keep it closed, for the most part, to the public."

"That's right, hotshot," Stan said. "But we do allow . . . certain gun clubs in the area to use it."

"I can imagine the types," Key said dryly.

"Oh, we're gonna give you a guided tour, Key," Ted assured him with a nasty grin. "If you can still walk after Stan gets done with you."

Key tapped on the metal of the cage behind Stan's head. "Did you eat your Wheaties this morning, pusgut?"

The man's teeth ground together in anger, and his face and neck grew red. He kept silent.

"You don't have to con me, Ted," Key said. "I know damn well you're not going to allow us to fight one on one."

Ted turned, looking through the mesh of the cage. "That's the only way it's gonna happen, boy. Just you and Stan. With no interference from any of us. Tonight, when the rest of the boys can get out here to watch."

"Including Lester?"

Again, both men laughed. "Yeah," Stan said. "I don't think he'd miss it for the world."

Outside the car, Key stood, flanked by guards, and watched as Stan Tabor showed off a bit, doing some footwork and shadow-boxing, huffing and puffing as his big fists smashed imaginary opponents.

Key thought: He knows how to box, but he's slow. And somewhat out of shape. He's used to bullying his way through life and whatever fights he's had. His size has always intimidated people. Key knew the type very well. If Stan's type can ever muster up the courage to volunteer for the military's special units, they're usually washed out very quickly.

Ted was looking at Key as Key watched Stan. "Don't worry about it, boy. I'm not gonna let Stan kill you. We gotta keep you alive so you can tell us who you're workin' for."

"That's very considerate of you, Ted."

"Lock him down," Ted told the men guarding Key.

The guards had taken Key's wallet, watch, change, and boots, giving him a pair of tennis shoes to wear.

Key paced his windowless room. Ten feet wide, ten feet long. A toilet, a sink, a wooden chair, and a bed. The wood floor painted a sickly green. The walls, three-quarter-inch plywood, painted a dirty white. The only door was a heavy, solid-core door, probably steel-enforced oak.

Key lay down on the cot and rested. He had been in jail, of one kind of another, in almost every country he'd ever merced in. Jail was nothing new to him. Neither was torture: Psychological or physical. He had endured both. And survived to become stronger from the experiences.

He mentally reviewed his present situation.

Grim.

The door to his cell opened. The two men he'd hammered on earlier, in the rain, stood in the open doorway. They grinned at him. Both of them had missing teeth and bruised mouths.

"We're gonna enjoy hearin' you scream, tough boy," one said.

Key stared at them until they slammed the door, leaving him alone.

Key stared at the ceiling. No one knew where he was. But, he'd been in worse situations and managed to wriggle out. He went over what he'd seen on his way in. The fence was no problem. It was not charged. Once on the grounds, the dogs would be the problem. On several past occasions, Key had been forced to deal with attack dogs. He knew he could probably handle one—with any kind of luck. But three or four attack dogs? No. So his first order of business would be to arm himself, then hunt for a way out. In that order.

It would be dark in less than an hour, according to Key's inner clock.

Should be dark now, if the government would leave time alone.

Key Lessard closed his eyes and went to sleep.

Chapter 6

The sounds of car doors clunking shut awakened him. Key slipped from the bunk and went through a short series of warming-up exercises, stretching his muscles. He was not hungry and would not have eaten had anybody offered him food. One, he was going to have to fight an ape and did not want anything heavy in his stomach. Two, the food might be drugged.

He sat down on the edge of the bunk and waited.

A deputy opened the door. "Let's go, Lessard. And don't get cute. If you do, I'll knock a leg out from under you with this." He patted the Pachmayred butt of a .357.

"Oh, I wouldn't dream of it," Key told him. "I'm looking forward to stomping your chief deputy into the ground."

The deputy looked at him in the dim light of the hallway. "Man, you're *nuts*! Stan Tabor's whipped two, three men at a time. I seen him do it once."

"Oh, yeah—who? Scared kids, frightened middle-aged men, and people half his size. Has he ever fought a warrior?"

"Man, Stan was a *football* player."

Key laughed at him. "I can't begin to tell you how impressed I am."

The deputy's expression was one of extreme exasperation. Key turned and walked up the hall.

"Wait a minute, goodammit!" the deputy said, hurrying to catch up. "You go where *I* tell you to go."

"Well, come on, then."

"Crazy son of a bitch!" the deputy muttered.

The room was huge; a combination auditorium/gym. Chairs had been placed around a roped-off square in the center of the room. Key guessed about seventy-five men were seated, some standing, around the square.

Key knew many of them. He should. He had gone to school with most. His eyes found Skip and his son, Jerry. Al Owens sitting right over there. Al had married—Louise. Yeah. Key knew them, but they were strangers to him now. Hostile, savage strangers. There was Lester, with his lip stuck out—literally. Les, Jr. with him. Niles Becker, Dexter Frank, Chris Litton, Wynn Carter, Ernie Hansen, Zack Moore. There they sat, waiting to see Key get his brains kicked loose. Ned Cosgrove sat smiling arrogantly at Key; he sat beside Paul Bennett. And there was Harry Bell and Jimmy Harris. All former classmates of Key.

Ted Gilbert lifted a rope and entered the square. He held up a hand for silence. When the crowd had hushed, he said, "Welcome, members of the Truth, the Faith, and the Lord. Men of the Faith, I have an apology to make to you all. What I thought was to be a valued associate has turned out to be a traitor." His eyes found Key and fired waves of hate. "A government agent sent in here to spy and destroy us." He pointed at Key. "And there he stands. Key Lessand."

Hate-filled eyes turned to stare coldly, deadly, at Key. Key stood in silence, meeting the hostile stares without changing expression.

"We found out his deception just in the nick of time," Ted said. "And now we're gonna see Mr. Traitor Lessard pay for the deceit. With his blood."

The crowd applauded that.

It was very difficult for Key to believe so many of his long-ago friends had turned so sour. But here they sat, living fact.

"Stan Tabor!" Ted yelled.

Stan stepped into the ring. Dressed in jeans and T-shirt and tennis shoes, the man presented a very formidable sight. Stan was big and heavily muscled, outweighing Key considerably.

"All right to take off my shirt?" Key asked the deputy.

"Fine with me. You're not going to be in that ring long enough to worry about it."

"I'll agree with that." Key slipped out of his shirt. He did not have on a T-shirt.

"Smart-ass!" the deputy muttered.

Key was heavily muscled, but his were not the power-pumper's type of muscles. More like a race horse. There was no unnecessary fat on Key. He was hard-packed muscle and bone. And a professional warrior who knew how to survive.

"Do I enter the ring now?" Key asked the deputy, who was looking at Tabor with ill-concealed and misplaced awe.

"Yeah. Go ahead."

Key slipped easily through the tightly strung ropes and stood in a corner of the ring. He smiled at Ted. "You'd better bet on me, sheriff," Key said, just loud enough for Ted to hear.

Confusion passed over Ted's face. For an instant, uncertainty marked the man's features. He shook his head and whispered, "You're a conceited fool, Lessard."

Key minutely shook his head. "No. Just a man who knows his limitations and capabilities—and one who had the balls to prove it without becoming a bully."

Ted flushed, knowing what Key meant. He stepped out of the ropes, catching his right boot on the bottom rope and almost falling to the floor. True to form, Ted was still a clumsy ox. He cursed softly.

Key laughed at him.

Ted's eyes, looking at Key, were hate filled. Outside the ropes, he yelled, "No rules, no rounds. Fight to the finish. Start it."

Someone clanged a cowbell, and Stan shuffled forward, snuffing and snorting and glaring at Key. Key met him in the center of the makeshift ring and kicked the man on his right kneecap. Stan dropped his guard and yelped in pain. Key slammed the knife edge of his right hand on the side of Stan's neck, hit him in the mouth with a short, hard-driven left hook, and then jabbed stiffened fingers into the man's eyes.

Blood spurted from a busted lower lip as Stan fanned the air with both hands and backed up, attempting to clear his vision. Spinning, Key kicked the man in the ass, sending him stumbling across the ring to fall heavily against the ropes. Before Stan could recover, Key was all over him with fists and feet and elbows.

Key drove his right fist onto the man's lower back, just above the kidney. Stan howled in pain. Key smashed an elbow onto Stan's ear. Bells rang in the bigger man's head, and he felt another gush of warm blood from a damaged and swelling ear. Stan turned in confusion just in time to feel Key's karate chop across his throat. Stan gagged and stumbled away, backpedaling away from Key.

He was not fast enough. Key seemed to be everywhere, for the most part, all over Stan.

Stan swung a big fist, catching Key on the side of the head, jarring the man to his toes. Can't take many of those, Key thought, stepping back for a second as the crowd jumped to its feet, roaring their approval at their hero's action.

Stan, mistakenly thinking he had Key on the run, came after him, grinning victoriously through his bloody mouth.

Key sidestepped and ducked a wildly thrown fist. He stuck out a foot and tripped the man. Stan fell heavily to the hardwood floor. The air whuffed out of him on impact.

Key brought his feet together, jumped up, leaving the floor, his knees bent, and dropped his entire weight down on the center of Stan's back. Key leaped to his feet as Stan screamed in pain, the scream choking off as vomit filled the man's mouth. Stan puked and passed out on the floor.

Key backed away and leaned against the ropes, watching Stan writhe in unconscious pain and sickness. His eyes searched the now silent crowd until they found Ted's face, pale with disbelief at the sight of his heretofore invincible hero. Ted nodded his head in surrender and rose to his feet, walking toward the makeshift ring. He climbed in and waved several men in with him, pointing to Stan.

"Get him out of here," Ted said.

The men in the big room were strangely silent. Key stood with his back to the ropes, his chest shiny from sweat. Ted walked to him. "You don't fight fair, boy."

Key met his gaze. "You said no rules, remember, Ted?"

"So I did, Key. So I did."

"Kill the son of a bitch!" a man screamed from the crowd.

"I don't think they like me very much, Teddy."

"If I'd let them, they'd tear you to bloody pieces, boy."

"Not before I killed the first two men to reach me."

Ted tried to stare Key down. He gave it up in a very short time. "You ain't gonna be so damned cocky this time tomorrow, Key."

"You're probably right, Ted."

Chapter 7

Key lay with his eyes closed. He wasn't sure he could open them. He didn't know what time it was, or really, what day it was. He hurt all over. Worse still, he didn't know how badly he was hurt.

The men who had taken turns beating him were all amateurs, and that was dangerous. An amateur can kill you; a professional can make you wish you were dead.

Suppressing a groan, Key opened blood-encrusted eyelids and crawled to the nearest wall of his cell. He pulled himself up to a sitting position. The coolness of the wall on his bare, bruised back felt good.

He tried to make his pain-filled, muddled mind work properly. Things were so jumbled. What day was it? He wasn't sure. He thought it was on a Monday evening when he fought Stan. But he wasn't sure. Assuming it was, today was — Thursday. He thought. Yeah, a Thursday.

With his fingers, Key carefully, very carefully, inspected his chest and ribs. He was bruised all over, that was for sure. But he didn't think anything was broken. No. There was a cracked rib. He could feel it.

His flesh was torn, in some areas, but despite it all, he'd been lucky.

If the beatings continued, his luck was going to run out, and Key knew it. In his weakened condition, Key could not stand up to many more hours of being hammered on.

But what to do?

He forced his mind to think survival; savagery. Raw hatred, fanned by thoughts of revenge, took over.

Thunder rumbled faintly, followed by the sounds of rain. All right, that was good. If he could get out of the cell, the rain would aid in his eluding the dogs.

Yeah, sure, he thought bitterly. But what a hell of a big *if*.

He found himself listening intently. For what? Then it came to him as his mind began to slowly clear away the pain clouds. Silence. The place was silent. The grounds gave off an almost deserted sensation.

He thought hard. He had managed to look out a window while being taken to—that room, last night. *Night*. And it had been night when he was dragged, literally, back to his cell. So it must be daylight outside. Most of the men of the TFL would be working.

He wondered how many guards were stationed full time at the complex? Not many, he felt sure. But how many was 'not many'?

Carefully, silently, Key inched his way to the door and placed an ear to the wood. He could hear nothing. He had done this a half dozen times before, and was always able to detect some sort of sound.

The building, at least this wing of the building

where he was held, seemed empty.

Key crawled back to the sink and turned on the water; very low output to keep down the noise. He bathed his face and chest several times, the cold water helping to wash away the remaining confusion in his head. After dousing himself with the cold water, Key felt refreshed and able to function, mentally and physically.

Now, a weapon.

Key's eyes, now that the dried blood, which had caked them before, had been washed away, found the wooden chair. He slipped toward it and began testing it, his strong hands seeking a weak spot. He found it and increased the pressure on the old wood. One long leg of the chair snapped. He now had a club about twenty-five inches long. A dandy head-knocker.

Now if he could just find a head to knock.

Preferably not his own head. His noggin had enough bumps on it.

He made up his mind. What the hell? All he had to lose was his life. He turned off the light in the room and knocked on the door.

Nothing.

He knocked again, louder this time. Pressing his ear against the door, he listened. The sounds of footsteps in the hall came to him. He eased away from the door, the club in his right hand held close to his side.

"What do you want, Lessard?" The muffled voice penetrated the wood and steel of the door.

Key groaned.

"Lessard?"

Key groaned again. "Doctor," he said weakly.

The man laughed. "Tough luck, boy. No deal."

"Bleeding," Key said. "I'm no good to Gilbert dead."

Silence. "Yeah. That's right. Be my ass if you died. Lemmie look at you. Stand back away from the door."

"I can't even get up."

Laughter. "I can believe that." A key grated in the lock. "You fuckin' hotshot Green Berets ain't as tough as you make out to be. You got hammered on pretty good over the past two, three days."

Three days? Had it been three days? Was today Friday?

The door swung open. "What the hell's wrong with the lights in—"

Key brought the chair leg down on the man's head with every ounce of weakened strength he could muster. He heard the man's skull pop under the impacting hickory; at least Key thought it was hickory. Whatever it was, it busted the guy's head wide open. Blood spurted. Key would see the whiteness of skull bone as the man hit the floor.

Muttering a low curse, leveled at the man on the floor, Key quickly fanned the man's unconscious body. He found a lock-back knife with a sharp blade, a snub-nose .38, and a dozen rounds of ammo for the .38. He took the man's wallet, money clip, and lighter. He had plans for the lighter.

Key quickly undressed the man, dragged him to the bunk, and heaved him up on the thin mattress, covering him with a blanket. The man—Key did not know him—was breathing badly. Blood was coming out of his ears and mouth and nose. He's dying, Key

233

thought. Badly brain damaged.

Fuck him! Key thought. He smiled grimly. A warrior's smile; a Viking smile. Key patted the man's shoulder, thinking, I'll give you a nice funeral pyre, member of the Truth, Faith, and Lord.

Key limped from the room and walked silently up the hall, stopping to listen at each closed door. When he could hear nothing behind the door, he carefully opened the door and looked in, inspecting each room.

Behind the third door, he struck pay dirt.

A weapons' and equipment room. Key carefully closed the door, leaving it cracked just a bit, and began selecting gear. He smiled as he picked up an Uzi SMG with folding stock. He wondered if the TFL knew it was made in Israel. He found an ammo harness and began filling twenty-five round clips with nine millimeter ammo, sticking the full clips into the pouch pocket. He filled a pack with blanket, tarp, flashlight, extra batteries, and spare clothing and socks. He put the .38 into the pack and selected a nine millimeter semiautomatic pistol with holster. He slipped that and a twin-clip pouch onto his belt, along with a long-bladed sheath knife. He dressed in jeans and cammo shirt and combat boots.

He was beginning to feel right at home.

He laughed softly as he pulled a gas mask down from the wall and checked the canister. Okay. He slipped it on. Might be getting a bit smoky around here before long.

He found several short lengths of rope and a can of camp stove fluid, highly flammable. He set the can and his pack just inside the door and stepped back into the hall, continuing his prowling. The wing was deserted. Working his way back down the hall, Key found his boots and wallet and money clip. He left his boots, clip, and wallet, after removing his money and driver's license.

Returning to his cell, he looked at the man on the bunk. Dead. He poured the flammable liquid around the room, on the pile of clothing taken from the dead man, and on the man. He struck a match and soon the room was blazing. He walked out into the hall, closing the door.

He set the Uzi on full auto and looked around him. Already, smoke was filtering out under the crack in the door. Thick, acrid smoke. He was glad he'd found the gas mask.

Key leaned against a wall for a moment, for he was very weak and tired and hurt all over. He knew from experience that a tired man is prone to make mistakes. He couldn't afford any mistakes. Smoke boiled around his boots. He could feel the heat building from the fire in the closed room.

He heard footsteps running in his direction. One pair of footsteps. Key stepped back into a room. Just as the man reached his location, coughing from the smoke, Key stuck a boot out. The running man, nearly blind from the smoke, tripped and fell hard, banging his head on the floor, stunning him, knocking the breath from him.

Key stepped out and bent down, looping the rope around the man's neck, and began strangling him. It's not as simple nor as easy as it looks in the movies, for the most part, produced and directed by people who wouldn't know real violence if it stepped up and spoke to them.

And if they did recognize it for what it was, the first thing they'd probably do would be to call for a lawyer.

As the smoke swirled around them, Key's breathing harsh under the mask, he held on for a full one hundred and eighty count, feeling the man slowly die beneath his hands. The guard's boots drummed on the wooden floor, sickening grunting sounds erupting from his closed-off throat. The man's tongue began protruding from his mouth, dark and swollen with blood. His eyes bugged out, changing color from the lack of oxygen. The dying man crapped and pissed his drawers. The smell was awful.

Key had done it, seen it, and smelled it dozens of times before. It was nothing new to him. He shut off his mind and choked the man to death.

He dragged the man to the closed door of what had been his cell and dumped him there.

Key could see nothing though the thick smoke. The rain continued to pour out of the sky. If anyone had heard the slight commotion, it had been dismissed as storm noise. Key slipped back up the hall, toward the exit.

He cracked the door and whistled softly. He heard the sounds of running dogs, their breathing harsh in the rain.

"Come on, boys!" he called. "Come on!"

He slammed the door just as the dogs reached it.

He couldn't do it. He couldn't trap those dobermans inside a burning building. He slipped out of that wing, through the smoke, and into another part of the complex. He went all the way to the extreme end of the farthest building, all connected by covered walkways. Making sure he had a way out, he opened the door and once more called for the dogs.

The dogs leaped in, slipping on the floor, nails clicking as they came.

Key shut the door and jumped out a window he had opened, slamming the window closed. Snarling, slobbering jaws just missed his hand.

"Fuck you," he muttered. He didn't like dobermans. He didn't trust them; had seen too many of them turn on their handlers.

But he couldn't burn them to death. Even if he did associate that breed of animal with the Nazi Party, concentration camps, and the SS.

He quickly scanned his immediate perimeter, getting his bearings. He slipped off the gas mask, started to toss it away, then decided to keep it.

The rain intensified, accompanied by licking lightning and rolling cadences of thunder. Key limped off toward the gate, staying close to the buildings. He was alert for guards. He saw none. He couldn't believe his luck was holding this well. And badly hurt he was, Key knew it was luck this time; more luck than skill.

There were several more cars and trucks parked around the complex, but Key knew for his plan to work, he would have to hoof it out. Taking a deep breath, Key walked openly and brazenly toward the main gate, expecting a bullet in the back at any moment. None came. He reached the gate and punched the red button. The gate slowly pulled open on the wheeled track. Key stepped free of the fence and punched the black button on the box outside the fence. The gate closed.

Key walked toward the woods at the rear of the complex.

It all seemed too easy.

Chapter 8

By the time he reached the wooded area smoke was billowing from the wing he had set afire. He kept on walking. He knew exactly where he was, and although he was not certain where he was going, he knew he had to put some distance between the TFL complex and himself.

He stopped on the crest of a small hill and looked back through the heavy rain. The rains had prevented the fire from spreading to the other buildings, but the wing he had set blazing was nearly gone.

Key was very tired and very sore and knew he was running a real risk of pneumonia in his weakened condition. He had no choice. He turned and resumed his walking, toward the river near the point.

Dark when he reached Rosanna's lodge. Due to the terrain, he had been forced to crawl whenever he came within eyeballing distance of any farmhouse. He was running a fever and alternately shaking with chills and burning up with fever when he slipped in through an unlocked window and stepped into the dryness of the empty lodge.

Using a flashlight, he located the bathroom and the medicine cabinet. He took several aspirin and two penicillin capsules, sticking the nearly full bottles into his pack.

In his stocking feet, he stood by the picture window for a moment, viewing his darkening rainy surroundings. Sensing something was out of place, he looked around him. The wall where the KC banner had once hung was bare, the flag gone.

Good. For the way Key was feeling had it been there, he might have burned the goddamned thing.

Walking to the bathroom, Key stripped and took a fast, very hot, soapy shower. He found a razor and carefully shaved his battered and swollen face. He then carefully cleaned up the bathroom. He put his muddy clothing and the towels into the washer and set the controls. Working in the dark, Key found the pantry and opened a can of beans and a small jar of dried beef, topping it off with crackers. He buried the garbage under other garbage in the plastic bag.

He carefully field-stripped his Uzi and cleaned and oiled it. He waited until his clothes and the towels were finished in the dryer and then stretched out on the couch. He dozed fitfully, warily, coming awake every ten or fifteen minutes to lie and listen for any sound out of the ordinary. At ten o'clock, he took more aspirin and penicillin, ate a small can of fruit, and laid back down on the couch.

He came awake several times during the night as headlights flashed on the road in front of the lodge. But the vehicles were traveling at a normal speed and did not stop or slow down at the lodge.

He was up at dawn, taking more medicine. His fever was nearly gone and he felt much better. He fixed bacon and eggs and toast for breakfast and then carefully washed the pan and plate, putting everything back where he'd found it. He wiped the countertop clean of crumbs and clicked on the radio, catching the news announcer in the middle of his reading.

". . . a fire destroyed a small section of the local sheriff's department's training area yesterday afternoon. The tragic blaze took the lives of two members of the sheriff's department, Deputies Oscar Harrison and Wallace Long, and a visitor to the complex, Mr. Key Lessard. Key Lessard is the son of local farmer Taylor Lessard. The bodies were badly burned, almost completely destroyed in the intense blaze. Each man was identified by various pieces of jewelry . . ."

Nice going, Ted, Key thought.

"Funeral services for the three men will be held tomorrow afternoon at the chapel of Barnes Funeral Home."

How does it feel to be dead, Key? That's what you wanted.

But who was the third man thought to be him?

Key didn't know; had thought there were only two guards at the complex. No matter.

Unless—

Ted was setting him up for something.

Key checked the house and lay back down on the couch, closing his eyes. He fell asleep. With a small smile on his lips.

"The doctors say we don't tell Miss Cat anything about Key," Taylor hold his children. "She's still in bad shape."

"I still don't understand what Key was doing out there," Claire said. She was still numb from the news of her brother's death.

"Neither do I, girl," Taylor said. "But I do smell a stinking rat in all of this." He did not tell his kids his feelings that Key was not dead. Taylor had been the only member of his family to view the awful burned remains of the body presumed to be Key's. In his heart, Taylor knew the body had not been that of his son. Nor was it the body belonging to either of the other two.

"What do you mean, Dad?" David asked.

But the father would only shake his head.

The other family members did not push it.

Rolf walked to a window and looked out. "Ted Gilbert's driving up. Got a hound dog expression on his face."

"That's an insult to a dog," Taylor said. "Rolf, see what the bastard wants."

Rolf met the sheriff on the porch and held the door open for him.

"Folks," Ted said, his hat in hand. "I'm sure mighty sorry about Key. County fire marshal says it was a short in some wirin' that started the blaze. For what it's worth to you all in your hour of grievin', it looks like Deputy Harrison was tryin' to get to Key's room to save him when he was overcome by the smoke."

Taylor had not seen Chief Deputy Tabor in a week. He wondered what had happened to the bully. "What was my son doing out there, Ted?"

"He had checked into a motel, Taylor," Ted replied. "It's my fault, and you all can feel hard at me if you want to. I won't blame you for it. I called him and asked why don't he come stay out at the trainin' site. Maybe show us some firearms procedure? Key agreed to do that."

Goddamned liar! Taylor thought. The man is lying through his teeth.

"Next thing I know, the fire department is answerin' the call. I can't begin to tell you all how sorry I am."

You lying son of a bitch! Taylor thought. Key would have called us and told us where he was staying . . . if he had gone out there of his own free will, that is. I don't know what is going on, but I'm damn sure going to find out. And I'm going to start by looking inside those boxes Key tucked away out in the shed.

"I guess that's it, folks," Ted said.

"Thank you for coming by, Ted," Claire said, showing the sheriff to the door. "We all appreciate it."

"Sure, Miss Claire. Everybody liked Key. Why, me and Key had patched up our differences and was buddies again. Just like back in high school."

And a hog can quote Shakespeare, Taylor thought. He walked out on the porch, watching Ted drive off, back to town.

About a half minute later, Whit Lockley drove by in his big Cadillac. Looked to Taylor like the banker was following Ted.

"Odd," Taylor muttered.

Taylor assured his kids he was just fine and shooed them all back to their houses. His own house empty, Taylor walked out back and into the shed. Squatting down, he opened the boxes Key had stored and sucked in his breath at the sight.

"What the hell was the boy going to do, start a war?"

He closed the boxes and restacked them.

He wondered where his son was.

Key left the lodge at dark, taking a five day supply of canned food with him. He had rearranged the remaining food in the pantry to cover, he hoped, the missing food. Since the supply was ample, he felt it might work.

During the driving of the back roads of Alton County, Key had noticed many deserted farms; there was one about five miles from the lodge. Although the rain had stopped and the night was pleasant, it took Key almost three hours to reach the deserted farm. His bruised rib — he had decided it was not cracked — was aching, and he was almost exhausted when he found the buildings and silo looming up stark and alone in the night.

He forced himself to eat a small can of pressed ham, washing it down with sips of water from one of several plastic jugs he had found at Rosanna's. After rinsing them out, he had filled them with water and tied a cord about the flanged neck for easier carrying. Key had always found it amusing to read books about the exploits of so-called mercenaries and all their up-to-date equipment they carried with them into the field.

Key knew only too well that mercs are usually forced to leave a country very fast, therefore one simply does not spend a lot of money on expensive and usually needless equipment, for you can't take it with you when you leave. Make your canteens out of plastic jugs. Use a reliable but cheap wristwatch—only a fool or a gross amateur wears a four thousand dollar Rolex into a mercenary-fought war; especially when the soldiers manning airports or other entrance or exit points will, in all probability, take it from you, along with much of your money, rings, and anything else that catches their eyes. A twenty dollar compass is fine. As long as it works. Key had once left a movie house after seeing the hero use the barrel of his rifle as a level for a compass sighting. The metal of the barrel will pull the needle off several degrees. Key had learned that that particular hero got shot in the end. Served him right.

A thirty dollar knife kills just as adequately as a three hundred dollar knife with all that bullshit stored in the handle. Key had known of mercenaries who left unfriendly nations—after the battle had gone sour—with their valuables shoved up their asshole.

Mercing is not glamorous work. Many men find that out the hard way. They get jailed, tortured, butt-fucked, or killed.

Key stretched out on his blankets in the loft of the barn and went to sleep.

Key did little except take medicine, eat, and rest for five days. On the fifth day of his self-imposed solitude at the deserted farm, he knew he was ready to make his moves. Deadly moves. For sure, he had to have more food; his supply was almost gone. His rib was still tender but almost healed.

The road that ran past the old farm place was not very busy with traffic, and the days had been boring. At night, when the winds blew, Key would lie in the loft of the barn and listen to the old windmill sing of better days on the prairie. The windmill (it had been there since Key's youth) alternately sang and hummed and squeaked as it caught the wind, its drive shaft disconnected, no longer bringing up water from the dry well. Its song was of days gone by, the melody directed toward the empty and somehow eerie-appearing buildings of the farm complex, the home that had seen generations of the same family come and go. The home and the land had watched life being born and the dead once more returned to the earth. The blades of the windmill sang a dirge for the farm family, that hardy breed of men and women who worked the land and endured as the land had done. Enduring winds and storms and flood and fire—and watching foreign competition, among other things, destroy them.

But the land was basically inert; the land did not care who worked it.

Or did it?

As a product of the land, Key understood the land far better than his city counterparts. The land, as any farmer can attest to, can be forgiving. The land does not know of low and unfair prices for what it produces. It does not know of the middlemen who lie between the farmer and the consumer. It knows, somehow, only the hard-working men and women who work the land and try to survive the hardships of their chosen vocation.

While the land did not know, Key knew that the TFL was not the answer to the farmers' problems. And meeting sheriff's deputies and state police and bankers with guns was certainly not the solution. Key knew the vast majority of police in Nebraska were not like the people in Ted's department. The majority were simply hardworking men and women who had a very disagreeable job to do.

Key didn't know the real answer.

His thoughts shifted away. He wondered how his funeral went. Did Cat know? Surely by now she did.

Dead. He was dead. But who was the man lying in that cold casket in Key's grave?

He would probably never know.

One thing Key knew he had to do: get back to the shed behind his dad's house and get his gear.

And he had to stay believed-dead until he could destroy the TFL.

He mentally reviewed the faces of those men who had been in attendance at the fight at the TFL's headquarters. Old friends no longer. Enemies, now. High school parties and football games and picnics and growing up together had to be pushed out of Key's mind.

He had met the enemy and knew them.

He left his pack and blankets and other gear hidden in the hay in the loft. He belted his ammo pouches around his waist and picked up his Uzi. He climbed down the ladder to the barn floor.

Key Lessard slipped out into the Nebraska night.

Since the funeral, Taylor Lessard had stayed close

to his house. He did his sleeping during the day; at night, he stood a lonely vigil in a darkened kitchen, sitting in a rocking chair by a rear window and watching the backyard.

For his son.

"We got us a night exercise, boys," John told the Alton County chapter of the TFL. "Live fire at a live target." He pointed toward a figure huddled on the earth, her nakedness highlighted by floodlights around the fenced-in area behind the TFL's headquarters.

The woman was in her mid to late thirties. The marks of her recent beating were evident on her body. Her rape and following shock marked her face and eyes. She knew there was no point in attempting any escape. She had seen the dogs earlier, on leashes, snarling at her. She'd rather have a bullet than be torn to shreds by those vicious animals.

She had been hearing rumors of how bad things were in this part of the state; had read newspaper accounts of the racist movement.

Having grown up in Lewiston, she had never believed the rumors.

But now she did.

"Where's Ted?" a man asked.

"He's . . . busy." John smiled.

Several other men laughed. They had all heard the screams of the man who had been with the woman when the school teachers had been stopped and brought to the complex.

"Ted is disciplining the man," John said.

"Yeah," Ned Cosgrove said. "Right up his asshole."

Ted's sexual aberrations had long been known and accepted by the men of the TFL. Understandably, since they were all deviant in one form or another.

"Always did want to fuck Lila when we was in high school," a man spoke. "Tell you what, boys: If her pussy was any better back then than it was an hour ago, I couldn't have stood it."

Rough laughter filled the floodlit night.

"Lonnie," John said, turning to the man. "See if you can put a bullet about two feet from the woman. To her right. Let's make her jump and holler."

"Show her who is boss, John?"

"Nigger knows that anyway," John said. "But it's always wise to remind them from time to time."

A rifle cracked. Lila jerked as the slug dug a furrow several feet from her. She bit her lip to keep from screaming.

She wondered who had fired the gun. She just could not believe her situation. She wondered what was happening to Simon.

And why this was happening to them both.

She had gone to high school with some of these men. And to college with two of them.

She wondered what had changed them.

Taylor Lessard watched as the shadowy figure moved from the barn to the shed. The old man smiled in the dark of the kitchen.

He could tell by the way the man moved it was Key. The figure moved as silently as a big stalking cat.

Whatever the TFL had done to Key, it had pissed

the boy off. Now the TFL would learn what happens when you make a warrior mad.

Should be very interesting in Alton County over the next week or so.

Very interesting.

Chapter 9

Key heard the shooting, but it was faint and very far off. He assumed it was coming from the TFL headquarters. He wondered what they were shooting at this time of night.

He thought for a moment, his mind made up. He touched the helmet he'd taken from the box. The steel pot was cold to his fingertips. He grinned. Look out, Hell's Angels, here comes Key Lessard with his steel pot for a motorcycle helmet.

He laughed aloud in the night. Two wheels would be just perfect. A motorcycle would be perfect for this type of terrain. A dirt bike especially. But where would he get one?

Hell, steal it! What else? Since he was dead and buried, he couldn't imagine going into the local Honda shop and buying one.

He stepped off the turn-row and walked over to the blacktop. He passed several houses before he found one that was dark. He prowled the garage and barn. Nothing. He walked on, passing several more lighted homes and inspecting the two more darkened homes before finding a motorcycle. It was a big bastard.

Bigger than what he really wanted.

He found several cans of green and gray paint and a brush, putting them in a gunnysack and tying that over the gas tank.

The gas tank.

He unscrewed the cap. The tank was full. He found a gallon can and filled it from the farmer's outside tank. He looked up at the tank. D. Frank was printed on the metal. Key grinned. Dexter Frank. Good ol' Dexter. Good ol' TFL member.

"Screw you, Dex!" he said.

In the tool shed, Key found some heavy wire cutters. He might need these.

He went into the house through the back door and found the phone. He dialed his Dad's number.

"Don't talk, Dad. Just listen. You know where the old Frankel farm is? The squeaky windmill. Yeah. Tomorrow, fill half a dozen five gallon cans with gasoline. Load up those boxes of mine in the shed behind the house. As nosy as you are, you've probably taken a peek at them." He thought he heard his father say something that sounded like 'smart-ass!' But he couldn't be sure. "Box up some canned food and bottles of water. Take everything out to the Frankel farm. As soon as you're there, act like you have a flat. I'll meet you. Be careful, Pop. Be sure you're not followed. Don't say anything about my being alive to anyone. Claire, Cat, Rolf, David—no one. Does Dexter Frank have a son? Now you can talk."

"Thank you, squirt. No. Two daughters. Both lard-asses. Why?"

" 'Cause I'm at his place. I'm just about to steal a

motorcycle."

"That's his. He never learned to ride it. Fell off a dozen times and then put it up. He probably won't even miss it. You sure the thing will start?"

"I'm about to find out. I hope to hell it does. Bring some money with you, too. And be careful; I'd hate to shoot your old ass off."

Key laughed and hung up on his father's extremely vulgar sputterings. He strapped his helmet on.

He had to jump off the bike from the battery of a three-wheeler. But he got it charged up and cranked and was soon roaring down the road, toward the Frankel farm.

He wondered about the shooting he'd heard earlier. On impulse, he cut down a gravel/dirt road that would bring him close to the TFL complex.

Lila was screaming as the bullets drew closer and closer. She had endured the rape silently, and she had made a vow she would not scream no matter what the men did to her. She would not give them that satisfaction. But that vow was long forgotten as fear overwhelmed her.

Lila watched as Simon was pushed and pulled, naked, out into the field. He walked as if in pain. He probably is, Lila thought. Same old Ted Gilbert. Perverted bastard. He had probably raped Simon. Ted was known to be sexually twisted. Been that way all his life.

The men were jeering Simon, calling him filthy names. Lila cocked her head. Was that a motorcycle she just heard? Surely not. She listened more intently.

Nothing. Must have been her imagination.

"What's the matter, Jew-boy?" a man yelled. "How come you walkin' so funny?"

Simon walked toward Lila, walking with as much dignity as the situation would allow. But his thoughts were as dark as the night outside the floodlit area. He just couldn't believe anything like this was happening in Nebraska. He had heard about the growing anti-Semitism in small pockets around the state, but he had always dismissed the talk as nothing more than hysterical nonsense.

Good God! Would it never end?

Simon thought about his family in Lincoln. He wondered if he'd ever see any of them again.

He thought not.

He began to mentally prepare himself for death.

Simon thought: I am going to die. That much I believe. But I shall not die without doing what I can to save a life. He spoke to Lila, just loud enough for her to hear.

"Lila, when I begin, you start inching toward the fence, a little bit at a time. One of us has got to get out of here to tell what happened."

"All right, Simon. But what are you going to do?"

"I am going to act a fool, Lila. Distract them. Get ready."

"Simon!"

But Simon had already begun dancing and jumping about, waving his arms, yelling obscenities at the TFL men. In Yiddish.

Lila began inching away, slowly making her way toward the fence that lay to her right.

No one had noticed the man dressed in field

clothes who lay on the outside of the fence. Using the wire cutters, Key opened a section of the fence big enough for Lila to crawl through.

"Wonder what the hell that boy's calling us?" Ernie asked, his eyes on the naked man yelling at them.

"I bet you it's nothin' nice, that's for sure," Wynn Carter said.

Key lifted the Uzi. The range was about two hundred meters: too far away for any accuracy from the short-barreled Uzi. But it was this, or nothing.

"Don't look around, lady," Key called softly. He still did not know who the woman was. Although she did look somehow familiar. "When I start shooting, you stay low and make it to the hole I've cut in the fence. With any kind of luck, I can get us out of here. You understand?"

She nodded her head.

"Your friend is a very brave man."

"Yes, I know."

Ted rejoined the group on the firing range. "Somebody shoot that son of a bitch!" he yelled.

Dexter Frank lifted his rifle and looked around him. "Me?"

"Yeah, you!" Ted said.

Dexter sighted Simon in and pulled the trigger. The slug caught Simon in the chest, knocking him to the cool earth. Simon lay still, alive.

Dexter giggled nervously. "I got him! I got him!" he yelled, jumping up and down.

Key pulled the trigger of the Uzi, holding it back, spraying the area with lead.

The men of the TFL hollered and hit the ground, hugging Mother Earth as the lead hummed and sang and howled over their heads.

Lila scampered through the hole in the fence and crouched beside Key.

Key shoved a fresh clip into the Uzi and paused to look at the woman. "Lila?"

She blinked, forgetting she was naked. "Key? Key Lessard? My God! Is it really you?"

"In the flesh. But let's save old home week for later on, Lila." He took off his shirt and gave it to her. She covered her bruised nakedness with it. "Run for the motorcycle in the timber, over there." He pointed. "Wait for me. Move!"

She ran into the near darkness, toward the thick stand of timber. She was so scared she was trembling.

Key burned another clip at the men of the TFL, reloaded, then shot out as many of the floodlights as he could. He ran for the motorcycle.

Ten seconds later, they were roaring out of the timber.

As the sounds of the motorcycle faded, the men of the TFL ran out into the field. One stopped and squatted down beside Simon.

Simon reached up and grabbed the man's neck with strong hands, holding on with all his strength. The man gurgled and bubbled and tried to break free. He could not.

Men beat at Simon with rifle butts, trying to break their comrade free from the death grip. Blood gushed from Simon's broken face. Still he held on. Simon reached up with one hand and hooked three fingers into the man's lower lip.

Simon jerked with all his strength.

He tore the man's lip completely off.

John stuck a pistol to Simon's head and pulled the trigger. Simon's hand fell free and lifeless to the ground.

The TFL man thrashed and howled in pain as his blood spurted.

"Goddamn!" Niles shouted. "We gotta get him to a hospital. Jesus Christ! He's bleedin' to death, boys."

"Drag that fuckin' Jew outta here!" Ted ordered. He looked toward the fence. Lila had vanished along with the sounds of a motorcycle. "Who the hell was that who grabbed the nigger?"

But deep in his heart, he knew.

Key Lessard.

Chapter 10

Key helped Lila up the ladder to the loft. Her skin was cold and clammy. He could tell she was going into delayed shock. He made her lie down and elevated her feet, covering her with a blanket. There was very little else he could do, for the time being.

"Lila, I'm going to hide the bike."

She looked at him through glazed eyes and nodded her head.

Key rolled the bike into a corner of the barn, tucking it away behind some rotting and rat-chewed sacks of what looked like corn. He climbed back up the ladder and sat down beside Lila, on the floor. Her eyes were closed.

"I'm no psychiatrist, Lila, but you've got to try to put what happened tonight out of your mind. I'm probably asking the impossible. But you've got to try. For the time being, you're going to have to mentally heal yourself. I can't take you to a doctor. Too risky. You can bet Ted is going to have this county, and the counties that border Alton, sealed off tight. And if you're thinking of going to the law, forget it. Ted is the law. Do you understand what I'm saying to you,

Lila?"

With her eyes still closed, she said, "Hopeless."

"No, Lila. It is not hopeless. It's a war, that's all."

She laughed bitterly. "That's *all*? The man says it's just a little war, that's all."

"That's all it is. And it's a war I'm going to win. Believe it."

She opened her eyes and looked up at Key. "I haven't seen you in twenty years, Key. But I've heard and read about your . . . exploits." Her voice seemed to be a bit stronger. "What do you plan on doing about Simon's murder?"

"I intend to kill every member of the TFL." Key said it coldly, flatly.

Lila's eyes widened. "My God! The man thinks he's Superman. But I don't see any phone booths around here, Clark."

Key chuckled. She had not lost her biting sense of humor. "No, I'm not Superman, Lila. Just a mortal man whose business is war, and I am a very good businessman."

She shook her head in disbelief.

"What happened tonight, Lila?"

"I got fucked in every way you can think of," she said harshly. "And I'm sure Simon was raped by Ted Gilbert."

"I suspected that. That wasn't what I meant. How did they, the TFL, get their hands on you?"

"Roadblock. Checking registration and driver's license, supposedly. Simon and I had been to a meeting at Kearney State. We were driving back home. Key, I don't understand the *point* of what happened. What is, was, the point?"

259

"I can only guess that the TLF wanted some live targets." Now he knew why the men at the gate that rainy morning had wanted him. For target practice.

Lila stared at him. Key could not tell if her color was returning or not. "You're not serious!"

"That's the only reason I can think of. Unless, this is just a guess; you and Simon have been vocal against the TFL."

"We're schoolteachers, Key. My God! I, we, didn't even know what those people were called. What does the TFL mean?"

"It's a hate group. The initials stand for The Truth, the Faith, the Lord."

"What a macabre joke."

"Yes."

"Goddammit, Ted!" Zack screamed the words. "That had to have been Key. I thought the bastard was dead and buried in the ground."

Ted fought back a growing sickness in his belly. "The son of a bitch is dead! Dammit, you saw the body in what was left of that bunk. We found his boots, what was left of his wallet, and his gold money clip." Ted was beginning to convince himself in his efforts to convince the others. "Now he wouldn't leave without those, would he?"

Zack shook his head. "I guess not. Yeah, you're right. 'Sides, if it wasn't Key who burned up, who was it?"

"Maybe I can answer that." A deputy stepped out of the darkness into the light. He held a piece of paper in his hand. "This just come over the wire.

From Kansas. They had a breakout at a jail down there the day before our place burned up. They caught 'em all but one. And this guy has folks up in Columbus. Our state patrol reported spottin' him down around Hebron, headin' north the night before our fire. The physical description matches the guy who got burned up in our fire."

"Maybe," Ted said. "But I still think it was Key."

"Ted," Niles said. "If Key is alive, he's got to be stopped and stopped damn quick."

"We got a three county area sealed off," Ted said. "Lookin' for that nigger bitch. If it was Key who grabbed her, we'll get them."

"You'd better," a cold voice spoke from the shadows.

The men of the TFL turned. Fell silent.

"If he's alive," Ted said, facing the man.

"He's alive," the man said. "And Key is the biggest threat we've got facing us at the present time."

Jeff read and reread the teletype message. He wondered if Key were really dead. He just couldn't believe a bunch of Nazi kooks would have the know-how to waste Key.

"You think it's Key?" the head of the CIA's K-section asked.

"I don't know. In my guts, I don't think so."

"You know we've been penetrated?"

"Yes. And we have two senators and a handful of representatives who are known to be sympathizers to the TFL."

"Wonderful," the man said dryly. "But we can't let

261

the oversight committee know we're working on this matter. They'd shit if they found out."

"Not to mention the press," Jeff added.

The section chief shuddered at just the thought. "If Key is alive, but presumed dead, it might work in our behalf to have him remain that way."

"I've thought of that. Yes. But Key might not go along with it."

"We haven't asked him yet."

"I don't think Key trusts us."

"Do you blame him?"

Key was up at dawn. Leaving Lila to sleep, he slipped from the loft and painted the motorcycle, streaking it gray and green. Using a tin can, he boiled water for instant coffee and took a cup to Lila. She was awake, watching him through large, still frightened eyes.

"Where am I?" she asked. "Beirut?"

Key recognized it as her attempts to joke. Same ol' Lila that Key remembered from high school. He smiled. Lila, it seemed, could bounce back from anything.

He wondered how many men had raped her.

He decided that would not be a polite question to ask.

"Sorry I can't offer you eggs Benedict, Lila. But how does a can of beans sound?"

"Grotesque. I'm not hungry, Key."

There was a flatness to her voice that Key didn't like. He was no stranger to seeing the aftermath of rape. He had seen it in every country he'd ever merced. With women of all colors, all faiths. Some could bounce back without apparent mental injury. Still others, it seemed, never fully recovered. He wondered what category Lila would fall into.

"Like it or not, Lila, you've got to eat. I'm not going to let you die from starvation on me."

"Yes, boss." She sipped her coffee. "What happens to Simon?"

"His body?"

"Yes."

Key decided not to baby her. "Somebody has probably transported the body clear out of the state, for sure the county, by now. It will probably never be found."

"I see. And Ted's people will have, by now, or are in the process of, repairing that part of the fence you cut out, right?"

"You're a fast learner, Lila. Yes."

She met his eyes. Her own eyes were savage in the early morning light. "You know I was in ROTC in college, don't you?"

"I didn't know, Lila." What was she getting at?

"I was a combat nurse in 'Nam."

"I see. I think. What are you trying to tell me, Lila?"

"That I'll stand and fight and won't run. Among other things."

"I'll hold you to that."

"I expect you to."

"What else?"

"That I qualified as expert with the M-sixteen and the forty-five pistol. That I was involved in two firefights while in 'Nam. Quite accidently. Obviously,

I was not a combat grunt. But I did kill—confirmed—three VC and wounded several others. I was highly decorated. I am a major in the Reserves."

"That's very impressive, Lila. And good to know."

"I thought you'd be interested."

Key smiled at her. "And are you trying to tell me you're ready to go to war, major?"

She sat up and faced him. "On one condition."

"Name it."

"You stash that stupid-looking helmet!"

He laughed. "Deal."

"Okay, white boy, deal."

"Well, then, come on, shine, let's do it."

And the classmates of twenty years past began laughing.

Chapter 11

At nine o'clock, Dad Lessard pulled up in front of the Frankel farm, set the brake, got out, and proceeded to jack up the rear of his truck. Key was already waiting in the weed-filled ditch that ran alongside the blacktop.

"I know you're watching me, boy," Taylor said. "But I can't see you. Talk to me."

Speaking low and very briefly, Key brought his father up to date.

Taylor cursed Ted and his department and those men who were a part of the TFL—men the man had called friend for years. "It don't surprise me," he said. "Some folks have gone plumb crazy. What about this Jewish fellow?"

"Buried with a half dozen sacks of quick lime over him, probably. Doubtful his body will ever be found."

"I hope you don't think the majority of people around here support crap like this, boy."

"I don't. But it goes back to that one bad apple in the crate."

"Yeah."

"How's Cat?"

"Much better. She knows about you; what was supposed to have happened to you, that is."

"No one must know, Dad."

"All right. Who was that third man in the building, son?"

"I don't know, Dad. The thought came to me that it might have been a government operative. I hope not. But if it was . . ." He trailed off into silence.

"You pays your money and you takes your chances . . . is that what you're saying, boy?"

"That's it, Pop."

Taylor was quickly off-loading the boxes and bags he had brought, concealed under a tarp in the bed of his truck. Lila was watching from the loft of the barn, ready to sing out if any vehicle came into sight.

"I got to say this, Boy: You sure picked a hard way of life."

"A hard world, Pop."

"I reckon. You plannin' on takin' on the entire bunch of these TFL people, son?"

"I most certainly am."

"Got your back up, huh?"

"Like a pit bull."

The father's smile was tight and hard. "You could just leave, you know?"

"Understand something, Dad," Key said from the ditch. "If I'm successful in this thing, the law will never see it my way. Then I'll *have* to leave. I'll be wanted by every law enforcement agency in the nation."

Finishing with his off-loading, Taylor removed the jack.

"I have to say this, son: Quit now. Come out of hiding and tell your story. Let the authorities handle it."

"It would be my word against theirs, Dad. It wouldn't wash in court. A few might be brought to justice, but the snake would just grow another tail. The TFL has to be stopped. And it looks like I've been elected to do the job." He thought for a few seconds. "Lila and me, that is. She's tough, and I believe she'll stand with me."

"I've been knowin' her since she was born. Her daddy was my doctor for years. All right, son. Do what you think you have to do. Where's your car?"

"Ted had it impounded. It's at the department's storage area. But before you say it . . . no. You can bet Ted's already covered his ass on that. You'll be getting it back. Probably soon. I have two choices, Dad. I can either run or stand and fight."

"Well, give 'em hell, boy!"

"Thanks, Dad."

Taylor Lessard tossed his son a key ring. " 'Bout twenty years ago, me and Roy Simmons bought a Jeep. It runs good. It's parked down on that piece of land I used to run sheep on. You know. Covered up with a tarp. I drove over there last night, after you called. Took a half dozen cans of gasoline and a new battery. Fired 'er up. She's a rough-ridin' bitch, but she's rock solid and in good shape. I put a case of dynamite in the back and some caps. Along with some other gear I thought you might need. I'm damn proud of you, boy. Watch your back trail, son. Take care."

He got in his truck without looking back at his son and drove away.

Key squatted in the ditch and watched his father's truck disappear from sight. There goes one tough old man, Key thought.

He looked in all directions and then looked up toward the loft of the barn.

"It's clear," Lila called. "I'm coming down to help you."

Together, they moved the mound of gear into the barn.

The gear looked over and stored, Lila said, "Is there anything in this mess that's going to fit me?"

"If you can make do."

"Honey, I'm black. I've been making do all my life."

"You're breaking my heart, Lila. Don't bullshit a bullshitter. Your father was a doctor and your mother a well-respected educator. You graduated from a prestigious university in the top five of your class, according to what I heard. Why you were in ROTC is a mystery to me, 'cause you damn sure didn't need the extra money. You've never picked cotton, chopped beans, wore flour-sack drawers, or tasted a chitterling in your life. And don't tell me you like this squalling crap currently called music, 'cause I remember your musical tastes. You like Chopin and Beethoven and Mendelssohn. So get off of it, honey."

For the first time since Key had pulled her away from the horror called the TFL, Lila's laugh was loud and genuine. "I joined the army to prove I was just as good as any damn man. And I proved it. But don't think just because my parents have money, I haven't had prejudices thrown up in my face, white boy."

They were playing the game they played back in high school.

"It's a cruel world, brown sugar."

"You're a prick, Lessard!"

"And a male chauvinist pig, too."

She laughed at him. "Get outta here. I have to get dressed."

Key and Lila rested during the remainder of the day, eating and napping the afternoon away. Lila was quickly bouncing back, at least outwardly. Key had no way of knowing how deep her mental scars went. Very deep, he suspected.

He had carefully watched her check out the M-16. She knew what she was doing, field-stripping the weapon expertly. He had given her the .38 he'd taken from the TFL headquarters, and she had tucked it in the waistband of the trousers Taylor had brought. She looked like a ragamuffin, with a piece of rope holding up her britches.

Lila had one problem: She was barefooted.

"We'll steal you some shoes," Key said.

"I've never stolen anything in my life!" she protested.

Key smiled and Lila braced herself. "You ever heard the old song about a nigger that don't steal?"

"But I caught three in my cornfield," she popped

back. "You're going to have to do better than that, Lessard. Outwardly, you've changed. But basically, you're still the same ol' Key."

"Oh? How so?"

She smiled sweetly. "Full of shit!"

He laughed. "Woman, thy tongue outvenoms all the worms of the Nile."

"I can't believe it!" She feigned great astonishment. "A mercenary who can quote Shakespeare. What other surprises do you have in store for me?"

"You'd be surprised at mercenaries, Lila. A great many mercs—so-called—are really very well educated."

"Then what happened to them—to you?"

Key fell silent.

She verbally prodded him. "Come on, Key. I know you made straight A's in school. All the way through. I know you had several top scholorships offered you for football. So what happened?"

"It was the roar of the real, the only beast—the crowd in the arena."

She cocked her head and looked at him. One could not call Lila black; not unless one had a vision problem. Lila was brown and very lovely, according to white standards, and that was all Key had to go on. "Blasco—Ibanez. Yes. I've read him. But so what?"

"Oh, I don't know, Lila. Call that last statement a cop-out, I guess. I just wasn't ready to come back. There was a restlessness in me that I couldn't contain. Farming just wasn't going to placate it. People are in control of their own destiny, Lila. Only a very stupid person blames others for their problems."

"Which brings us to? . . ."

Key shrugged his heavy shoulders. "Nowhere. Why do you ask?"

"Isn't this TFL group blaming others for their problems?"

"Yes. Just like a lot of black groups who are very vocal, wouldn't you say?"

"Of course. But don't change the subject, please."

"I didn't. Not really."

"This is weird, Key. Takes me back twenty years."

"Lila, understand something, if you will, for I know you can. The TFL does not, by any stretch of the imagination, represent the thinking of the majority of citizens. I hope," he added. "Oh, hell, I know it doesn't. Like other hate groups — and believe me, I have encountered a number of them around the world — they're made up of very shallow-minded people. Hitler got started the same way, and then the infection spread to encompass more intelligent people. And the same thing could happen in the good ol' U.S. of A., Lila, Believe it."

"Hell, Key! Obviously, it is happening."

"To a degree. And it's spreading, Lila. The minorities had better get their shit together and join the mainstream."

She glared at him. "How about the right to be different, Key?"

"That still exists, Lila. I hope it always will. But when one is in the minority discretion is the catch word."

"I think there is a lot you're leaving unsaid, Key."

"You're right."

"What you're saying is: When this is over, and if

271

we're successful, we're going to have to go underground, on the run, right?"

"You got it."

She smiled mischievously. "The underground railroad rolls again."

Key looked heavenward. "Oh, shit, Lila!"

Just after supper, which he prepared and ate alone, Taylor Lessard felt an urge for a smoke. He looked around the house. Out of cigarettes. And at his age, Taylor didn't give a damn about the warning on the side of the package. If he wanted a smoke, he wanted a smoke.

He walked out onto the porch and made up his mind. He walked through the night to his pickup and backed out of the drive, pointing the nose of the old truck toward the glow of lights from Lewiston. Halfway there he was stopped at a roadblock. Chris Litton, Wynn Carter, and two Alton County deputies stood by the cars pulled across the road.

Taylor stuck his head out and yelled, "What the hell's going on here, boys?"

"Checking for criminals," one of the deputies said, walking up to the truck.

Checking for Lila, you mean, Taylor thought. And my boy. "Well, as you can see, I don't have Billy the Kid or Bonnie and Clyde with me. So would you kindly move those vehicles blockin' the road and let me through?"

"Keep your pants on, old man," Billy Barstow, the younger of the deputies, said. "And watch that smart

272

mouth."

Taylor looked at the deputy, not believing the young man's words. He had gone to school with this loudmouth's *grandfather*. Sheriff Faulkner would have never tolerated this punk in his department. But then, a lot of things had changed over the years. Not many of them to Taylor's satisfaction.

"Boy," Taylor said. "I respect the law. But I expect the lawmen to respect me, as well."

"Shut up," Billy told him. He was thinking about Ed and his missing lip. He wondered if the doctors had been able to sew it back on. And what did the guys who carried Ed to the hospital say about the accident?

Taylor opened the door and got out of the pickup. Rage filled him. He, and others in Alton County, had sat back on their butts and watched the sheriff's department go from a good office to a sour one. Like most people in the county, he knew, but could not prove, that Ted and the TFL had scared off any decent opposition that was thinking of running against Ted. He had watched a handful of kooks and nuts and perverts slowly strangle the county in a fist of fear. He had watched Ted fire all the good, hardworking deputies and replace them with rednecks and bullies and assholes.

And it was time to do something about it.

"Boy," Taylor said to the deputy. "Don't you tell me to shut up. I'm not a criminal. I am trying to hold my temper 'cause I respect that badge you're wearing. But you get off my back, son."

Taylor had no way of knowing, yet, that it was all a

setup, ordered by the leader of the TFL to smoke out Key.

Billy laughed at him. "Old man, you best shut that trap of yours before I haul you off to jail for disobeying the orders of a peace officer."

"*Peace officer*!" Taylor blurted. He had to laugh at that. "Deputy, either charge me or let me through. Right now."

"Fuck you, old man."

Taylor flushed with anger. He took a step toward Billy.

Billy shoved him back, slamming Taylor against the fender of his truck. "Old bastard thinks he's a badass, boys."

Taylor Lessard's temper finally reached the boiling point. He knew only too well what this young man really was: a two-bit punk who enjoyed hammering on folks with his billy club. Just like all the other deputies in Ted's department. They all used their badges to force sex with ladies passing through. Either put out or go to jail, girls. Every deputy on the force was what the folks down South called white trash. Billy's idol was Stan Tabor. And that should tell the whole story.

Taylor planted both booted feet on the blacktop, reared back, and knocked the deputy sprawling with a hard right cross. Billy landed on his butt. He looked up at Taylor through astonished eyes. Blood leaked from a busted mouth.

Billy began cussing Taylor. "Get that son of a bitch!" he shouted.

And Taylor knew it was all over for him. He

realized then this entire scenario had been a setup to draw Key out of hiding. He looked to his right. "You no-good pup!" he said to the man standing in the shadows by the side of the road.

"You shouldn't have interfered," the man told him.

"I've suspected for a long time," Taylor said.

"And now you know for sure." The man smiled at him.

Taylor opened his mouth to speak to—

Pain exploded in his head. Taylor Lessard plunged into a falling, seemingly never-ending, painful darkness.

Chapter 12

Key looked toward the east as a sadness touched him. The emotion came unexpectedly, almost overpowering with its thrust.

He had felt the same way when she died, and he was far away.

Key wondered what had happened.

Lila picked up on his mood shift. "What's wrong, Key?"

He looked back at her in the darkness of the loft. "I don't know. A feeling. I can't explain it." He once more lifted his eyes to the east. He wondered what had brought on this dread-filled sensation. He had experienced it several times in his life. Always, it meant someone close to him had died.

Key picked up his Uzi. He glanced at Lila. "You feel like staying alone for a time?"

"Not really. But I don't think I'm going to have much choice in the matter, right?"

"Right. I'm going to find out what's going on around here."

"Key," she said softly. "How long do you think you're going to last riding around the county on a motorcycle with a submachine gun strapped across your back?"

"As long as it takes me to finish this private little war. I'll push the bike a few hundred yards down the road before cranking it. You stay low and out of sight. I may come back in the Jeep. I don't know. I do know that something has happened; is very wrong. I may be very late in returning."

"And if you don't come back?"

"You're on your own, kid."

"The man is a veritable paragon of concern."

"Yeah, and I worry about you, too."

"Cretin! Be sure and put the cat out when you return."

He grinned, his very white teeth flashing against his burned-in tan. "I'll sure do that. By the way, I'll see if I can't steal you some shoes."

Although there was no need for it—the nearest neighbor being about two miles away—Key pushed the bike down the road before cranking it. The night was moonlit and star filled, and that was Key's only illumination as he rode without the headlight on. He had cut the wire, since the light automatically came on when the engine was cranked. He rode slowly, not really knowing where he was going, but knowing in his guts that something was very wrong.

Key had noticed during his driving of the back roads of the county that a great many people rode three wheelers at night—many of them on the roads, disregarding the laws against that. That would work in Key's behalf, for people had grown accustomed to the snortings and rumblings of three-wheelers and motorcycles and would pay little or no attention to

277

the sounds of his motorcycle.

He left the road several times, riding into the fields at the sighting of distant headlights. No one spotted him. He pulled off the road and took a series of turn-rows when he reached the outer edge of Lessard land. He parked his bike and walked up to Rolf's back door. It seemed that every light in the house was blazing.

He called in a whisper for the dogs, and they came to him, recognizing his sight and smell. He spoke to them softly, calming them, petting them.

The dogs trotted off to do whatever it is that dogs do in the night.

Key slipped up on the back porch and listened.

The conversation chilled him, angered him, sickened him.

". . . was Dad doing out at night anyway?" Key caught the last bit of Claire's question.

"And what the hell was Whit doing out here at night?" David asked.

"Yes," Martha said. "It seems very odd that Whit would just 'happen along,' and find the body."

"There has never been a mugging in this part of Alton County," David said. "At least not that I can remember."

"I don't believe Dad was mugged," Claire said. "I think someone deliberately killed him."

"Why, sis?" Rolf asked. "I agree with you, but why? Dad would have never picked up any hitchhiker. That's for sure."

"Why are a lot of things happening?" David asked, his voice tired. "First Key, then Dad. Goddammit, who is next?"

"And who is doing it?" Rolf asked.

"We all know that." Claire's reply was bitterly spoken.

"Careful, Claire," Martha warned.

"Oh, to hell with being careful!" Jenny lashed out. "I'm tired of being careful. Dammit, it's time for all of us to fight back."

Rolf looked at his wife. "If you got something else on your mind, honey, say it, please. It's past time."

"Look," Jenny said, pacing the large kitchen. "For the last couple of days, Dad had been very happy; humming and cheerful—right? There was a mysterious, mischievous light in his eyes. Like . . . well, like maybe he knew something all of us didn't—right?"

They all agreed she was correct. Come to think of it, they had noticed that, too. But . . . so? they asked her.

"I slipped up to Dad's house twice, at night, after Key was supposed to have been killed. Dad was sitting in the dark, in the kitchen, in a chair, watching the backyard. All night long. I don't think Key is dead at all. And I think Dad knew it. I believe Key contacted him. I think Key is out there, and he's going to fight the TFL."

"By himself?" Glen blurted.

"Probably," Eddie said. Until now, the older of Taylor's grandchildren gathered with the adults had been silent.

Rae said, "I think that the Taylor family had best stay close to home base for a time—until this is over. I think there is going to be a lot of trouble in Alton County."

The parents listened to their kids talk.

279

Key listened from his quiet place on the back porch.

"I read a book about something like what's happening around here," Eddie said. "I think somebody is trying to pull Uncle Key out of hiding; make him do something rash. But with Uncle Key, I don't think it's going to work."

"Yeah," Rae agreed. "I just hope granddad wasn't followed last night."

"What are you talking about, sister?" David asked his daughter.

"He took off somewhere last night. He was gone about three hours. He put some boxes in the back of his truck before he left. A lot of boxes."

"Which way did he go?" Rolf asked.

"North. I watched his headlights turn off at Robin Road."

"But there is nothing up that way," Eddie said. "And I mean, *nothing*."

Claire rose from her chair. "All right. Let's get down to the distasteful part: When do we bury Dad?"

All agreed on the day after next.

Key picked up a pair of tennis shoes from the back porch, and an old blouse and jeans that belonged to Jenny. He slipped from the porch and made his way back to the motorcycle. He pulled out, heading for the Jeep his father had told him about.

When he arrived at the tarp-covered Jeep, Key had to smile, despite all the sadness. His dad had told him he had left some other gear—he wasn't kidding.

Taylor had hooked a small, two-wheeled trailer to the Jeep. Leave it to the old man to cover all angles, Key thought.

Key muscled the motorcycle up on the bed of the trailer and roped it down. He then inspected the back seat of the Jeep.

A rifle and shotgun lay on the back seat. A .308 and a twelve gauge chambered for magnum loads. Boxes of shells lay next to the weapons. There was a portable radio and extra batteries. Binoculars in a case. The floorboards of the back seat were filled up with cans of gasoline. A case of dynamite and caps. Cans of food and bottled water. Boots and assorted clothing.

Taylor Lessard wanted Key to have a fighting chance of winning this war.

Key cranked the Jeep and listened to the engine for a moment. It ran without a skip. Key suspected his dad had put in new points and plugs.

He dropped the Jeep into gear and pulled out, heading back to the Frankel farm. He tucked the Jeep away and climbed up the ladder to the loft.

"You're back earlier than I expected," Lila said. She studied his face for a silent moment. "What's the matter, Key?"

"The TFL killed my dad."

"Oh, God. I'm sorry. How did it happen?"

He told her all he knew. "Dad lived a good life," he said with a sigh. "He told me he missed Mom. Well, they're together now."

"You really believe that, Key?"

"Yes. Don't you?"

She shook her head. "I don't know. I used to go to church and believe in all that. After a while, it became very illogical to me. If there is a God, Key, I don't believe He would be so tolerant of the ills of this world. I just don't."

"You're certainly entitled to your opinion, Lila. But I'll stick with my beliefs. Oh, I found you some tennis shoes."

"Don't change the subject. You're a mercenary, Key! You deal in war and death. You've dealt pain and suffering and death all over the world. I'm not being critical of you, personally. It's just that I can't but see the two very opposite philosophies joined, that's all."

"God liked His warriors, Lila. Some say Michael was God's mercenary." He smiled. "You think Nat Turner went to heaven, Lila?"

"If there is a heaven, yes, I certainly do. He was fighting against injustice."

"And what am I preparing to do here in Alton County?"

She waved her hand. "Never argue religion or politics, my father used to say."

"Or women, my father used to say."

"Toss me my damn shoes, Lessard!"

Key handed her the tennis shoes and started for the ladder.

"What are you going to do now, Key?"

"Paint the Jeep."

The day dawned very bright and very hot; one of those much talked about Nebraska summer days, where the mercury would hover around a hundred and five. Key stood in the loft, looking out at the dawn, his thoughts as dark as the day was bright.

Red dawn, the thought came to him. How many of

these dawns have I seen on the day of imminent combat? And how many more will I see?

He shrugged that question away. No one but God can answer that, Key.

But do I really care how many more days I have left me?

He was thoughtful for a moment. Yes, he sighed, he cared. But he didn't care enough to stop what he thought he had to do here in Alton County.

He looked back at the sleeping Lila. She stirred restlessly as the temperature began its relentless climb. He walked over to her and shook her awake.

She looked up at his grim warrior's face. "What's wrong, Key?"

"Nothing is wrong. Everything is wrong. Let's go to war, major."

Chapter 13

"I don't believe this!" Lila said, her words flung back by the rush of wind into the open Jeep. "We've got two or three hundred people looking for us and here we are, riding along in an open Jeep as if we're going on a picnic."

He smiled at her. "Do you think I'm nuts, Lila?"

"I don't think your elevator goes all the way to the top, Lessard. For sure."

"You always do what the enemy least suspects, Lila. I haven't shaved in over a week. I've got a pretty good start on a beard. You haven't been back here for any length of time in years. I think we can pull this off."

"I think you're *off*, all right."

But she was smiling.

Key laughed.

"Where are we going, Key? Or do you have any idea at all?"

"We're going to the Dexter Frank home."

"Dexter was one of those bastards who raped me."

"I know."

"What are we going to do at his house?"

"Burn the goddamn place to the ground."

"On top of everything else, the man is a pyromaniac."

"Burn, baby, burn," Key said with a straight face.

Lila gave him a sour look, muttering something under her breath. Key couldn't catch all the words. Part of it rhymed with a trucker's brother.

They could not help but pass several vehicles. Some of the drivers waved, as country folk are prone to do, whether they know the other driver or not. One man waved and shouted, "Hi, Lila. Give 'em hell, Key!"

"Right," Lila said. "Great disguise we have going for us, Key. We're practically invisible."

Key wondered if his mock funeral had fooled very many people at all.

"Who was that guy, Key?"

"I don't know."

"White man and a black woman riding around the county. I mean, *really* Key!"

He looked at her. "You're not black."

"Well, what the hell am I then?"

"Cinnamon."

"Drive the damn Jeep, Key!"

He chuckled during the short drive to Dexter Frank's house.

When they got there Key got out of the Jeep and prowled the house. No one at home. He wondered where Dexter's family was. No matter. He was just glad none of the women were at home.

"Beautiful home, Key," Lila said. "Must have cost a couple of hundred thousand dollars."

"Dexter had two or three good years and went hog-wild. Didn't put anything back for the bad years. Piss on him."

"Very eloquently put, Key."

Key poured gasoline around the inside of the house and outbuildings. He backed the Jeep out of the drive and lit the fuse on several taped-together sticks of dynamite, holding it for a moment while Lila squirmed on the seat beside him.

Finally she blurted, "Will you *please* get rid of that damn thing?"

"But of course, dear." Key tossed the sputtering stick at the house and floorboarded the gas pedal.

The explosion rocked the Jeep and sent pieces of the Frank house several hundred feet into the hot morning air. The large gas tank by the barn blew like a bomb. Key cut off the road and tucked the Jeep into a stand of timber. The gray and green and brown Jeep was almost invisible. He uncased his binoculars.

"What are we waiting for?" Lila asked.

"I like to watch fire trucks."

The first vehicle to come roaring up the road belonged to Dexter Frank. Key watched him through the high-powered, fifteen by sixty field glasses. Dexter looked very angry, his expression changing to astonishment as he slid to a stop and got out of his truck, looking at the wreckage that he had once called home.

Dexter jerked off his pearl-gray cowboy hat and threw it on the ground. He kicked the hat, then jumped up and down like a spoiled, angry child. Ted Gilbert pulled up, with Stan Tabor driving. The men got out. Stan seemed to be walking very carefully. Ted tried to calm Dex down. It was a futile effort.

When the fire trucks arrived, there was little the firemen could do except stand about, watching what was left of the house and barn and sheds burn themselves out. The firemen hosed down the smoking ruins and left.

Dex and Ted and Stan stood off to one side, talking. Key would have given a hundred dollars to hear the conversation, for he suspected most of it was about him.

Lila broke the silence. "You're smiling, Key. Why?"

"One giant step for mankind," Key replied, not taking the binoculars from his eyes.

"*Humankind*," she corrected.

"Yes, Gertrude." A wicked smile was playing around the corners of Key's mouth.

"I don't think I'm going to like the reasons behind that smile, Key."

"You want to have some fun, Lila?" He reached for the .308.

"Oh, sure." Her reply was decidedly dry.

Key took the .308 from the case and checked the loads. He had no way of knowing at what range his dad had sighted it in, but Taylor had always liked the long shot, so Key guessed at two hundred yards. Key could compensate for that. He filled his pockets with ammo and slipped from the Jeep. He tested the wind. No wind. Good. He looked at Lila.

"You'll miss me terribly while I'm gone?"

She rolled her eyes. "Like the roses miss the dew, Lessard."

Key laughed at her.

He was not being disrespectful of his dad's death.

287

Key knew Taylor would approve of this — and appreciate it.

He slipped out of the timber and belly-crawled for a hundred yards, until easing up onto a slight rise, just above the planted field. He watched as what he assumed to be Dexter's wife pulled up in a new Lincoln Town Car. All two hundred and seventy-five-odd pounds of her. She wobbled and hollered and squalled as the fat shook. Key could not recall her name, but he did remember that she had been such a trim, pretty girl in high school.

He wondered what had turned her into such a lard-ass.

He felt a very swift moment of compassion for Dexter. Fleeting. Like lightning.

Even from four hundred yards away, Key could hear her shrieking. "Goddamn niggers and Jews done this, Dex!" she roared, her voice similar to that of a drill sergeant addressing the troops — during a hurricane.

She finally ran out of races and nationalities and religions to blame and plopped her fat ass back into her expensive car and left.

All present seemed relieved.

Key lifted the .308, sighted in the bar lights on Ted's car, and pulled the trigger.

He completely missed the lights, the slug wanging off the roof of the car and howling wickedly off into the hot air.

"Holy shit!" Ted hollered.

Key quickly adjusted the scope and sighted in the bar lights. He blew a fist-sized hole in the lights, sending bits and pieces of plastic and glass flying.

"Jesus Christ!" Stan yelled, looking wildly around him.

Stan jerked out his pistol and began blasting the hot morning, not knowing which direction the unfriendly fire was coming from.

Key laughed at the antics of the men.

He quickly refilled the five-round magazine and sighted in the left front tire of Ted's car. He blew the hubcap off, sending the round metal spinning and clattering on the gravel. He flattened the rear tire of the squad car and went to work on Dexter's truck, flattening two tires and pocking the windshield.

Dexter, Stan, and Ted were now belly-down in the blast-littered front yard. Behind them, the house smoldered. Key put two rounds into the dirt, close to the sprawled men, laughing as they squalled in fright.

Key began putting slugs into the engine of Ted's car, hoping to hit the battery and knock out the radio. He did more than that.

He set the car on fire.

The gasoline in the carburetor and fuel line exploded, blowing the hood off. The hood just missed the men hugging the ground.

Behind him, Key could hear Lila's laughter as she watched through the binoculars.

Key reloaded and waited.

"*Key!*" Ted yelled. "Goddammit, boy, I know that's you out there. Now, shit, Key! Cain't we talk about this, partner? Now, come on, Key. You got to see our side of this thing. They's two sides to every story, man."

Key had never seen it fail: Hate groups were all the same. Cowards when the chips went down. Big-mouth, night-riding, hooded cowards.

Key's reply was several rounds into the sooty dirt in front of the men. Once again, they hollered in fear. He reloaded and went to work on Dexter's truck, firing at the engine. Smoke began curling up from under the hood.

Key quit when the barrel of the .308 became too hot to touch. He edged backward, off the rise, and began running for the Jeep, jumping in behind the wheel.

As he cranked the engine, he said, "Want to make a pass by the boys and give them a taste of five-fifty-six ammo?"

"You're driving."

Key spun the wheel and roared out of the timber, bouncing over to a turn-row. At the blacktop, he cut to the left and floorboarded the gas pedal. Lila was ready with her M-16, on full auto.

As they drove past the three men, Lila leveled the M-16 and held the trigger back, spraying the area with lead.

When they were past the smoking ruins of house and barn and cars and trucks, Lila said, "That wasn't too smart, Key. Now they'll know we're in a Jeep."

"We'll correct that tonight."

"How?"

"By stealing something else to drive."

Key and Lila lay in the loft of the barn and listened to the radio news from Lewiston's local station. The fire at Dexter's house was mentioned, but nothing was said about the one-sided firefight on any of the three newscasts they monitored.

Clicking off the radio, Key said, "We've got them on the defensive. Ted can't afford to go public with our being alive. That's one for us, but it puts us in a bad situation."

"Worse than what we're already in? How, for God's sake?"

"Now they have to kill us. They have to keep looking for us until we're dead. They've got to pull out all the stops."

"You're just a well of good news, aren't you, Key?"

He grinned. "Ol' cheerful Key. The class clown."

"Key made goddamned fools of you all." The man spat the scornful words at Dexter, Ted, and Stan. "He put you on the run and he knows it."

"Well, what in the hell would you have done?" Ted blurted, flaring up at the leader. "Dammit, man, we didn't even know where those shots were coming from."

The founder and leader of the TFL waved Ted's remarks away. "No matter. I know Key. He won't run. He's in this until the end. I want every man you can muster covering the grounds outside the cemetery tomorrow. If there's a way in hell he can do it, Key will attend the funeral. If we let him slip through our fingers this time, we're going to have a full-scale battle on our hands."

"I thought that was what I was in today," Dexter said sourly.

"Not yet," the man replied. "But if Key gets his way, you soon will be."

"A lot of folks in the county know Key is alive," Ted told the man. "And they're on his side."

"Then they can come to his funeral. Kill him!" The man turned and walked out the door.

Chapter 14

Key had carefully brushed away any tire tracks leading into the barn, just making it back inside the barn before a sheriff's department airplane growled into sight, coming out of the sun.

Ted was pulling out all the stops in his search for Key and Lila. Key imagined the man must be close to panic by now. And he wondered if the local leader had chewed Ted's ass.

Key suspected he had.

But who was the leader? Key didn't have a clue. But he felt it was somebody local. Whit? Maybe. The signs pointed in that direction.

Twice, Sheriff's Department cars had rolled slowly down the road in front of the Frankel farm, two men to a vehicle. The men had looked the place over but had made no attempt to pull in.

The third Sheriff's Department car pulled into the drive and stopped.

"Now what?" Lila whispered. They lay in the loft, near the hay door.

In an almost silent reply, Key clicked his Uzi onto full automatic and looked at her.

She got the message.

"Billy Barstow and Walt Lewis," Lila whispered. "Two rednecks if there ever was a pair."

"Will Barstow's boy?"

"Yes."

"I seem to recall that Will was one of the last KKK members in this area."

"That's right. And Walt was very vocal in attempting to reform a chapter of the Klan around here about ten years ago."

"How successful was he?"

"The same men who now belong to the TFL joined. So the rumor goes. Hard to tell behind those hoods. But when they tried to march in Lewiston, the townspeople threw rocks and bottles at them."

Walt and Billy got out of the car and looked around. "I don't see no tire tracks in the dirt," Walt said, his voice carrying to Key and Lila.

"Naw, they ain't here. Knew they wouldn't be. Barn door wide open. No tracks. He's close to the river — bet on it. Hell with it. Let's sit and rest for a minute. Damn sun is fierce, boy."

The two deputies squatted in the shade of the barn, directly beneath Key and Lila. Walt Lewis laughed. "That was a funny sight the other night, wasn't it?"

"What?"

"Shootin' that Jew-boy."

"Yeah. We'll have to get some more of them for target practice. I'd like to have me another round with that Lila, though. She had some fine pussy."

"Well, I hope she moved her ass more with you than she done with me. She just laid there like a log while I was humping her."

Key noticed Lila's hands tightening knuckle-white on the M-16.

Another car pulled into the drive. Niles Becker, Wynn Carter, and Lester Kidd got out, walking up to the deputies. Yet another car pulled in right behind the second car, Harry Bell getting out.

Class reunion, Key thought.

"Well, Key's hid out pretty good," Lester said. He squatted down. "We can't find no sign of him at all."

"We'll get 'em," Billy said. "He'll show up at that old fart's funeral tomorrow, for sure."

Key listened, the only emotional sign displayed was a slight narrowing of his eyelids. His thoughts were something else.

"Was the old man carryin' any money?" Lester asked.

" 'Bout a hundred dollars," Billy said. "We split it up. Niles got the old man's watch, and Matt took his ring."

"Old bastard popped you pretty good, didn't he?" Lester asked maliciously, looking at Billy's slightly swollen mouth.

"Not near so much as Key whipped your ass, Kidd," Billy responded.

Lester flushed, stood up, and opened his mouth to speak. "Knock it off," Niles said. "You all heard what the man said. No bickering among ourselves. We can't afford it. Goddamn, but that was a lousy thing Key done to Dexter's house."

"Lost everything," Walt said. "Man works hard all his life and some nigger-lover burns him out. I just can't figure Key."

Harry Bell said, "Key is no nigger-lover. Don't none of you kid yourselves."

Billy looked at the man. "You mind explainin' that, Harry?"

"Sure. We backed him into a corner, that's all. If we'd left him alone, none of this would have happened. We beat him up, tortured him, never could break him, and all we succeeded in doing was pissing him off. Now we got a man-killing grizzly bear prowling around. Nathan pulled out about an hour ago." He dropped that in matter-of-factly.

"Nathan?" Walt asked. "What do you mean, pulled out?"

"Just that. Took his wife and kids and loaded up the car and van and took off. The leader don't know that yet, and I don't want to be the one to tell him."

"Nathan is a coward!" Lester said.

"No, he isn't," Harry contradicted quietly. "Nathan was a Marine in 'Nam. He isn't a coward. He's just using good sense. Key was a paratrooper, a Ranger, a Green Beret, a French Foreign Legionnaire, and a world-class mercenary. Key's got more combat know-how than all of us put together. He's a survivor. He's a killer. He's a tracker. He's a stalker. And I think we all screwed up bad. I did a little checking on Lila, too. She's a major in the Army Reserves. A decorated hero out of Vietnam. Oh, I screwed her the other night. My dick was in it, buy my heart wasn't. I don't have a thing against Lila. Never have. We were good

296

friends in high school. What we all did the other night was wrong. Made me sick. But don't misunderstand me—I'm in this just as deep as any of you. I won't back out or run. I know we have to kill Key and Lila. And if I have to do it personally, I will. But when this is over, I'm out of the TFL. I told the man that."

"You're yellow, Harry," Billy said.

Harry sighed and ran his fingers through his thinning hair. "No, I'm not, Billy. Public opinion, at least around here, is turning against us. Things are going sour. Townspeople really got upset about Miss Cat. A lot of folks didn't like her, but a lot of them that didn't like her thought that snake business was a crappy thing to do. Now her family has sent some hard-eyed ol' boys in from Chicago. Snooping around, asking questions. Seems the Monnets own a top-flight security agency—right up there with the Pinkertons. There isn't but three, four investigators in here, right now, but I don't want to jack around with none of them." Harry fell silent.

"Shit!" Niles said, summing up the feelings of most present.

"All this talk is just between us, boys," Harry said. He rose from his squat with a grunt. A pistol was stuck in his waistband, a deputy sheriff's badge pinned to his shirt.

Harry walked to the barn door and stepped in. Key had knocked out a wall between two stalls and had hidden the Jeep there, covering it with a tarp, hoping the murkiness of the barn interior would aid in the deception.

Harry looked around, then looked up. He met Key's eyes, looking down at him. Harry nodded his head minutely and walked back outside. "Place is empty, boys. Come on, let's go. We got to do it."

When the cars had pulled away, leaving a cloud of dust to settle around them, Key said, "Harry looked right at me. He covered for us. I thought Harry had too much sense to get mixed up with something like the TFL."

"He didn't rape me, either," Lila said. "I thought it was because he hated blacks. Now I know differently."

"That was interesting about public opinion."

"Don't count too heavily on the citizens, very many of them, helping us."

"Yeah, I know."

"Why didn't you just kill them all?" Lila asked. "You had the chance."

"Then we wouldn't have learned anything."

"We could have tortured them!" she replied, a savage edge to her voice.

Key was certainly no stranger to torture, both on himself and others. He was curious, however, at the heat in Lila's voice.

"I can't speak for all the women who have been raped, Key. But I'd be willing to bet a very large percentage of them would have agreed to carve up their attackers . . . with a very dull knife."

"First rule of guerrilla warfare," Key said. "Never get captured by the women."

"I had a friend who was raped; like me, gang-raped. She never really got over it. It leaves scars that

298

are unseen."

Key opened his mouth to speak. He closed it. There was nothing he could say.

Chapter 15

Key and Lila watched the sun boil down in the west, the fading rays bringing a promise of some relief from the intense heat of the summer's day.

"What do you have planned for us tonight?" Lila asked

"Not us, Lila. Me. Tonight I go into town."

"And do what?"

"I want to see what Lewiston's new factories produce."

She looked at him. "Office supplies," she said matter-of-factly. "I have friends who work in them."

Key blinked. One mystery exploded by two words. Ken had been right. "Office supplies?"

"Yes, Chairs, desks, filing equipment. Nothing sinister about that, Key."

"Except the TFL owns them."

"So if you blow them up you put several hundred people out of work."

"I wasn't planning on blowing them up," he said peevishly. "Just checking them out."

The look she gave him stated silently that she didn't

believe that for a moment.

He shrugged. "Well . . ."

"That's what I thought. Key, who told you the TFL owns the factories here in Lewiston?"

"I got the impression Coach Warner was implying it. Maybe I was wrong."

She shook her head. "No, you're probably right. Say, come to think of it, those factories all have government contracts. That mean anything to you?"

"It means that TFL might well have high-level contracts in our government."

"Wonderful," she said sarcastically. "So now that you're not going into town, what's on the agenda?"

He smiled.

"Uh-oh!"

"Key, I didn't mean you any harm!" Paul Bennett said. "I swear it, man. Don't do this to me. I'm begging you."

"Beg? That's what you and the others tried to get me to do back at the complex, when you were hammering on me, wasn't it? But I wouldn't beg, ol' high school buddy."

"Goddammit, Key, I was just doing what the others were doing. You got to understand."

"Oh, I understand, Paul."

"Dammit, Key, you were a traitor to the cause!"

Bennett's wife was visiting her relatives upstate. They had one son, one daughter, both attending summer school at the university. Paul's was the third house they had visited that night; the others had young kids present. Key did not wage war on kids. He

301

would leave that to the PLO and IRA. Paul Bennett stood in his backyard, in his underwear. He was shivering from fear, the sweat shiny on his face and arms and legs.

Key's laugh was void of humor. "A traitor to the cause, Paul? you're a fool. What did you people do with Simon's body?"

A sly look sprang into Paul's eyes, the moonlight reflecting off the fox-like glint. You'll let me go if I tell you?"

Key stepped forward, shifting the Uzi from right to left. He hit Paul flush in the mouth with a big, hard fist. The man was knocked sprawling.

Paul looked up at Key through glazed eyes. He spoke bubbling words through a bloody mouth. "We'll get you, Key. Someday, someway. The TFL will get you. We're worldwide, man. In every white country. Death to all non-whites!" he yelled.

Disgusted, Key tied the man's hands and feet and dragged him out into his cornfield. He dumped him on his butt.

"You're a fool, Paul. You've been duped into believing a truckload of crap. The Jews aren't your enemy. Just like any other race or religion, there are good, bad, and indifferent among them. Like Baptists or Episcopalians. Can't you see that?"

"You're the fool, Key," Paul spat the words along with a mouthful of blood. "If America is to survive, all nonwhites and non-Christians must be killed. We will persevere, Key. You're walking around dead, man."

Key left the man babbling and shouting his racist slogans. He walked back to the house and poured gasoline around the interior, jerking down the drapes and saturating the expensive fabric with gas. He trailed a stream of gasoline outside, waited until the fumes had drifted away, and dropped a match into the gas. In less than two minutes, the expensive home was blazing.

Paul was howling and cursing Key and Lila from the cornfield.

"Let's go," Key said.

"You going to leave that bastard alive?" Lila asked.

"You want to shoot him?"

For an instant, Key thought she might take him up on the offer. The she cursed softly and walked back to the Jeep, her shadow long from the flames of the fire.

Driving away, Key said, "All that hate is going to burn you up, Lila."

Her eyes were savage as she looked at him. "You ever been butt-fucked, Lessard?"

"Fortunately, no."

"Then shut up."

Far in the distance, they could hear the wailing of the fire trucks.

Key knew better than to try a repeat of that afternoon's ambush. This time, Ted and his men would be ready. Key cut across country, using dirt roads, until coming to a small grocery store/gas station. Al Milton owned it. Al Milton had been one of those watching Key and Stan slug it out at the TFL headquarters. Al had been one of those who had tortured Key.

Key rousted Al and his wife, Vivian, out of bed, in their nightclothes, and herded them out the back door of their house, which sat alongside the store.

Vivian cursed Key in a steady, nonstop barrage of profanity. Spotting Lila, she began directing her profane hatred toward Lila.

"I remember you in high school as such a goody-goody churchgoer, Vivian," Lila said. "You seem to have changed a great deal."

"Nigger whore!" Vivian spat the words at Lila, then literally spat at Lila. Her spittle ran down Lila's face.

Lila calmly wiped her face clean and then decked the woman with a balled right fist. Vivian's more than ample rear end bounced off the grass.

Fortunately for Vivian, she decided to keep her filthy mouth shut.

"I farmed all my life, Key," Al said quietly. "Just like my dad. I lost it all three years ago. The same year dad died. If it hadn't been for my taking over the old store, I don't know what me and the wife would have done."

"I understand that losing your land was not entirely your fault, Al. But what is entirely your fault is putting all the blame on others. Then you decide to join the TFL and hate everybody. Take part in killing and raping and torturing. Spread fear around the county. Did all that get your farm back for you, Al?"

"You just don't understand, Key. We've got to drive out the nonwhites. Kill them, if we have to. It's a consipiracy, Key. The—"

Key waved him silent. "Yeah, I know, Al. I've heard it. If you're stupid enough to believe all that, you deserve to lose your land. You should sit on street corners and sell pencils."

"You gonna burn me out, Key? Like you done

Dexter?"

Key did a mental turnaround. "No, I'm not. I'm going to give you another chance, Al."

"What do you mean?"

"Pack up and get out."

"You can't run me out of my home, Key. You don't have the right."

Key lifted the muzzle of the Uzi and stuck it under Al's chin, lifting his head. Al began sweating. Key could smell the man's fear. "This gives me the right, Al. You can arrange to sell the place when you get situated. I would suggest California. And, Al? . . . "

Al met his gaze through very frightened eyes. "Yeah?"

"If I ever see you around here again, I'll kill you. You understand?"

"I understand. And I understand something else, too, Key: You're *crazy*! Man, you're the one who ought to be getting out. You can't fight the TFL. Not if there was a hundred of you. We're spread all over the world. We'll get you, Key. Bank on it."

"You got kids, Al?"

"One. A boy. He's been gone two years. He took off; refused to join the KCs. I don't know where the little asshole is. Don't care."

"I'll give you thirty minutes to pack, Al."

Key cut the phone lines leading to the Milton house and watched as Al and Vivian hurriedly packed. Key escorted the man and woman to their car. "Don't come back, Al. I meant what I said."

"I could just drive into town and tell Ted where you are," Al said.

"You might. But not if you have any smarts. You

see, Al, I have nothing to lose. I'm committed to breaking the back of the TFL, and I know it can't be done legally. That leaves me only one road to follow. I'll be on the run for the rest of my life, Al, and I know it. What difference does it make to me if I have to burn this entire county back to the ground?"

"You always was crazy, Key Lessard!" Vivian hissed. "But you've changed. You always took up for the underdog when we was young. Well, Key, *we* are the underdog now."

"There is truth in what you say, Viv. But you're blaming the wrong people for your problems. There is no conspiracy, Viv. John and the others have duped you all."

"You *lie*, Key!" she yelled at him.

"Shut up, Viv," Al said. "Just shut your trap."

"Big man!" she shrieked at Al. "Gonna join the TFL and that'll be the end of all our troubles. You had a gun by the bed. Why didn't you use it on this bastard when he broke in? Huh? Huh?"

"Oh, shut your goddamned mouth!" Al put the car in gear and drove off.

"He gave in without a fight," Lila said. "I can't believe it."

"People who join hate groups are basically cowards, Lila. But Al won't stay gone very long. Right now, he's running scared. Tomorrow this time, he'll be wondering why he cut and ran and probably check into a motel and think about it. If Viv will shut up long enough. I'll give him a week—he'll be back."

Key looked at Lila. "I want you out of this, Lila. While there is still time. I made a mistake bringing you into it. I also made a mistake burning people out.

All I'm doing is driving people deeper into the grips of the TFL. I keep on, public opinion is going to turn against me."

"Us," she corrected.

"No. Just me. I think I know of a way to get you clear and to use the TFL's tactics against them. Expose them for the cowards they really are." He began to smile.

"Uh-oh. I've seen that smile before."

"Yeah, you have."

"What have you got up your sleeve, Lessard?"

"I think you'll enjoy it, Lila."

"That remains to be seen."

Chapter 16

"I love it, Key!" Lila laughed, looking at Billy Barstow.

"You sumofbitch!" Billy squalled. "You tricked me."

Key had gone looking for a deputy, any deputy. He had found Billy. He flagged the man down, popped him a short right to the jaw, and drove him out into the country. There, Key stripped the man.

Billy now was handcuffed to a tree, his hands high over his head, his toes just touching the ground, the cuffs looped over a limb.

"You know the editor of the *Sentinel*?" Key asked.

"Sure," Lila said. "George McCallon. You remember him."

"Yeah. Go find a phone and give him a call. Tell him who you are and what happened to you. Tell him I'm alive and to come out here, and bring a camera with him."

"Lessard!" Billy squalled. "You bassard! This ain't decent."

"Shut up, short-dick," Lila told him.

"Been a long time, Key," George said, shaking hands with Key. "I wish this meeting was taking place under more pleasant conditions."

"Me, too, George."

"I kind of had a hunch you weren't dead. From all I can read about you, Key, you're a hard man to kill. What's up tonight?"

"Billy Barstow." Key shone his flashlight at Billy. George's eyes followed the beam. He began laughing.

Billy did his squirming best to hide his nakedness, but everytime he twisted, the cuffs bit into his wrists and he hollered. Billy began cursing. He cursed them all. "We'll get you, McCallon! Just like we got Henry Ran—" He abruptly closed his mouth.

McCallon's eyes narrowed in hate. He looked at Key. "Just like they got poor Henry Randolph," he said quietly. "The dirty bastards!" He lifted his camera and took a half dozen very quick flash shots. Billy squirmed and yelled.

"You cock-suckin' nigger-lover! You print them pitchers and I'll sue your ass."

"Well, in that case, let me be sure I've got some good pictures—excuse me—*pitchers*!" McCallon took two dozen more shots, from every angle. Billy squalled and hollered each time the flash popped.

"Are you really going to publish any of those, George?" Key asked.

"You're damn right. If one develops out that doesn't show his tally-whacker." The editor grinned.

"You get me off this goddamn tree!" Billy yelled.

"And that there's an official police order, McCallon."

George told Billy to commit an impossible act upon himself, ending with, "I don't have the key, Billy."

"*Key*'s got the key!" Billy yelled.

"Put a little beat behind that and we could do the funky chicken," Lila said.

"You black whore!" Billy shrieked. "You think this is funny, don't you? If you think that gang-bang was rough the other night, you just wait until I get my hands on you. I'll cut your tits off!"

"You're hearing all this," Key reminded George.

"Every word, and I'll testify."

"Unlock these cuffs!" Billy yelped.

"I threw away the key," Key yelled.

"I got to pee!" Billy shouted.

The trio ignored him. George said, "Don't attempt to attend your dad's funeral, Key. The rumor is that Ted is massing every man he can muster to surround the cemetery."

"I'm 'bout to bust!" Billy squalled.

"I won't, George. Time for that later. Funerals are barbaric anyway. Our last holdover from paganism. George, how much is it going to take for the people to rise up against the TFL?"

"Not much, Key. A lot of people believe the TFL killed your dad."

"Yeah, so do I."

"How about Lila?"

"I want her out of this. But who do I trust?"

"None of the Sheriff's Department here, that's for sure. How about young Ben Cosgrove? Do you know him?"

"Yes. And I trust him."

"I've got a mobile phone in my car. You want me to call him?"

Key grinned. "Yeah. That should be very interesting."

Laughing at Billy, George walked to his car.

Ben Cosgrove almost had a heart attack. "It's my sworn duty to arrest you, Key!" he said. "I mean, I'm glad to see you. I'm glad you're still alive. But I *got* to arrest you. You can't do this to a cop."

Key met his gaze with very cold and unfriendly eyes. "You really want to try that, Ben?"

"Hell, no! But what else can I do?"

"Take Lila and put her under protective custody, in the care of men you know you can trust. Take her statement." He glanced at Lila. "Who is your attorney?"

She told him.

"Know his phone number?"

"Sure. In Lincoln."

George said, "You want me to call him, Key?"

"If I can arrange it, Key, how about holding her in Lincoln?" Ben asked.

Key met Lila's eyes. "It's up to you."

She jerked her thumb at Ben. "You trust this cop?"

"Yes, I do, Lila."

"All right, Key."

"I got to piss, man!" Billy hollered. "This ain't right, people. I ain't no hog to be trussed up like this."

"Shut up, Barstow," Ben told him. He looked at Lila. "He's one of the men who raped you?"

311

"Yes."

Ben was thoughtful for a moment. "I've got to call my captain. We've got to be one hundred percent right on this thing. And under no circumstances can we allow Lila to get into the hands of the Sheriff's Department personnel in Alton, Pike, or Bishop Counties. Lila, this could be very dangerous. I have to tell you that."

"I know. And I understand."

"Let me talk to my captain," Ben said. "Okay to use the phone in your car, George?"

"Help yourself."

"Oh, Lord!" Billy squalled. "It's runnin' down my leg!"

The captain of Nebraska State Police, along with a sergeant, listened to Ben, to George, to Lila, and finally to Key. The captain listened without any expression change, but his eyes kept drifting to the Uzi held casually and expertly in Key's hands.

When all had finished, the captain said, "Miss? . . ." He looked at Lila. "What is your last name?"

"Jordan."

"Miss Jordan, you had nothing to do with the burning of the Frank or Bennett homes?"

Key had carefully rehearsed Lila. "No," she said softly.

The captain asked her several more questions. He finally nodded his head. "Cosgrove, arrest that . . . *peace officer* over there." His words were filled with contempt. "Charge him with kidnapping, assault, rape, and murder. I'll add about a dozen more

312

charges when I get to the station."

"I didn't do all them things by myself!" Billy hollered. "I was obeyin' orders, that's all. I ain't takin' this fall alone."

"That's what I'm counting on," the captain said, speaking so Billy could not hear him. "Barstow is a weak sister. He'll roll over."

"He'll do what?" Lila asked.

"Spill his guts." He looked at Key. "You, Mr. Lessard, present quite a different problem for me."

"You mean you don't know what to do with me, right?" Key asked with a slight smile.

The top cop returned the smile. "Oh, I know what to do with you, Mr. Lessard. I'm just not certain I have enough men with me to accomplish that objective."

"Billy is going to break wide open, captain," Key said. "You're going to get his statement and jail several of the TFL's little fish. But you're not going to even upset the top men. Their ass is covered. Bet on it. Why not leave them to me?"

"I didn't hear any of that, Mr. Lessard. And neither did any of my men." He sighed. "Mr. Lessard I am going to take Miss Jordan to my car. Sergeant, I want you to take Deputy Barstow to your car. Cosgrove, start taking Mr. McCallon's statement. All that is going to take about five minutes. During that time, Mr. Lessard, if you were to slip away, that would be terribly unfortunate. But you are a very resourceful man; you've probably managed to elude authorities before. However, Mr. Lessard, if you are still present when we finish with our tasks, I will arrest you. And I will charge you with arson, kidnapping, theft, at-

313

tempted murder, illegal possession of an automatic weapon, and several other charges. It could turn bloody. I would hate that. But I've arrested tougher boys than you in my time. Although offhand I can't think of any," he muttered.

Key grinned. "See you around, captain."

"God, I hope not!"

Chapter 17

He grabbed the ring of keys George tossed him. "Take my car, Key. Good luck."

Key drove straight to Lewiston. Straight to Cat's house. He jimmied the lock on the kitchen door and walked in.

He was standing over her bed when she opened her eyes and looked up at him.

"Key!"

He bent down and kissed her. "Hi, babe."

"Am I dead? Are you a ghost?"

"You're not dead and I'm no ghost. How you feeling?"

"A hundred percent better now that you're alive. But —"

"Just listen for a minute." Very succinctly, he brought her up to date.

"I've had dealings with Captain Martin. I can't believe he just turned you loose."

"Believe me, I was just as surprised. Cat, you know an attorney in Lincoln name of Carl Nolan?"

"Yes. A very fine old man. Why?"

"You feel like doing some work?"

"As long as it doesn't entail much walking, sure."

"First thing in the morning, get in touch with Nolan. He was my dad's attorney. Whatever monies Dad might have set aside for me, have them transferred to this overseas account." He gave her a slip of paper. "The police will never break the back of the TFL. Not doing it legally. But I can—and will. I'm going to need some people I can trust. That's you, and this Mr. Nolan, too. Dad stressed that . . . I think. I have a feeling the TFL has deep government contacts and a feeling that I'm going to have to go on the run. That suits me just fine. I wasn't cut out to be a farmer. You know what I'm saying, Cat?"

"Yes," she said softly. "But I don't have to like it." She felt for his hand and gently squeezed it. "Key, have you really thought this out? If you start killing, no matter how bad the TFL is, a jury would have no choice but to convict you. You'll be running for the rest of your life. Oh, I know that you can go back overseas and work as a mercenary; probably with impunity and probably for the CIA . . . but is that what you really want?"

"No." Key spoke from both his heart and mind. "It isn't. Part of me would kind of like to try settling down. With you."

Tears sprang into her eyes. She could feel the love in his voice.

"Cat, hear me out. Perhaps a peaceful existence is not my destiny. Every member of the TFL is just as guilty as the man who actually beat my father to death on that road. And I'm convinced they did it. Every one of them. But yet, I'd be willing to bet that if the police do find out who killed Dad, that person will not receive the death penalty. Call me a foolish, rash, revengeful man. You'd be right. But the TFL is going to pay for what they did to Dad, to you, to Henry Randolph, to Lila, to Simon, all the unknown others, and to me. And they're going to pay in blood."

"You don't have to convince me, Key."

He smiled at her in the darkness.

"I own a place up in California, Key. Up in the Trinity Mountains, north of Redding. It's between the Shasta National Forest and Clair Engle Lake. If you can't come back to me before this matter ends . . . Well, hand me a pen and paper."

She carefully wrote out directions to her cabin and told him where the keys were hidden. "I have a friend who lives a couple of miles away. I'll tell him you're coming out. I'll write to you in care of him. You two will get along well, I'm sure. He's a cantankerous old goat, but as loyal a friend as I've ever had. Now you take this writing tablet and hand over power of attorney to me."

Key wrote what she dictated and dated and signed it. "Got any money in the house?"

"Several thousand dollars over there in a wall safe." She pointed and gave him the combination.

"You know your father has sent men in from Chicago?"

"They've been to see me. They'll probably contact you. Take their offer of help."

"All right. Use some of my money, Cat, buy me a good used truck. Two gas tanks. Use Nolan if you think he can be trusted. No hurry. I'll be around for about a week more. Register the truck in your name and stick a paper in the glove box stating I have full use of the vehicle. Use the name Dave Martin. I have a valid international driver's license in that name. I'll get back to you, Cat, one way or the other."

He kissed her. Very gently. "I love you, Cat. I wish it could be different. And I really mean that."

"Someday, Key," she said softly.

"Someday. Yes. Keep that in mind."

Then he was gone into the night.

Harry Bell was waiting for him in George's car. Or what was left of Harry was waiting. He had been horribly tortured. His fingers cut off, his face beaten into bloody strips of flesh.

Key started up and drove off into the night. It was callous, he knew, but he had to get Harry away from Cat's house.

"Talk to me, Harry," Key said.

Harry gasped for breath, a painful wheeze. "John decided to make an example of me. Somebody who was at the . . . Frankel place . . . told John what I'd said." He moaned. "The entire membership of the local chapter and those of Pike and Bishop Counties met out at the headquarters late this afternoon. Watched me tortured. Evil, Key. They're all evil. All of them. Some of them, probably all of them, really enjoyed watching me scream. Some of them gave . . . Ted and John and . . . Stan instructions as to what to do next. They thought they'd killed me. Dumped me in a ditch. I played dead. Crawled to . . . Miss Cat's. Hoped you'd be there. Hid for several hours, waiting. Get them for me, Key. Please. Key . . . the leader of the TFL—all chapters—is . . ."

He passed out on the back seat.

Key pulled in at Zack's service station and used the outside phone. He called the state patrol. Captain Martin had just walked into the headquarters.

Quickly, Key told the man what had happened to Harry Bell and where he was.

"I've got a unit not ten minutes away, Lessard. Key? If you're there when my man arrives, he'll try to arrest you."

"I'm gone."

When Key looked at Harry, the man was dead. Harry's mouth was gaped open, gasping for that last breath of air that he didn't quite manage to suck into his lung.

"Hell of a homecoming party, Harry," Key said. "Band isn't worth a shit. But it's about to liven up, ol' buddy. Real soon."

Key turned and walked into the darkness.

Chapter 18

Dawn broke when Key crawled into the loft of the Frankel barn. He had hot-wired a car, leaving it some five miles from the barn. He laid down on the hay and closed his eyes, falling asleep almost instantly. When he awakened, it was noon, and very hot.

A good day for killing.

Key set about checking his weapons, carefully cleaning each one. He stored the rifle and other gear in the barn, and carried the shotgun, the Uzi, the dynamite, and grenades down to the barn floor. He planned to swipe another car and come back for the rest of his gear.

He looked around him. "Time to pick up the tempo," he said aloud. "The drummer is dragging the beat."

"Need some help, Lessard?" The question came from behind him.

Key spun around, the Uzi lifting, his finger on the trigger. Two men stood by the corner of the barn. They both lifted their hands to show him they were unarmed.

"Monnet Security, Lessard. You better ditch that

motorcycle. It might be hot by now. Take one of our cars. They're rental cars, but what the hell? Mr. Monnet is CEO of the company."

"Thanks. How'd you find me?"

"Plain old legwork. Took us four days. I've fought in 'Nam, Africa, and the Mideast. But this is the worst bunch I've ever seen. You wanna deal us in on this or is it a private war?"

"For the time being, it's private. But hang around." He grinned and they both returned the grin, catching his drift.

"Lessard, if you come out of this thing alive, the TFL is going to be hard on your ass. They won't try anything with Monnet Security; we're too big. But you, that's different."

"You got something on your mind?"

"Mr. Monnet has. You come see him when this is over. If you make it out alive, that is."

"His daughter and I already have plans."

"Lucky you," the man said with a grin. "See him anyway. Okay?"

Key nodded. "Either of you have any idea who the leader of these goons might be?"

The Monnet men looked at one another. The second man nodded at his partner. His partner told Key.

Key's face tightened. It was worse than he expected.

Key bathed in the waters of a long unused hog trough and carefully shaved around his beard and trimmed it. He put on clean clothes from the inside out. He laid his Uzi on the front seat beside him and slipped the rented car into gear.

As soon as he touched the accelerator he knew this was no standard car. He got out and raised the hood. Nothing but motor from side to side, radiator to firewall. He lifted the trunk lid. A racing stabilizer was bolted to the floor of the trunk. There was a police band radio and CB under the dash.

Key pulled out, heading for Lewiston.

The people who gathered in Roy Maxwell's barn were a cross section of rural America: small businessmen and carpenters and painters and druggists and bricklayers and farmers and everything in between. And to a person, they were angry.

And they were armed.

Roy waved the crowd silent and climbed up on a bale of hay. "All right, folks, settle down for a minute. Now we all know that Key is alive. And he's fightin' the TFL. By himself. We know that Lila Jordan was kidnapped and raped by Ted and his bunch, and a friend of hers, a Simon somebody or another, was killed. Harry Bell is dead. Mr. Bradbury down at the funeral home says Harry was tortured to death. It's gone way too far, people. And it's our fault. We let it get out of hand. Oh, we thought it was funny back seven, eight years ago, when Ted was first elected sheriff. We didn't know he was part of it. Everybody just figured Ted wanted to strap on a gun and go struttin' around the county, actin' like one of the Earp boys. We didn't figure he could do any harm. That's what we get for figurin'.

"What makes me feel sad is that we—all of us—

322

allowed the situation to get this far. We had a good, tight little town here, whites and blacks and Jews and Hispanics all workin' together. We ain't *never* before had no incident of racial problems. Not until this goddamned TFL stuck its ugly head up. If it hadn't a been for Scott Steinberg givin' me credit at the store years back, my kids wouldn't have had *shoes* to wear. And there's precious few of you here that can't say the same thing. But we just sat back and watched in silence as he was burnt out and run out. That makes me feel so ashamed I want to puke, and then ask the Lord for forgiveness.

"And today we put Taylor Lessard in the ground. One more good man gone, thanks to the nuts and bolts and cranks of the TFL. It's time to fight, boys. Way past time to pick up guns and fight for what we know is right. Now, I didn't always agree with Taylor's assessment of what brought on the farmer's present situation, but he was entitled to his opinion. Farmer's got a right to the nice things in life same as any other man. That's beside the point.

"Point is . . . are we going to fight?"

The interior of the barn thundered when a hundred shouted: "Yes!"

Roy waved the men back to silence. "All right. But we can't just go out and start shootin' willy-nilly at everything that moves. And here's something else, too: Bad as I had to admit it, the boys in the TFL do have some trainin' that we don't. Oh, we had it when we was in the army, but for me, that's been more'n thirty-five years ago. Now I know all of you that was in Vietnam; you boys line up over there." He pointed, and the younger men began lining up against a wall of the barn.

Roy said, "James, you was a captain in the Green Berets. So you're in charge. Pete there was a Marine Corps sergeant. Chuck was a Paratrooper. Hal was an Infantryman. Steve, you was a Marine. There's about a hundred of us, so that'll be four groups of twenty-five each, with James commanding the overall group. Let's get to it and make our plans."

"Good, God, but I'm glad to see you alive, Key," Whit said.

"That right, Whit?"

Key had boldly driven his car into the driveway of the Lockley home and entered through the back door. Linda had uttered a slight scream and almost fainted at the sight of Key. She recovered and came to him, putting her arms around her old classmate.

She backed up and sniffed daintily.

"I bathed in an old hog trough," Key told her.

She smiled. "I never would have guessed. Would you like to use our shower, Key?"

"No. I'll smell worse than this before it's all over. But I would like a drink of whiskey."

Whiskey poured over ice, Key sat down, his Uzi beside him on the expensive couch. Whit smiled at him.

"You thought it was me fronting the TFL, didn't you Key?"

"Yeah, I did. It all pointed in your direction, Whit."

"I thought so. I could have told you differently, but you wouldn't have believed me, would you?"

"Probably not. How in the hell did he get mixed up in something as slimy as the TFL?"

"He's power hungry, Key. And he owes a lot of money to a bank in Lincoln. And he's trying to keep a couple of girlfriends in cars and cash. He also hates you."

"Hates *me*? Well, I sure as hell never knew that."

"He didn't feel you had any right to any Lessard land. You being gone for years, and all that. I don't know any of this for fact, Key. It's pure hypothesis, but I think I'm correct. And," Whit sighed, "I think he is insane."

"Is that an assumption, Whit?"

"No. He's had several breakdowns, small ones. Lewiston is a small town; news gets out. And," he said and sighed again, "he just doesn't like blacks and Jews and . . . other minorities. How do you explain that, Key? I can't. He wasn't raised that way. He just took a wrong turn somewhere back along the line."

"How did he keep his . . . troubles from the family?"

"By lying. A mentally disturbed person can be awfully devious, Key."

Key had nothing to add to that.

"Now we have another small problem, Key."

"Oh?"

"Roy Maxwell is gathering a group of men out at his place. To fight the TFL."

"It's about time for the men in the county to find their balls."

"Key, you've been gone a long time. But the law was the law when you were here. You haven't been gone that long."

"Sometimes, Whit, the law is not adequate, and people have to take the law into their own hands. If you don't like it, Buddy—stand aside."

"I'm not a coward, Key."

"I never said you were."

Whit slowly unbuttoned his shirt, exposing a long, jagged scar that ran from his right shoulder all the way across his chest, angling down and disappearing near his hip. "Tet," he said.

That told Key the whole story. "I didn't even know you were in the service, Whit."

"I was no glory boy, Key. Just a Grunt. I may be out of shape, but when push comes to shove, I'll shove back. Hard."

Key stood up, a feeling of warmth spreading over him. "You think you can still plug that hole, Tackle?"

"You're damn right!"

"Well, let's do it."

"For Coach Warner."

"And Kathy."

Chapter 19

Key, with Whit riding beside him, took Linda over to Cat's house. "You stay here until this is over," Whit told her.

"Yes, dear."

Whit couldn't get into his old field pants; his belly was just too big. He finally gave it up and slipped into a jump suit. But his Mini-14 was real and so was the ammo belt around his waist, filled with loaded clips. And the Colt .45 semiautomatic pistol hooked onto his harness was real enough.

"I'd hate to tell you what you look like," Linda said, just before the men left.

"John Wayne?" Whit said hopefully.

"Well . . . to me, you do."

Whit kissed Linda, Key kissed Cat, and the men pulled out, driving openly through the suddenly very quiet town.

"Tell me the truth, Key. What do I look like?"

"Orson Welles."

"Same ol' Key. Honest to the core. I feel like an idiot.

"You won't after the first shot is fired," Key assured him.

"I'm ready," Whit said quietly.

And Key knew he was.

"Matt Rivers," White said, pointing to a man in uniform standing on a street corner by a Sheriff Department car.

"Rivers was a bully and a thief when I left here," Key said.

"He hasn't changed much either."

Key pulled over to the curb. When Rivers saw who it was, he almost swallowed his dentures.

"Take a message to Ted," Key told him. "Tell him I'm going to kill him."

Matt's mouth opened and closed several times, but no words came out.

"Rivers!" Whit spoke sharply.

"Yes, sir, Mr. Lockley?"

"Bend down here."

Rivers bent down and stuck his ugly face into the car. Whit leaned over Key and punched the man on the snoot. Rivers fell backward, banging his head on the door on his sudden way out. He landed on the sidewalk, on his ass, his nose bloody.

"Carry your ass, Rivers!" Whit told him. "If you know what's good for you."

Laughing, Key dropped the car into gear and pulled out.

"Sir?" A state policeman approached Captain Martin.

Martin looked up. "Yes, Knowles?"

"Armed men are gathering in Alton County, sir. Vigilantes."

"Is that right? Where'd you hear that?"

"Message from Sheriff Gilbert. Just received it, captain."

"Sheriff Gilbert is a classic example of a fool, Knowles. Are you certain you received any communication from Alton County?"

The highway cop looked at his CO for a long moment. Then he smiled. "Come to think of it, sir, no. Communications are down in Alton County. I don't know what's going on in there."

"Well, that's unfortunate, Knowles. We'll have to get over there and see what's going on — in the morning. Maybe in the afternoon."

"Yes, sir."

"Where is Cosgrove?"

"Alton County, sir."

"If by chance you do manage to contact him, tell him I said to keep his ass down."

"Yes, sir."

"Of course, he won't. But I think when the dance opens, he'll figure out the best thing he can do is hunt a hole. I hope."

"He thinks Key Lessard hung the moon and stars, sir."

"He's going to grow up in a hurry hanging around Lessard."

The jailer looked up. First into Key's very cold, mean eyes, then into the muzzle of the stubby little Uzi. He thought for a very quick moment as to what would be the best course of action to take. He took it.

"Yes, sir? Could I help you, sir?"

"You can turn everybody in this jail loose," Key told him. "And then you can haul your ass out of here."

Whit had looked over the jail register and found no dangerous criminals booked. Only simple drunks.

"Yes, sir, Mr. Lessard. A very splendid idea indeed. I'll do that right now."

"And if you push the wrong button, I will pull this trigger. You wouldn't like that."

"No, sir. I most certainly would not. I shall take great pains not to push the wrong button."

The jail was soon emptied. Key wondered where the other deputies might be. Aloud.

"Among other things, they are looking for you. And there seems to be some sort of problem with a mob."

"I see. I bet you know a lot about what goes on in this jail, don't you?"

"Yes, sir. And if I talked, the TFL would track me down and kill me. No matter where I went."

Key got the message. "Get out, keep going, and don't come back."

"Consider it done, sir."

The jailer hauled his ashes.

Key lifted the muzzle and put a full clip into the radio equipment, forever silencing transmitter and receiver.

"What the hell is going on around here" a man yelled.

Key and Whit stepped out of the office to face the portly gentlemen.

"Whit?" the man said. "Good Lord, man, are we at war? Have the Russians landed?"

"No, the TFL has," Whit replied. "Mayor, I believe you know, or have heard of, Key Lessard."

"But . . . you're *dead*!"

"Not hardly," Key assured him. "Which side are you on, mayor?"

Whit answered for the mayor. "The mayor is a fence-straddler, Key. He walks around with his eyes closed. Something a lot of us have done for too long a time."

"I won't take umbrage at that, Whit. It's the truth. Mr. Lessard, there is a bounty on your head. There are about three hundred heavily armed men looking for you. The man who kills you gets fifteen thousand dollars — cash."

"Other than Ted and his people, and the ones I personally know, how can I tell them from friendlies?"

"Unfortunately, you can't, Mr. Lessard. But there are men in here from Pike and Bishop Counties. Many of then Sheriff Department personnel."

331

A door slammed in the rear of the jail. "Get home, mayor," Key told him.

"I think not, Mr. Lessard." The mayor went to a gun cabinet and chose a sawed-off shotgun. He checked it for loads. Full. He stuffed his pockets full of shells. "I've been blind for too long, sir. It's time to make a stand for decency."

"Your ass, mayor," Key told him. He faced the corridor.

"The goddamn cells are empty!" a man's voice rang out. "That damned Lessard's been here."

"I want that fifteen thousand," another man spoke.

"I wanted to screw that Lila 'fore they dropped that grenade in on her," the first man said. "Pity. That was a good-lookin' head—for a black girl."

"Lila is dead?" Whit whispered. "I thought she was in protective custody."

Choking back a battle cry filled with rage, Key stepped around the corner and leveled the Uzi, knee-high. He pulled the trigger. Lead bounced and howled and whined around the concrete and steel walls. The two deputies were knocked to the floor, their legs mangled.

Key ran to the bloody mess and jammed the muzzle of his nine millimeter into the crotch of one man. The man screamed in protest and pain.

"Lila Jordan?" Key hissed. "What happened to her?"

"Lord, man! Don't pull that trigger. Sheriff Buckman from Bishop County sent some men into Lincoln. They had an informant on the state patrol. Told

332

'em where Lila was being kept. Way out in the country. They killed her—not more than an hour ago."

"Captain Martin know yet?"

"I doubt it. She was held 'bout fifty miles north of Lincoln. They killed the cops guardin' her, too."

"The informant's name? Goddamn you, you'll beg me to kill you if you lie to me."

"Hands up, Lessard!" The voice came from Key's right.

Without hesitation, not knowing who the man was, Key turned and shot him three times in the chest, the nine millimeter slugs knocking the man backward. Due to the muzzle rise, the third slug took the man in the center of the face.

The mayor puked on the floor.

"The state patrol informant?" Key snarled the question at the wounded men.

"I don't know, Lessard. I swear I don't."

"I'm calling Martin now," White said. "Got him." Briefly, he explained, then hung up.

"What did Martin say?" Key asked.

"He cussed and hung up. It sounded like all hell was breaking loose at the headquarters.

A rifle cracked. The mayor slumped to the floor, a bloody hole in his chest. The shotgun clattered to the floor.

Whit turned and began pulling the trigger of his Mini-14, clearing the doorway of all living things.

"I don't know any of them," Key said, looking at the sprawl of dead and wounded in the doorway.

"I do. They're from Pike County. We're going to be badly outnumbered, Key."

"You want out, Whit?"

"You have to be kidding."

"Whit, what we're doing is against the law. I have nothing to lose. You have everything to lose."

"I refuse to bow down to Ted Gilbert and his ilk," the banker replied. "I'd rather die."

"Bear in mind, Whit, that you might get your wish."

Chapter 20

The Pike County sheriff, Owens, and his men were stopped cold by Roy Maxwell's fighters. And the sheriff didn't like it.

"Stand aside, boys," Owens ordered.

"You have no authority in this county, Owens," a farmer reminded him. "So why don't you just take your scummy TFL crew back to Pike and keep it there?"

"I don't think you really know what you're saying." Owens looked at the man in the glare of headlights. "You all better make it easy on yourselves and stand aside."

Owens's men were slowly fanning out toward the ditches on both sides of the road. Maxwell's men raised their weapons.

Sheriff Owens began to sweat. "Now, boys," he cautioned. "You fire on a peace officer and you boys are in deep trouble."

"Tell your men to stand still, sheriff!" Pete told him.

"No way you boys can win this," Owens said. "You know that. We all have long memories."

"Meaning what, sheriff?" a man called.

"Billy Barstow and Lila Jordan are dead. State has no case. All you got is Key Lessard, and he'll be dead 'fore morning. Even if he makes it, nobody is going to believe the word of a damned mercenary. Think about it, boys."

Maxwell's men stirred and looked at one another.

"Join us," Owens urged. "The Truth, The Faith, and The Lord is the only way out of this mess. Pledge your hearts to us. Together, we can make this nation what it used to be."

"What happened to Billy Barstow?" a man called.

"The state patrol killed him."

"You're a liar, sheriff! One of your men, or Gilbert's, or Buckman's killed him to shut his mouth. To hell with you, Owens!"

A deputy raised his rifle and shot the man in the chest. The night exploded in gunfire. The men took cover behind their cars and trucks and began blasting away at each other. They would do so until dawn, when the Nebraska State Patrol would finally arrive.

Chuck's group of Maxwell's fighters met the Bishop County sheriff and his men at the county line.

"That's far enough, Buckman!" Chuck said. "Just turn your ass around and carry it back to Bishop. We don't need your kind in Alton County."

Buckman figured himself a man of much action and few words. He pulled his .357 and shot Chuck in the belly.

Old Roy Simmons leveled his ten gauge goose gun and fired both barrels. The blast literally tore the

Bishop County sheriff in half.

The night pocked and sparked and flashed as the men quickly took positions behind cars and trucks and settled in for a firefight.

David and Rolf had sent their families out of the county immediately after the funeral. David now stood in the den of his house and watched Rolf slip out the back door of his home.

David wondered where his brother was going.

"The state patrol will be in here in full force by dawn," Whit said. "If we're going to break the back of the TFL, we'd better get cracking."

"Are the roads leading in closed?"

"Yes. Just spoke with James Carlton. He's leading a group of men that are in the process of closing the roads. Most of them should be closed off by now."

Key and Whit were talking via CB.

Whit said, "Two groups of Alton County men are holding off men from Pike and Bishop Counties. All we've got to worry about is the local group of TFL people."

Key smiled at the *all* part of Whit's transmission. He lifted his mike. "Whit, go to Cat's and stay there. Don't argue. I think the women are in danger, and someone needs to be there to protect them. That's you, Whit."

Reluctantly, the banker agreed. "Good luck, Key."

Key hung up the mike, rounded the corner, and almost ran into Walt Lewis, coming dead at him in a patrol car. Key spun the wheel and cut down a side street, Walt right behind him. Key saw the spark of Walt's pistol. His back window suddenly had a hole in it. Key spun the wheel and did a state-trooper turnaround in the street, the nine millimeter in his left hand. He poured half a clip into Walt's window. As he roared past, he could see Walt's head flung back, his mouth open, blood leaking from a hole in his forehead.

Key's police band radio crackled. "All units, all units. This is Sheriff Gilbert. Lessard is in town, driving a blue two-door Dodge. Get him, get him."

A car pulled up alongside him. Four men in civilian clothes. Armed. Key recognized them. TFL members. He jammed on the brakes and backed up, turning around. He reached for a grenade and pulled the pin, holding the spoon down. He braked suddenly, and the car behind him swerved to miss ass-ending him. Key tossed the grenade into the street. The grenade blew just as the TFL car rolled over it. Flames erupted as the gas tank blew, quickly enveloping the entire car.

Key roared away, leaving the men to grow accustomed to the heat.

Key sped down a deserted street, the night behind him illuminated by the greasy flames from the burning car.

Stan Tabor's unit crossed the intersection just ahead of Key. Key's smile was a savage thing to see. He floorboarded the gas pedal, pulling in behind Stan. Key picked up the mike to the police radio.

"Hi, Stan! Guess what's about to happen to you?"

"Get away from me, you son of a bitch!" Stan

screamed into his mike, the words rattling the small speaker. "You're crazy!"

"You have two choices, Stan. Give yourself up and tell all, or die. Make up your mind."

"I'll see you in hell, Lessard!"

"Distinct possibility, Tabor." Key placed the Uzi between the outside mirror and the car door. It was a poor brace but better than nothing. The Uzi has poor controllability on full auto, something Key knew only too well. But Key wanted to give Tabor a twenty-five round present.

He pulled the trigger and held it back.

The hot brass pinged off the steering wheel, burning Key's hand where it hit and falling to the floorboards of the car. The rear window of Tabor's car exploded and splintered as pieces of Tabor's head bounced around the interior of the patrol car. Blood splattered the shattered front window of the car. Tabor's patrol car slewed off to the left and crashed into a light pole.

Key drove on.

He had to see somebody, and he wasn't looking forward to the meeting.

He came to a roadblock, manned by Alton County deputies. He stopped a half block away and watched as armed civilians surrounded the roadblock. As he watched, Key inserted a full clip into his Uzi, chambering a round.

The civilians, some of whom Key recognized, disarmed the deputies and handcuffed them, placing them in the caged back seat of their own patrol cars. Some of the deputies were from surrounding counties.

Key backed up, turned around, and headed out the other way. The sounds of gunfire had faded in Lewiston as the TFL members either ran away or surrendered.

Key headed out of town, toward the TFL headquarters. Just as he was pulling up to the main gate, John attempted to drive out. Key blocked his exit.

"Going somewhere, John?" he called.

John cursed him.

"Oh, now, John," Key said with a smile. "You shouldn't feel that way. I thought you were such a religious man."

John's profanity increased, the filth pouring from his mouth.

Key pulled the pin on a grenade and drove up to John's car. He released the spoon. "I have something for you, John."

He chucked the pineapple through the open window and drove on, listening to John's screams for about two seconds. A crumping, splatting sound ended John's screaming. The car mushroomed as John was splattered all over the interior.

Key drove through the open main gate and up to the complex, parking and getting out. He hooked several grenades onto his harness and shoved several sticks of dynamite into his pockets, along with caps and fuses.

"Key!" Ted's frantic voice sprang out of the darkness. "We can work something out, buddy. I have money. How much you want to let me go?"

Key remained silent, trying to pinpoint Ted's location. There! He slipped away from the car and made his way toward the building.

Ted flitted from window to window. Key could see the shotgun in the man's hands. It would be easy to kill him, but Key had other plans for Ted.

"How much you got, Ted?" Key called, dropping to the ground as the words left his mouth.

Ted's shotgun roared, the buckshot singing over Key's head. Key took that time to race for the building, slipping in a side door.

"I got you, you son of a bitch!" Ted shouted. Then he giggled. An odd sound coming from the big man's mouth.

As silently as a stalking spider, Key slipped toward Ted.

"Does it hurt, you bastard?" Ted yelled. He once more giggled. "Son of a bitch," he muttered. "You screwed up everything I ever wanted. My girl, football, everything!"

Key slipped to the floor, belly down on the hardwood, and tossed an inactive grenade in Ted's direction. Ted jumped about a foot off the floor at the noise and squalled like a young girl. He blasted the corridor with shotgun rounds, some of the buckshot coming alarmingly close to Key.

He heard Ted shuck an empty and heard the click of the trigger hitting nothing. Key lunged to his feet and ran toward Ted, knocking the man sprawling with a hard shoulder. Key kicked him on the jaw, stilling him.

When Ted came to his senses a few minutes later, he was standing on a board, the board laid across two saw horses. The TFL was in the process of rebuilding the burned part of their complex. Or had been rebuilding.

Ted had a noose around his neck, the other end of the tightly pulled rope tied on a rafter.

Ted cut his eyes to Key. Key was smiling at him. "Key, for God's sake. Get me down. This board's gonna break!"

"Probably will," Key answered.

Ted noticed then he was naked from the waist down. "What happened to my pants?"

"Well, I was going to shove a stick of dynamite up your butt, Ted. But that would have been too quick a death. Even though it's what bastards like you deserve. This way will do."

"Whooo!" Ted hollered. "Don't let me die, Key. Please. I'll tell you everything. Everything. Name names . . . everything!"

"Too late, Ted. You know it wouldn't be admissible in a court of law."

"Then I'll testify!"

"And I'll clap hands and sing 'When The Roll Is Called Up Yonder'."

"You goddamn heathen! How dare you mock religion!"

Key laughed at him. "*You* are calling *me* a heathen? You're a joke, Ted. A very sick joke." He leaned on the board. It creaked.

"Whoo! Whoo! Don't *do* that!" Ted squalled.

"Name names, Ted."

"And you'll let me live?"

"No. But I'll give you a quick bullet."

"Fuck you!"

Key left the man cursing him. He began his search of the complex. He found computer software and tape recordings and file cabinets full of dossiers. He carried them all to his car and put them in the trunk. Key began setting the complex on fire. He stepped back into the main building and looked up at Ted.

"Last chance, buddy-boy."

Ted cursed him.

Key leaned on the board.

"Waaahhh!" Ted shrieked.

"The fire will be here in about five minutes, Ted. I'd take that time to pray, were I you. You'll either hang or burn to death."

Ted began stamping his bare feet on the board.

"Whatever turns you on, Ted."

Key had just walked out the door when a cracking sound came from behind him. Ted's panting abruptly stopped, ending in a choking gurgle.

Key drove out the gate, past John's weird-shaped car. He had a couple of more stops to make. And then?

He didn't know.

Chapter 21

David was sitting on the front porch of their father's house when Key turned into the drive. There was a shotgun on the floor beside the rocking chair.

Key walked up to the porch, stopping about ten feet from his brother. "It's all over now, David."

"For these counties, maybe," David agreed. "But the TFL will get you, Key. No matter where you run, and you're going to have to run. They'll get you. We're much larger than anyone believes."

"I'll take my chances. Why, David? Why'd you have Dad killed?"

"He began to suspect. He was going to have me cut out of his will."

"Dad told you that, personally?"

"No. But he was. I know he was."

"Wrong. I read the will, David. A copy of it is right in there, Dad's house. In the study."

"You mean—"

"Yeah, David. I mean you were going to come into lots of money."

"Well, I'll be goddamned! I had the old bastard killed for nothing."

"I can't believe you're saying those words, David."

David ignored him. He giggled. Spittle oozed out of one corner of his mouth. "He always did like you best, Key."

"Christ, David! Let me take you to a doctor. To a hospital. You're sick, brother. But you can be helped. I'll speak for you. I swear it."

"No hospitals for me. Too late, now. Lester and his foolish boy took off, Key. Running like frightened rabbits. I don't know where they went. I never could tolerate Lester. Is Ted dead?"

"Yeah. So is John. So is Stan. A lot of others."

"You've been busy."

"I have the Jesus Files in my car."

"I figured as much." He lifted his right hand. He held a .44 revolver. His father's old .44. It was a cap and ball converted to cartridge more than a hundred years back. But it was not chambered for modern ammunition.

He had his eyes on the shotgun and didn't notice the .44. But he knew the old pistol had not been fired in more years than he could remember. He had one chance.

"I'm gonna kill you, you traitor!" David said.

Key saw the fat gleaming round noses in the cylinder. Modern ammunition.

David jacked the hammer back. "Good-bye, baby brother," he said with a smile.

He pulled the trigger.

The pistol exploded just as Key dived for the ground. When he raised his head to look up at the porch, part of his brother's head and right hand and arm were splattered all over the porch.

Key stood for a moment, knowing it was over for one of them and just the beginning for another.

He stepped over his brother's body and went inside to use the phone to call the cops.

Never was a cop around when you needed one.

Chapter 22

Captain Martin stood with the commanding officer of the Nebraska State Patrol. Men and women from the State Attorney General's office stood close by. The governor of the state had just helicoptered in in a swirl of dust.

"What's the count so far?" the governnor asked.

"Twenty-two dead and climbing," an aide told him. "We've got people going over the tapes and dossiers Patrolman Cosgrave gave his captain. The Jesus Files, that mercenary called them."

"What mercenary?" the governor asked.

"Key Lessard."

"Oh. Yeah. Him. Where is he?" The governor knew where Key had gone. The governor had had a long distance call from a friend of his in Washington, D.C. before leaving his office. Talking with someone from the CIA made the governor very nervous. The governor was reminded of his past connection with a certain infamous project during the early days of the Vietnam War. It would do for that to be made public.

Absolutely not!

No charges were to be filed against Mr. Lessard.

None at all. Understood?

Oh, my, yes. A hero, that's what Mr. Lessard will be.

Good.

"Mr. Lessard is gone, governor. I don't know why. As far as I know, there are no charges against him."

"Keep it that way."

Chapter 23

"I'm assuming your end of the line is secure, Key?" Jeff said.

"Monnet Security checked it all out, buddy."

"Well, not that it matters. Incredibly, there are no charges against you in Nebraska."

"Jeff, you never could lie worth a damn! I see the company's fine hand all over this thing."

Jeff laughed. "Well, maybe. But the TFL's got big money on your head, buddy. Big bucks."

"That's no surprise. Bring me up to date, will you. I've been sort of, well, busy."

Jeff's laughter was just a bit obscene. "Yeah, sure you have. Well, your brother was buried in the family plot. Off to his lonesome. Lester killed himself in South Dakota. His son, Lester, Jr., went underground along with his sister, Betty. They've dropped out of sight. Simon's body was recovered in Pike County. His widow says she would like Lila to be buried in their plot. Your brother, Rolf, was named to take over as sheriff in Alton County. I think he might run come time. He'd be a good one. A lot of people are in jail, and a lot of people think you should be, but various members of the TFL have rolled over, squalling their guts out. The state's attorney general's office doesn't think you could be convicted. So you're clean."

Key knew that. Cat's father had stepped in, and the elder Monnet swung a lot of weight.

"How about the factories in Lewiston?"

"Owned by the TFL. Several banks have now taken them over. They'll keep on operating, and I don't have to tell you how that came about."

"So the TFL does have high-level contacts in Washington." Statement, not a question.

Jeff's silence told it all.

"How big is the TFL, Jeff?"

"Big, boy. Awesomely so. Worldwide. You want a job fighting them? You'll damn near have a free hand."

Key turned to look at the woman lying on the bed in the penthouse apartment in the Windy City.

Cat patted the empty space beside her.

Key laughed. "I already have a job, buddy."

He hung up.

WILLIAM W. JOHNSTONE
THE ASHES SERIES

Available wherever paperbacks are sold, or order direct from the Publisher. Send cover price plus 50¢ per copy for mailing and handling to Kensington Publishing Corp., Consumer Orders, or call (toll free) 888-345-BOOK, to place your order using Mastercard or Visa. Residents of New York and Tennessee must include sales tax. DO NOT SEND CASH.